"Still certain you want to go with me? It may be dangerous," Colin warned.

"It's definitely dangerous," Isabella said.

"I'm talking about the life-or-death kind of danger."

"I'm not afraid. Besides, you told me you thought it would be safe enough for a few more days." She linked her arm with his.

Colin shook his head. "Isabella, you're dangerous in too many ways to count."

She laughed. "I don't think I've ever had a man consider me dangerous. Now you—I'll bet every female you meet sees a streak of danger in you," she replied.

"I wouldn't hurt a woman. You should know that."

"Ah, but you're a threat to a woman's heart." Her voice was warm and sexy.

"Careful, Isabella," Colin murmured, meeting her gaze with his own. "You're asking for trouble."

She smiled. "I'll take my chances."

Dear Reader,

It's fall and the kids are going back to school, which means more time for you to read. And you'll need all of it, because you won't want to miss a single one of this month's Silhouette Intimate Moments, starting with *In Broad Daylight*. This latest CAVANAUGH JUSTICE title from award winner Marie Ferrarella matches a badge-on-his-sleeve detective with a heart-on-her-sleeve teacher as they search for a missing student, along with something even rarer: love.

Don't Close Your Eyes as you read Sara Orwig's newest. This latest in her STALLION PASS: TEXAS KNIGHT miniseries features the kind of page-turning suspense no reader will want to resist as Colin Garrick returns to town with danger on his tail—and romance in his future. FAMILY SECRETS: THE NEXT GENERATION continues with *A Touch of the Beast*, by Linda Winstead Jones. Hawk Donovan and Sheryl Eldanis need to solve the mystery of the past or they'll have no shot at all at a future…together. Award-winning Justine Davis's hero has the heroine *In His Sights* in her newest REDSTONE, INCORPORATED title. Suspicion brings this couple together, but it's honesty and passion that will keep them there. A cursed pirate and a modern-day researcher are the unlikely—but perfect—lovers in Nina Bruhns's *Ghost of a Chance*, a book as wonderful as it is unexpected. Finally, welcome new author Lauren Giordano, whose debut novel, *For Her Protection*, tells an opposites-attract story with humor, suspense and plenty of irresistible emotion.

Enjoy them all—then come back next month for more of the best and most exciting romance reading around, only in Silhouette Intimate Moments.

Yours,

Leslie J. Wainger
Executive Editor

Please address questions and book requests to:
Silhouette Reader Service
U.S.: 3010 Walden Ave., P.O. Box 1325, Buffalo, NY 14269
Canadian: P.O. Box 609, Fort Erie, Ont. L2A 5X3

DON'T CLOSE YOUR EYES
SARA ORWIG

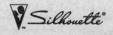
Silhouette®

INTIMATE MOMENTS™
Published by Silhouette Books
America's Publisher of Contemporary Romance

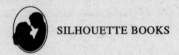 SILHOUETTE BOOKS

ISBN 0-373-27386-X

DON'T CLOSE YOUR EYES

SARA ORWIG

lives in Oklahoma. She has a patient husband who will take her on research trips anywhere from big cities to old forts. She is an avid collector of Western history books. With a master's degree in English, Sara has written historical romance, mainstream fiction and contemporary romance. Books are beloved treasures that take Sara to magical worlds, and she loves both reading and writing them.

Chapter 1

Keeping to the shadows under the trees, the tall man dressed in black blended into the Texas night. Beneath the pale sliver of April moon he dashed across the manicured lawn while unerringly following the map he had memorized.

Under a leafy oak, he paused to check that the hunter was not the hunted. If he spotted anyone following him, he would abort his mission and try again some other way. He waited in the humid darkness before he ran again.

In an elegant, gated community of the small town of Stallion Pass, he went over fences with ease. As he crossed the lawn of a three-story, red-brick Georgian mansion he noted few lights in the upper-story windows and hurried to the back of the house.

With a knowledge of the yard and house gained from his surveillance he crept to the back wall where two wires came out of the ground and ran up to a small box.

Pulling out his pocketknife, he cut the phone lines to disengage the alarm.

Moving to the side of the house, he hid his backpack behind a spirea and removed a glass cutter from his pack.

There was a faint scrape when he cut away a circle of glass and then unlocked and opened the window. The man hoisted himself up, over the sill and into the darkened room.

The bright beam of the tiny penlight in his hand revealed oil paintings, antique guns, a glistening silver candelabra and elegant furniture. He whistled softly in appreciation. The furnishings in this one room were worth a small fortune, he knew.

With practiced stealth, the man eased into a dark hall and headed toward the sweeping staircase. As he dashed towards the stairs, a door opened. Light spilled out and a woman stepped into the hall, colliding with him.

Instantly, without thinking about it, his training kicked in. He caught her, spun her around and covered her mouth with his hand as he pinned her arms to her sides.

"I'm not going to hurt you. I'm—"

She stomped on his instep, sending a flash of pain through his leg. At the same time, she jabbed an elbow into his middle, knocking the wind from his lungs.

"You wildcat!" he snapped as he dodged knees aimed at parts he wanted to protect. He had never slugged a woman and he wasn't going to start with the lady of the house, but in her defensive fury she was trying to gouge out his eyes.

"Ouch!" he exclaimed, a kick to his shin sending a flash of pain through him as she scraped her fingers across his cheek.

"Dammit!" he snarled, wading in to wrap his arms around her to crush her against his chest.

Another tactical error because, for one stunned second as she struggled against him, he forgot the fight, the danger and his mission.

He was conscious only of soft curves, enticing perfume,

silky tendrils of hair and female hips gyrating against him, causing reactions entirely different from what the struggle they were having should elicit.

His guard was down, lost in the proximity of a warm, soft body. His only thought, Desirable female. Very desirable.

Too late, he felt his gun leave the waistband of his jeans at the small of his back only to be thrust into his ribs.

"Let me go!" she stormed.

Careful to avoid any sudden moves, he released her.

She had his pistol aimed at him. If she had been a man, he could disarm him. As it was, she stood too close to protect herself. He'd never been able to strike a woman and he wasn't willing to take any chances now. He didn't want to make this situation any worse.

"Careful," he cautioned. "Are you Savannah Remington? I'm a friend of Mike's. I'm here to see him."

"*Friends* don't break into houses. Get your hands on your head and don't move," she ordered, stepping away from him.

"Don't call the police," he urged. They stood in the unlit hallway, but his eyes had adjusted to the dark and he could see that she was a beauty. She wore cutoffs and a T-shirt that hugged fantastic curves. "I was in the service with Mike," he continued. "I'm a friend. I thought I might have someone following me so I needed to get into the house to see Mike under the cover of darkness."

"I don't believe you," she said, edging away from him.

"I'm telling the truth." He glanced beyond her and saw what she was trying to reach. A cell phone, plugged in to be recharged lay on a nearby table.

"Don't call the police. I'm Colin Garrick. You can ask—"

"Colin Garrick is dead," she said flatly and took another

step. She was inching back, now definitely too far away for him to attempt to retrieve his pistol.

"I am Colin. Really. Everyone thought I was killed but I survived."

"I'm calling the police and they can learn your identity."

"Give me a minute and listen!" he exhorted. "Someone is after me, which is why I broke in—I'd hoped to find Mike. Where is he?"

"He's not here," she said, still cautiously easing away from him.

"I promise you, I'm who I say. I've known Mike since we were little kids," he persisted, rushing his words in an effort to get out information that would convince her of his identity. "We grew up together, went to the service at the same time. If you're his wife, you should know things about us when we were kids, where we lived—"

"I'm not his wife. I'm the baby-sitter."

"Look, can we have this conversation without you holding a gun aimed at me?" She didn't lower the gun.

"Who are Mike's best friends?"

"Boone Devlin and Jonah Whitewolf were his best friends when he was in the service. I don't know who his friends are now."

"What was Jonah's wife's name?" she asked, still leveling the gun at him.

"Kate," he answered, and the woman's eyes narrowed.

"Did Boone Devlin have any brothers or sisters?" she asked.

"He had eight. Nine kids in his family counting him. Ken, Zach, Izzie—" As he talked, he saw her eyebrows arch. She blinked as if deeply surprised and he hoped he was getting through to her.

"If you're Colin, you gave Zach Devlin a special present on his nineteenth birthday. What was it?"

For a moment Colin went blank and a sense of panic

gripped him. Boone's younger brother Zach's twenty-first birthday had to have been years ago. Even at the time, the gift hadn't been a big deal, Colin was certain.

If she went for the phone, he would have to stop her then get out and away without talking to Mike. He tried to remember the gift, thinking of Boone and his younger brother. Her eyebrows arched higher, and he could see his chances of convincing her slipping away.

"My first rifle," he snapped the second he recalled the incident.

To his relief, her eyes widened and she stared at him openmouthed. "You're Colin!" she whispered and he was surprised by her shock. They were total strangers. "No one else could know about the rifle except you and Boone," she said.

"My pistol—" he reminded her.

"Oh!" She lowered his gun, turned it and held it out to him. "You're really Colin Garrick," she repeated, still sounding stunned.

"That's right." He tucked the pistol back into his jeans and got out a handkerchief to wipe blood from his cut lip. "You must take martial arts."

"How did you get in?"

"I cut a windowpane. I'm sorry, but I need to be careful. I don't want to bring any more danger to Mike than I already have. That's why I slipped in this way. Will he be home soon?"

"Why didn't the alarm go off? I had it set and switched on," she said.

"I cut the wires. You don't have a phone now. Sorry."

"I should have known. You guys—" she said, shaking her head. "They think you're dead," she repeated.

He dabbed at his neck and saw more blood on his handkerchief.

"Come with me, and I'll get something for your cuts,"

she said and turned. He followed her, watching the sexy sway of her hips and remembering the feel of her pressed against him. He shook his head as if to clear it. It had been a long time since a female had stirred his desire and this was not the place or the time for that to happen.

When she switched on a hall light, he admired the oil paintings on the walls, the polished hardwood floor and the crystal chandelier. "It's difficult to picture Mike in this house," Colin remarked. As he looked around, his attention riveted on the woman.

In darkness she had been attractive. In light she was stunning. Her flawless peaches-and-cream skin was perfection. Lush curves and long, shapely legs made him remember exactly how it had felt to hold her close against him. Enormous, thickly lashed, luminous blue eyes gazed at him with a disturbing sharpness.

Her thick, lustrous brown braid didn't look as if a hair of it had been ruffled; he knew he looked as though he had survived a dogfight. He had the beginnings of bruises, his shirtsleeve was torn and he was bleeding from various and multiple scratches.

He realized he was staring at her. She was looking just as intently at him, which surprised him. But then everything about her amazed him, including her swift resistance and his getting tossed onto his backside.

"They don't know you survived," she repeated, her gaze going over him intently, a furrow wrinkling her forehead.

"For a long time *no one* knew otherwise," he said, still scrutinizing her. Standing only a few feet away from her, he could detect her enticing perfume.

"When will Mike get home?" Colin persisted, trying to pull information out of her and wondering why Mike would tell the baby-sitter about him or his days in service, much less about the gift of his old rifle to Zach.

"Tomorrow," she answered, and Colin swore under his breath.

"You're bleeding," she said. "We were going to do something about your cuts." She led him down the hall into a large yellow-and-white bathroom with chairs, potted plants and a sunken, black-marble tub with gold fixtures. Motioning him to a chair, she opened a cabinet to retrieve small bandages, ointment and gauze. As she did, his gaze roamed freely over her. She took his breath. The thick braid was dark brown and he could imagine her hair hanging free.

She walked back to him and as their gazes met, he could feel the tension snap between them. Startled, emotions tore at him. He hadn't felt this electricity with a woman in years. Not since— Abruptly he yanked his memories from the past. He didn't want to feel anything now. He couldn't afford to.

"If you'll turn around, I'll clean the cut on the back of your neck for you."

He stood. "I'll shower and wash all these cuts, then you can help me with the ones on the back of my neck."

"I didn't know you were a friend," she said, studying him as if he had dropped from another planet.

"That's all right. You just defended yourself and did a damn fine job of it."

She nodded and left, closing the door behind her. He let out a breath and wiped his sweaty brow because she sent his temperature soaring.

Feeling stings all over his neck, hands and face from scratches she had inflicted, he showered, relishing the hot water pouring over him. If she didn't teach martial arts, she could. Someone had taught her well and she must practice. Her reactions had been as quick as his, if not quicker. He had surprised her when she'd stepped into the hall, but she had caught him off guard when she'd fought back. He had to give her credit, she had handled the unexpected confrontation better than he had.

Colin dried and dressed again in the same clothes. He opened the door to call to her and paused, realizing he didn't know what to call her. She'd been waiting in the hall and as soon as he opened the door, she sauntered toward him, entering the large, steamy room.

He moved to sit in the chair to let her put antiseptic on the scratches on the back of his neck. "I don't know your name."

"Yes, you do," she said.

Startled, he stared at her. While her blue eyes twinkled, she smiled at him, which was pure delight. He almost wanted to smile in return. Puzzled, he said, "You said you're not Savannah Remington. Do I know you?"

"Yes. If you're really Colin, you do."

"I wouldn't have forgotten *you*," he said, the words out before he thought.

In the depths of her eyes desire flickered and the silence between them dragged out as their gazes locked and sparks danced between them. She was beautiful, mysterious and unpredictable, and he was certain he had never met her before in his life.

He rubbed his head. There were blanks—times when memory had failed him—but she couldn't have been any part of that period in his life. If she had, she wouldn't want to tell him about it now. Not with a smile.

As the silence lengthened, his gaze lowered to her full, red lips and he wondered what it would be like to kiss her. He shocked himself. She caused him to long for things he hadn't wanted in aeons. He moved closer to her, his gaze traveling over her features while he searched his memory.

She was far too beautiful for him to have forgotten her. Perplexed, he shook his head. "I can't possibly know you."

She laughed, a merry sound that wound warm tendrils

around his stone-cold heart. "Remember an afternoon when you and Boone were on leave and went to the state fair?"

Dimly he recalled the incident. They'd had to take Boone's kid sister and a little brother along. He stared at her. "There's no damn way—"

"Yes, there is," she replied, amused. "I'm Isabella. And don't you dare call me Izzie."

"You can't be little Izzie," he said, remembering a skinny kid who was all arms and legs and big eyes with braces on her teeth. "You're Isabella Devlin," he said, suddenly feeling as if someone had punched him in the middle.

He hadn't seen Mike or Boone or Jonah for years. Isabella, Boone's little sister, had been part of that earlier life of his. Other than his parents and brother, this was his first contact with his past since that explosion in that faraway land. Five years—an eternity in which his life had changed totally.

Emotions that he thought were as dead as he was supposed to be and often felt, surfaced, catching him off guard and tightening in his chest.

"Isabella," he said in amazement, grasping her shoulder. "Those guys are like family. In some ways closer than my family because of what we did together…" His voice faded as his fingers clutched her shoulder. "Isabella," he repeated in amazement.

Impulsively she reached out, wrapped her arms around him and held him.

Colin embraced her, inhaling her perfume, feeling a tie to his past with his best friends. Emotions tore at him; hurt for losses, relief to be with someone he could trust. Isabella—little Izzie—part of the Devlin family. He realized how tightly he was holding her and released her, stepping back.

She smiled and gestured for him to sit in the chair. "You don't look the same, either."

"No, I guess I don't," he said, his back to her. "I've had a lot of reconstructive surgery to put me back together. Damnation, you're Izz—Isabella. No wonder you were a handful. Boone taught you how to protect yourself, didn't he?"

"Yes, he did. And sometimes we still practice. I work out."

"You're baby-sitting Mike's baby?"

"His regular nanny was ill, and Mike and Savannah had a trip planned, so I said I'd stay," Isabella explained as she dabbed antiseptic on his scratches and put gauze and bandages over the deepest cuts. "Sorry, Colin," she said when she knew his cuts stung from the medication.

"That's okay."

"There. I'm done," she said briskly, putting gauze and antiseptic away. "We can go sit somewhere and you can tell me what's going on. Would you like something to drink? Or to eat?"

"Oh, yeah. I can't remember when I last ate," he said, falling into step beside her. Her head only came to his shoulder. "For someone so small and dainty, you pack quite a wallop."

"Thank you. I tried."

He laughed wryly. "Evidently, I need practice."

"You were very old-fashioned and gallant. You could have hit me at any time and ended the battle."

He smiled at her and was caught again as an electrical current stirred every nerve in his body, a reaction he didn't want in the first place and sure as hell didn't want now that he knew who she was. "It's hard to equate you with Boone's kid sister," he said in a husky voice.

"I grew up," she said, her voice breathless, making his pulse skip. Their gazes were still locked and they had stopped walking and were simply standing, staring at each other.

"If you'd given me the rest of the year, I never would've guessed who you are."

"I haven't changed *that* much," she answered, looking up at him with crystal-blue eyes that mesmerized and held him.

"Yes, you have." He sighed. "I know I have, too. At least they fixed me up where I don't scare little kids."

"No, you'd never scare children."

Silence ensued, a taut stretch in which his heart hammered and he felt himself come alive in ways he'd thought were impossible. "We were headed somewhere," he reminded her.

Taking a deep breath, she turned, but not before he saw her cheeks flush. "The kitchen. It's at the end of the hall here on the main floor."

"Do you live with Boone instead of in Kansas?" he asked.

"The family home is gone. Mom died four years ago, and we're all scattered now. I've lived in California, but Boone talked me into moving back here. I'm living in his guest house on his ranch while my house is built in Stallion Pass."

"I heard the guys all inherited from that fella we rescued—Frates."

"That's right. You would have been in the inheritance, but they thought you were dead."

"I was."

When she looked at him sharply, he shrugged. "I might as well have been dead. For a long time I was near death. I had surgery after surgery, but they finally patched me up. It's a long story."

"Go ahead and tell me," she said. "I'm interested and I know Boone will be."

Colin couldn't resist and caught her braid in his hand. "Isabella. I just can't believe it's you. Are you married?"

"No. There's no man in my life. And you're changing the subject."

His gaze drifted over her features. "Must be your choice, then."

"You were telling me about what happened to you. You said you had operations."

"Yeah," he said as they entered the kitchen. He paused, taking in the oak cabinets, earth-colored ceramic flooring, burnt-orange-tiled countertops and copper pans hanging from a pot rack above a tiled island.

"Sit down. I'll get you something. What would you like to drink? Mike has everything—beer, milk, tea, coffee, soda."

"I'll get a beer and if you have sandwich fixings, that'll do."

"You can have a sandwich or what I had tonight—prime rib, baked potato—which will take no time in the micro-wave oven."

"You twisted my arm," he said, his mouth watering over the thought of prime rib. "I've been on the run and haven't been visiting four-star restaurants. I haven't eaten anything since about five this morning." As he started toward the refrigerator, she walked toward the pantry and they brushed against each other.

Colin reached out to steady her and this time the tension that streaked between them sizzled. Inhaling, he turned away, clamping his jaw tightly closed as he yanked open the refrigerator door, took out a cold beer and uncapped it.

"You won't join me?" he asked, pulling out a chair at the long, oak table. Watching Isabella bustle around the kitchen, he looked at her long, bare legs again, still surprised at the changes in her. Izzie.

"No, as I said, I ate earlier," she said. "But I'll have a glass of iced tea with you."

She opened a cabinet and stood on tiptoe to try to reach

a glass pitcher on a high shelf. When she did, her T-shirt pulled tightly across her full breasts and Colin inhaled, his temperature rising another notch. He stood and crossed the room, reaching up to get the pitcher and hand it to her, his fingers brushing hers when he did so.

Again something flickered in the depths of her eyes. He knew she felt that sparkling electricity, too.

He clenched his teeth and turned away. He didn't want to feel sparks if she were a total stranger much less someone he had known for years. Years and another lifetime ago.

He sat and ran his fingers along the cold beer bottle, then raised it to hold against his hot temple. He tried to keep his gaze anywhere except on her.

Giving him a speculative look, she said, "I don't suppose you're checked into the Stallion Pass Grand."

He shook his head. "I'll get out of here. Stop worrying."

"Where will you go?"

He thought about what he would do next. "I wanted to see your brother and Jonah while I'm here, but I want to see Mike first. I don't have to, I just wanted to. We go back a long way."

"You can stay here," she said.

"After what I put you through, I figured you'd want me gone."

"I know Mike and Jonah. You four guys were really close. They'd want you to stay," she said, getting ice and pouring tea for herself. Having washed a potato and put it in the microwave oven for him, she put a thick piece of prime meat in the oven. "I don't mind you being here."

"Thanks. I'll take you up on that offer. It'll be paradise after where I've been."

In minutes she had the prime rib, a steaming potato with butter and grated cheese ready for him, along with generous slices of French bread. She sat across from him.

"You said you were concerned about being followed. How likely is it that you were?"

"Not likely," he answered. Then dug into his dinner with relish.

"I've got someone after me who wants me dead," Colin explained, picking his words carefully. "If he had been following me that closely, I wouldn't be here talking to you. He wouldn't have waited until I got here. I've been damn careful—which you may not believe since you almost pulverized me."

She smiled and shook her head. "I said before, I know that you could have stopped me. You just didn't want to hit a woman. It sounds like you're involved in some serious stuff, right up to your chin. Are you bringing trouble to my brother and Mike and Jonah?" she asked bluntly.

"That's the last thing I want to do, which is why I went to so much trouble to keep my tracks covered and to slip into this house and contact Mike at night when no one else would see me. I don't want to increase the danger to any of them."

"'Increase the danger,' she repeated with arched eyebrows. "So why did you come then? Why do you want to see them?" she asked with curiosity.

He knew she was worried about her brother. "I need to warn Mike, Jonah and Boone. I know I'm in danger. I think the three of them might be in danger, too."

Chapter 2

"Why would they be in danger?" Isabella demanded, chilled enough to rub her arms. Colin's smoke-colored eyes were as cold as marble. None of her brother's and his Special Forces friends were prone to exaggeration and she might not have seen Colin in years, but she doubted the man would be here without a good reason.

"All of them have been out of the military, away from that life, for a long time now," she commented while Colin ate his dinner. "They have their lives and have been in the spotlight with this inheritance. Their lives are open and if anyone wanted to find them, it would be an easy thing."

"It's something that goes back to the explosion when everyone thought I'd been killed." Putting down his fork, he gazed beyond her, a distant look coming to his eyes as if he had forgotten her existence or even where he was. "I died then in many ways," he said so quietly that she had to lean closer to hear him; she was certain he had forgotten her presence.

"For a long time, I didn't want to live." With each word his voice grew more harsh, increasing the coldness surrounding her. "I still don't care if I live or not, but I'm concerned about my friends. I don't want anything to happen to them."

As he talked, she studied his rugged yet appealing features. She had seen all the scars on his chest and back, but he was lean and muscular and looked incredibly fit. She was responding to him physically in a way she shouldn't be. For all she knew, the man was married. Yet he certainly was sexy, dressed in black from head to toe. Dangerous and tough. There was no denying what those smoke-colored eyes could do to her pulse....

"That last mission I was on was covert. The four of us were to rescue an agent who had been taken hostage by a criminal terrorist."

She remained silent. Boone never talked about his missions, especially that one, and she had only a sketchy knowledge of what had happened five years ago.

"I was the first to get to the building where they held the hostage. The other guys were behind me. As I went in, someone detonated a bomb. The hostage and I were closest to it."

"That's dreadful!" she exclaimed, half not wanting to hear what had happened and half of her needing to know.

"Someone had tipped the guys off. If the bomb had blown seconds later, all of us would have been killed."

"But why didn't anyone know you were alive?"

"When the car bomb exploded, I was directly in its path. The others knew they had to run for it. Mike, Jonah and Boone probably would have looked for me, but they saw me take the blast. They had to run for it. From what I pieced together later, the news reports had listed five men killed in the explosion, one unidentified. So, they would have assumed I was dead.

"From what I learned later, when the local authorities found us," Colin continued, "they thought I was dead, but then someone detected a heartbeat so they rushed me to a hospital."

His attention returned to Isabella and he focused on her as if realizing her presence again. "I was told all that much later. I had amnesia and to this day do not remember one thing from the moment of explosion until long afterward. Long, long afterward."

"Colin, I'm sorry," she said, reaching across the table to squeeze his hand. Instantly his fingers closed over hers and he held her hand firmly, his gray eyes focusing intently on her. Electricity streaked from his touch over every cell in her body.

"You make me feel like I'm home even more than when I saw my family and really was at home."

"I don't know how that can be," she answered, her pulse quickening. She had reached out in sympathetic gesture, but the instant his hand had closed over hers and he'd looked at her, the contact transformed into a fiery, physical awareness. She didn't react this way to other men and she didn't want such a response with a man who was danger personified. Besides, as she dimly recalled, Colin had a fiancée in his past.

He was not wearing a wedding ring, but she would not be surprised to hear that he was married by now.

"Why didn't you let your family know you were alive?"

He dropped her hand. "It's a long story," he said in a tone so filled with bitterness she was sorry she had asked.

"So you got over the amnesia," she prompted, wanting to hear the rest of his story and why her brother and his friends might be in danger.

"Somewhat," he said, taking another bite of potato. "I remember most everything except the explosion and a couple of weeks afterward."

''That was a long time ago. Why does it matter now?''

''The ringleader of the terrorists escaped the blast, but I'm sure he doesn't want me to live—I'm the witness who can identify him if I can just remember what went down. My memory is gone. No one knows when it might fully return. If it does, I may also know enough to identify a double agent who was involved. *Someone* tipped the terrorists about our plan to rescue the hostage, who was a U.S. agent. There's a good chance the spy was one of our own men and he wants me dead.''

''How do you know a double agent was involved?''

''Someone had that meeting set up to kill us and the hostage. If we had all gone in together as we'd originally planned, they would've succeeded. Someone arranged things a little too well—it had to be an inside job.''

She shivered. ''That's dreadful. Someone you worked with set all of you up?''

''Right. The CIA suspect they have a double agent high up in the ranks. Secrets are getting out that have hurt them. Men like us have been killed because their cover has been blown.''

''That's dreadful, but if my brother and Mike and Jonah weren't there with you and the hostage, why are *they* in danger?''

''For that, we need to go back to when I was injured. After the explosion, I was in a foreign hospital for over a year. It was a while before I knew who I was.''

''You were an American. Didn't they try to contact someone about you?'' she asked.

He stopped to take a long drink of beer, wiping his mouth and eating a bite of roast. After a moment he continued. ''When I began to remember enough to know who I was, I contacted—'' He stopped abruptly and looked away. A muscle worked in his jaw and she realized he still was emotionally entangled in the memories of his past.

She was uneasy, a chilling fear growing that even though he didn't want to bring trouble to them, he had. But maybe, as he was trying to tell her, the trouble was already here and his news would help alert Boone, Jonah and Mike.

Colin was silent so long, she wondered if he had forgotten what he was saying. "You said you contacted—whom?" she prompted him. "The army?"

"No. Danielle, my fiancée. She was my first thought when I regained my memory. I thought if I could just reconnect with her, I'd be okay. But she had gotten married. The hostage exchange was to take place in one of those obscure Eastern European countries near Russia. I was brought into the hospital with no identification and no memory. Since I could speak fluent Russian and no authorities or military were looking for me, I was pretty unimportant. Those people had their own civil war going on and there was so much unrest and turmoil going on that I was hardly worth any interest at the time," Colin said quietly between clenched teeth. He had stopped eating and was staring into space again. "After that I didn't care then whether I lived or not. Nothing made sense. To most of the world, my family, my friends, the army, I was dead. So, as far as I was concerned, I was dead."

"That's terrible! Colin, your family was so hurt. They were at Mike's wedding and they were still grieving."

"I know and I regret their hurt. I was in and out of surgery, had to go to therapy, had setbacks. Then, because of the political situation, I was put into prison. I didn't care and wanted to die."

"Things went from bad to worse for you!" she exclaimed, knowing how tough all four men were and amazed that Colin had succumbed to grief. Then she realized how vulnerable he would have been with a memory loss and injuries and on medications and totally cut off from family and friends. "I'm sorry."

"No need for you to be sorry. You had nothing to do with any of what happened. I finally managed to contact the military. They got me out of there and to a hospital on a U.S. base in Germany."

"Why didn't you contact your family at that time?"

"I hurt and didn't care to live, and for a time, didn't know whether or not I would survive. If I didn't get well, I didn't want my family to go through losing me twice. Maybe it was wrong, but my thinking was fuzzy. Half the time I was medicated too much to think clearly."

"So what happened?"

"Once the military got into it, things changed. I got good medical care and had a lot of reconstructive surgery. Actually, they did a fair job on my face. They had to rebuild my cheekbones and my jaw and my nose."

"They did a great job. You don't have any visible scars on your face at all." Isabella reached out and touched the tips of her fingers to his cheek. "Actually, you're still a very good-looking guy," she said lightly.

He focused on her to the extent that she wished she hadn't admitted the last. That she hadn't touched him.

"Thank you," he replied. "I suspect you're saying that because I'm Boone's buddy and you've known me forever. But that's all right."

Isabella had been talking with him not quite an hour, yet she could see he had become bitter, cynical and hard. She was saddened by his words, because even in this brief time, she could tell that Colin was not the man she'd once known. She remembered that day at the fair. Boone had ridden the roller coaster with Vince while Colin had ridden with her. Colin had been a fun-loving, carefree, easygoing man who'd always laughed a lot and made the others with him laugh. Now he wouldn't even smile.

"Go on, Colin. Finish your story," she said, dropping her hand back to her lap and sipping her tea.

"The military wanted me to keep my survival quiet, even from my family. Special Forces started me working again on ferreting out the CIA double agent. I was flown to Langley and looked at pictures of everyone in the agency, studied their whereabouts at the time of the explosion, talked to psychiatrists. Doctors did all sorts of things to trigger my memory. Most of it gradually returned. Everything in my life except the explosion and about a month afterward. To this day I don't remember the blast. When, and if, my memory does return, it might not help. On the other hand, I may have seen something that would help identify the spy."

"So where do Boone, Mike and Jonah fit into this?"

Colin finished eating and pushed back his chair. She stood to remove his plate and clear the table.

"Sit down, Isabella. I'll help in a minute."

She sat again. "Go ahead with your story."

"Not long ago, I was in Virginia. Someone tried to run me down. They came close enough to put me back into the hospital with bruises. Someone was trying to kill me, which meant whoever the double agent in the agency was, knew about me. That knowledge narrowed the possibilities. He knew I was still alive. We assume he was bound to know that my best buddies were Mike, Boone and Jonah."

"So they think you might have let your friends know what you knew."

"Possibly. They obviously don't know enough to act on their knowledge or they would have already. As long as no one knew I was alive—including my family and friends—then they were safe. But now someone knows Mike, Boone and Jonah might have information that will help me trigger my memory. It's a long shot, but not out of the question. And the person involved is desperate. To try to run me down when I was with an agent is the act of someone on the edge, determined to get rid of me. I was fine being dead, if it meant everyone else was safe. But now someone knows.

And I've got to see if I can remember what happened before my family is put in danger.''

"So that's why you're here," she said, thinking about the danger the men could be in. As well as their families just for being with them.

"I'm sorry if I've frightened you. You may want to pack and get out of your brother's guest house for a time,'' Colin said.

Isabella shook her head. "Don't be silly, I'm not any more afraid than Boone will be. If there's danger, I'll be careful.''

"The men may not be in danger, but we don't know. I want to warn them in case they are.''

"What about your family?''

"I've contacted my family twice since then. The first time was right after Mike's wedding. But they were never involved in my work and seeing them didn't help my memory lapse. I was with them only briefly.''

"They have to be overjoyed you're alive.''

"Yeah, but I don't want to bring danger down on them needlessly. The last time I saw them, I slipped in and out the way I hoped to do here. I'm hoping my parents are in less danger because they weren't part of my military life. But I can't risk staying with them, risking my family. I've been away from home a long time. In my adult life, I've been with Boone, Mike and Jonah more than with my parents and being with them may trigger that last bit of lost memory.''

"I hope for your sake, seeing your friends does jog your memory.''

"The person after me is desperate. Agents have been killed because of this spy. I want to catch him.''

Once again a chill slithered down her middle. "I guess you need to see my brother and the others. I think I can safely say they're in for a shock.''

"Thanks for letting me sleep here tonight," Colin said.

She merely nodded, thinking about the gaps in his story. "It's been five years. That's a long time."

"Little things trigger bits of memory. If I can recall what happened in that house and who I saw, I might be able to end this whole thing and stop running. Also, my enemies may suspect these guys here know more than they actually do."

"So you avoid phones, a paper trail, all that stuff."

"Every bit of 'that stuff,'" he agreed.

"Let me pick up a little," she said, rising and gathering up dishes. "If you want, we can go sit in the other room to talk."

"Sure. It's good to see you again, Isabella," he replied, standing and gathering the rest of the dishes to help her. "In fact, it was downright agreeable after the first ten minutes."

"Well, what were you expecting when you broke into a house?"

"I expected to find Mike and to talk to him and leave. But then, life is always full of unexpected twists and turns."

They cleaned together, restoring order to the kitchen, and then Isabella motioned toward a door. "Let's sit in the family room."

When he walked beside her, she was conscious of how tall he was. "So where do you go from here?"

"You don't want to know. It's better if no one knows."

"Do you trust anyone?" she asked, wondering about his solitary life. He was ruggedly appealing with dark, brooding, craggy looks. What was it about him, she wondered, that attracted her? When they looked at each other or barely touched, sparks all but danced in the air. She couldn't understand the unwanted, volatile chemistry between them. He was not the man to take home to the family.

Not in the next hundred years. He was solitary, dangerous, in trouble, cynical, brooding, hurt. Everything undesirable, yet when he had held her close in his arms to try to stop her attack, she had felt an electrifying charge that she couldn't recall experiencing with a man before.

Now, as she strolled beside him, she tried to focus on what he was saying to her.

"I trust Mike, Boone and Jonah. For their own sakes, there are things I won't tell them, because they're better off not knowing."

"Do the doctors ever think your memory will fully return?"

"They don't know. But they didn't know about some things that have already happened," he said.

She gazed at his full lower lip, the slightly full upper lip, a sensuous mouth. Unbidden images of his mouth on hers had her pulse beating faster. She tried to stop unwanted thoughts and to concentrate on their conversation.

As she switched on a light in the family room, he paused to look at the room. Trying to see it through his eyes, she also glanced around at the cozy room with its leather furniture and huge fireplace, thick, patterned area rug and mahogany furniture.

"Mike's mansion is elegant," Colin said. "I'm pleased for him. I hope he's happy."

"He and Savannah seem blissful, and they love little Jessie."

"I'm glad for him and the life he's found here." Colin sat in a winged chair and Isabella sat in a corner of the brown sofa, tucking her legs beneath her. When he stretched out his long legs, her gaze drifted down the length of him and then up again to find him watching her.

While a blush heated her cheeks, she was at a loss for conversation.

"Bring me up to date about my friends, Isabella," Colin said. "I have only sketchy information."

"Okay, Mike has a security business, and Savannah still practices law although she's home a lot with Jessie. Jonah inherited a cattle ranch and he and Kate live there," Isabella replied, but her thoughts were more on Colin.

"I heard Jonah has a son."

"That's right, Henry. And another baby on the way."

"So he and Kate got back together. Miracles never cease. I suppose the bone of contention between them is gone since he's out of the service. What about your brother?"

"Boone just married Erin, the manager of the horse ranch that he inherited."

"All the guys are married," Colin said, once more bitterness clearly filled his voice. "And you're not. So what do you do, little sis?"

"I'm a photographer. I have a shop in Stallion Pass."

"Do you enjoy it?"

"I love it. As a matter of fact, why don't you let me photograph you, Colin. You have an interesting face."

He shook his head. "If I didn't know you were Isabella, I'd be highly suspect of your request."

"You have an interesting face," she protested.

"That's the first time I've ever been told that. I'm sorry, but no, I don't let anyone take pictures of me. Too dangerous to have them around. I don't want anyone who's looking for me to pick up my trail."

"What if I take a few pictures of you and keep them to myself until this is over?"

He locked his hands behind his head. "It may not be over for years."

"Then I'll keep your pictures hidden. Let me take them. You'll be a grand subject."

"Sorry, Isabella, but the answer remains no. Photograph Jonah or Mike."

"I have pictures of all of them already."

"My answer is still no."

"Let me know if you change your mind," she said, certain that he would.

"You're a bit stubborn, aren't you?"

"No more than you are," she replied easily.

"Tell me about your life, Isabella," he said. Every time he pronounced her name, it sounded different from when anyone else said it. Everything about Colin was unique. Sympathy created a strong tie to him. Also, was she empathetic just because she had known him for years and remembered who he had been?

She did know he held a dazzling appeal for her, and he must have felt something, too. She had glimpsed his reactions, heard his voice drop to a husky note. But Colin was the last man on earth she would want to find captivating. He was hard, cynical and cold. She was appalled and saddened that he hadn't seen more of his family or let them know sooner that he was alive. Still, she could remember Colin as the happy person he had once been. His harshness was easier to understand when she considered the trauma he had experienced.

No matter what the reason, it was an incredible loss and waste for him to give up on life. She looked at his thickly lashed, smoky eyes. They were startlingly pale and intense against his dark looks. Locks of black hair fell over his forehead. He was thin, the hollows in his cheeks dark shadows beneath the prominent bones. He was ruggedly handsome and she knew he would photograph spectacularly. In a picture, the brooding look in his eyes would tell its own story.

"Remember when you rode the roller coaster with me?" she asked, wishing she could get a smile out of him.

One dark eyebrow climbed and he stared at her. "I sort of recall that day. Don't be insulted, but that wasn't high on my list of unforgettable moments. You were a skinny little girl. How old are you now, Isabella? Seems like you ought to be about nineteen, but I guess that's not right.''

She laughed. ''Don't you know you're not supposed to ask a woman her age? But then, to you, I don't qualify as a woman. You still see a skinny kid.''

''No,'' he answered solemnly, giving her one of those somber looks that stole her breath, ''you definitely qualify as a woman, Isabella.'' He stood and moved to the sofa beside her and leaned forward to take her braid in his hand. ''A very beautiful woman,'' he said in a husky voice.

She couldn't move or take her breath. How could he have such an effect on her when he neither intended it nor cared and it was unwanted on her part?

''I know you're a hell of a lot younger than I am.'' He began to unfasten her braid. ''Your hair is long. Let's see it out of that braid.''

She felt faint tugs against her scalp as she watched his hands at work. He had well-shaped fingers, thick wrists, strong-looking hands. Tiny scars spread across the backs of his hands and wrists and upper arms. He had pushed up the long, black sleeves of his knit shirt and his forearms were sprinkled with short black hairs.

He smelled soapy and clean. He glanced up at her and met her gaze and tension running between them jumped another notch.

''You shouldn't have to run all your life,'' she said.

''I don't intend to,'' he replied grimly, giving her a hard look. She wondered to what lengths he would go to stop the killer. ''If I can't get my memory back, there are places in the world where a person can go and live and never see another living soul.''

''You weren't meant for that kind of life, Colin!'' she exclaimed. ''What a waste that would be! You can't become a recluse.''

''Being a hermit isn't a bad life.''

"To never love someone else, never have a family—"

"I don't see *you* with a family. Are you in love with someone?"

Startled, she blinked at him and was mildly annoyed. "No, but I'm out in the world and I enjoy people, and someday in the future I might have a family. Even if I don't, I have a full, active life. I'm not hiding from the world."

"I'm not exactly going to hide from the world, just from a killer," he said as if explaining the situation to a child. He shot her a dark look and she knew she had touched raw nerves and hurt him.

"Colin, I just remember how friendly you were. I'm prying and being as pesky as a little sister, I guess." She smiled at him and he touched the corner of her mouth, a touch that sent fiery tingles to the center of her being.

"Your intentions are good, but you know the old saying about hell being paved with them. Watch out, Isabella. I'm not a lost cause you need to save. I know what I want."

He finished unbraiding her hair and began to comb his fingers through the long locks that fell to her waist. Her straight hair now held slight waves from being plaited for hours. He caught up a handful and rubbed the strands across his cheek. "You have beautiful hair."

"Thank you," she whispered. He'd leaned close enough that she could see the faint dark stubble on his jaw. His short hair was thick, an unruly tangle above his forehead.

"So tell me about your life. What have you done since that roller coaster ride?"

"I went to the University of Southern California on a scholarship and got into photography and found my field. By my senior year I was making so much money with my photography that I dropped out of college."

"You must be good at picture-taking."

"Good enough," she answered in amusement. "After another couple of years I had my own business, and it's grown.

Then when Boone settled here and liked it so much, he talked me into moving my business to Stallion Pass. Photography is something you can do anywhere, and a lot of people come into Stallion Pass for one reason or another. In a lot of ways it's like a resort town.''

"So where is the romance in your life?''

"At the moment it's nonexistent.''

"Which I find surprising. All right, who was there, and why is he gone?''

"There was someone a while back, but he wanted to get serious and I didn't. I'm not ready for marriage.''

"Why not?''

"My business. Right now that's more important. It won't always be, but it is now.''

"Well, maybe you just haven't met the right guy.''

If he weren't so solemn, she would think he was teasing her, but he looked incapable of teasing anyone.

"Maybe I haven't.''

"Any other guy, any other time?''

"In college—same deal. He wanted to get married and I didn't. I have my plans for my business.''

"Sorry I won't be around long enough to see some of your photographs.''

"Well, you can see at least one or two because I've taken some of Mike's little girl, Jessie.'' She was aware Colin still toyed with her hair, combing it through his fingers, letting it slip over his hand. "Colin, why didn't you go into the witness protection program?'' she asked. "You could have had a new life that would be almost like normal.''

"The killer is someone high up in the Agency. He would know where I am and who I was. I can handle a solitary life and I won't have to worry about what's behind the next tree or around the next bend. Or have government agents constantly after me to do something. I've served my time with the government and I want to end it soon.''

"Living in solitude for the rest of your life is like a prison sentence," she argued, hating to see him give up on life.

"Solitude isn't always bad. So what do you take pictures of?" he asked, turning the conversation away from himself.

"People, mostly. I do all sorts of portraits. A lot of babies and little children, newborns. I do weddings. I like it all. I had one assignment with a national magazine that took me to Patagonia and I loved it. I've had some showings of my photographs in galleries."

"So, where are you building this house of yours?"

"Near this one. I'll live close by. I bought an old house and had it torn down and I'm rebuilding what I want."

"You wasted a house?"

"I didn't want it, but I like the location and there aren't any more lots available right around here."

She heard the hall clock chime and then, an hour later, she heard it chime again. She liked talking to Colin, yet the whole time, she still felt an underlying sadness over the changes in him and the life he led. When the clock chimed three, she noticed the time.

"It's getting late. Let's go find you a bedroom. I need to go to bed. Jessie is up about seven in the morning. She won't care what time I went to sleep." Isabella stood. "So how safe are we tonight? We don't have an alarm now, and one pane is out of one of the windows."

"I'll stay down here and guard you," Colin decided. "I left a backpack outside behind the bush by the window. I'll go out and get it."

"Let me get it for you," Isabella suggested. "You tell me where you put it, and that way you won't be outside where anyone can see you."

He nodded and led the way to the room where he'd entered the house. He pointed at the bush. "My backpack is there."

"I'll get it. I'll have to call someone to come out and fix the alarm tomorrow."

"Mike needs to get a different type of alarm. A lot of men can do exactly what I did. It was almost as easy as walking through the front door."

"I wonder if that's true at Boone's and Jonah's," she mused.

"At least they're out on ranches. That's more challenging, but not impossible to break into. Wouldn't hurt for all of them to take a close look at their security."

"I'll get your backpack." She raised the window and put her leg over the sill.

"What are you doing?" he asked.

"Going out the way you came in. It'll be easier." She slipped outside and dropped to the ground, retrieving the backpack and turning to hand it to him through the open window. He reached down to lift her inside, his hands picking her up under her arms. She placed her hands on his forearms and felt the muscles knot.

He swung her inside with ease and set her on her feet, looking down at her. They stood in the darkened room. Her eyes had adjusted to the dark and she was certain his had, also.

"You're as light as a feather," he said.

She didn't want to move away, her hands still resting on his arms. His hands slipped down to her waist. She wondered how long since he had kissed a woman. Was he going to kiss her now?

Chapter 3

He stepped back, inches farther from her. "You've got your life, Isabella, and I have mine. Don't conjure up things that aren't there."

"You're scared to let go and live again. Talk about waste—"

"I'm not complicating my life or yours anymore than I already have," he said, and she knew she should leave him alone.

Wordlessly, she moved away and he picked up his backpack.

"You know where the bathroom is. I'll show you one of the downstairs bedrooms. We should be safe."

"I agree. But I'll still sleep on the sofa. I'm a light sleeper."

She led him to a bedroom and switched on a small lamp. The four-poster was covered in white eyelet and she couldn't imagine Colin in the fancy bed. And she knew she shouldn't try. She eyed the backpack. "Those are your things?"

"I travel lightly," he said. "Clothes wash and I don't need much to get along."

"I think there are clothes here, and Mike probably has some that would fit you. You're thinner, but about his height. There may be a robe in that closet."

"I don't need a robe," he said. "I'm all right. Go to sleep and don't worry. I'll hear anything that's amiss."

"Well, if someone breaks in, don't be so polite this time. You hit the intruder."

"Now wouldn't that have been terrible if I had hauled off and struck you?"

"Me, yes. Someone breaking in here, no."

"Don't worry. It won't be anyone friendly coming after me, and I won't hesitate," he said, touching her hair. The light was a soft glow and they were standing close. Once again, her heart began a drumroll. His smoky eyes darkened as he stood looking at her.

She tilted her head to study him and touched his jaw lightly. "You should live where there are people who care about you, get back your old life."

"Never." He shook his head. "I won't go through that pain twice in my life and I won't ever trust a woman with my heart again, not after Danielle," he said harshly, his gray eyes growing glacial.

"Half the world takes love lightly," she said in exasperation, wishing she could reach him. "People marry and divorce with tears shed and short-term pain. You four guys fall in love with someone and it's a forever deal. Jonah didn't want to live without Kate. He didn't date. He was bitter. Now you're the same way, torn apart over your fiancée after all this time."

"You've never been in love, Isabella, not really in love. Those guys who wanted to marry you and you didn't want to, you weren't in love. You don't know what it's like. And it is a forever thing. One love, always."

"If it had been a 'forever thing,' for your sweetheart, she wouldn't have married someone else. Get over Danielle, Colin. It was over for her a long time ago. Life is wonderful and people are marvelous and caring and exciting. Stop trying to be the walking dead and come back into life." Isabella knew she should stop, but this was probably the last time she would be alone with Colin. Tomorrow morning she would be busy with Jessie. Then she expected Colin to be with Mike and the other guys and then gone forever.

"I'll bet you've never been a coward about anything else in your life," she said. "But you're scared to live."

"You're scared to love!" he snapped back, a muscle twitching in his jaw.

She blinked and then stared hard at him. Slowly she shook her head. "No, I'm not," she said. She stepped close, wrapped her arms around his neck, stood on tiptoe and kissed him.

Stunned, he was caught off guard as much as he had been the first few seconds he had accosted her in the dark hallway when he'd broken in. When her tongue slid over his, his insides clenched, his heart thudded and he came to life.

His arm banded her waist. Standing in the middle of an inferno could not heat him more. Holding her tightly in his embrace, he leaned over her while he kissed her in return. She wouldn't call him scared again.

The desire was like an explosion. Something he hadn't felt in so long, it shocked him. His body had been as numb as his heart. But he was coming back to life in a rush.

Passion raged like a roaring bonfire. His heart thudded and he ran his hand down her back, over her buttocks, pulling her up tightly against him as he kissed her long and thoroughly.

Anger, lust, a staggering hunger for her mouth rocked him and he poured himself into kisses that were the first real ones in too long to remember. Her kisses were hot and sweet and unbearable torment.

Then he remembered that he was holding Boone's sister in his arms.

Colin raised his head, gazing down at her as she opened her eyes. Fire burned in depths of blue, accelerating his pulse. It was an effort to release her. Her lips were red, her long hair cascaded around her face and over her shoulders. Her nipples pushed against the tight T-shirt and her breathing was as ragged as his as they stared at each other.

"You're off limits." His voice grated. "I haven't—" He broke off his words.

"I shouldn't have pushed you, Colin," she said. Her eyes were huge. "Just don't let go of life. You are much too wonderful to do that." She turned and left the room, and he watched her go. His pulse pounded. He had not kissed a woman since Danielle.

He hadn't felt alive since that explosion, but he had drifted through pain and daily living, not caring if he was numb to everything, not caring if he was only half alive and in danger or about anything else that came his way. Only this past year had he decided he wanted out of Washington, away from the military and all authorities. He wanted peace and quiet, and a simple life. He didn't want to hurt his family further or to bring danger to them.

The last thing he'd planned to do before going into his isolation was to warn his buddies of the danger they might be in.

Now he was on fire with longing he hadn't felt in years. This kid sister of Boone's had stormed into his body, making his heart pound harder, awakening him to needs that he thought were dead and over. Little Izzie. But she wasn't "little" Izzie any longer. She was a beautiful, desirable, stubborn woman.

He didn't want to be on fire with longing. He didn't want to think about her kiss that had all but melted his insides.

But Colin suspected he wasn't going to be able to forget her kiss anytime in the near future. He wiped a hand across his mouth, wishing he could erase her kiss, wishing they hadn't goaded each other into such a heated confrontation.

She was like a miniature tiger. There should have been warning signs. Do Not Surprise Or Taunt. Big blue eyes and hair in a pigtail. Deal With At Your Own Risk. She should have been sweet and pleasant and afraid of him as most young women were.

Maybe that gutsy daredevil blood in Boone ran in his whole family. Boone. Isabella was his kid sister. "Just keep reminding yourself," Colin whispered to himself. He needed to keep his hands off Boone's sister. He would never have thought this would be a problem.

Instead it was a monumental dilemma—one that kept his pulse racing even now, long after she had sashayed out of the room with that sexy walk of hers.

He groaned, raked his fingers through his hair, then rubbed his knee. His old injuries were acting up after the earlier struggle with Isabella. But he also ached in places he hadn't hurt in years. And the desire, hot and elemental, angered him.

She had brought him back into life like igniting a fire— Could he put out the flames? Could he go back as he had been, numb, unemotional, not caring? He swore under his breath and walked through the downstairs of Mike's mansion.

Colin switched off lights until the entire lower floor was bathed in darkness. His eyes adjusted, and he strode to the window he had broken, gazing outside. But his mind was still on Isabella and her kiss.

She was the first woman since Danielle to get through to him. He didn't want Isabella Devlin clouding his thinking or stirring him to yearnings he thought were long dead. He wouldn't be here long. He was here to pass on a warning and to vanish once more.

From what she had told him, she didn't know anything about love. She knew plenty about kissing. And fighting. And shocking him into awareness.

"Dammit, get out of my thoughts!" he whispered. Raking his fingers through his hair again, he remembered combing his hand through her long, silky hair. She had smelled delectable…tasted luscious…and he wanted to forget every second he'd spent with her tonight. He heard a thump overhead and looked up. Everything had to be all right.

Uneasy, he turned and went to the foot of the stairs. All was dark at the top and he climbed slowly, carefully, not making a sound. In seconds he could see the upstairs hall where one small wall lamp burned. Doors opened off the wide hallway in both directions. He knew there was a third floor to the mansion. He hadn't asked Isabella where she was sleeping.

He climbed a couple more steps and saw a door open a crack, light spilling out. He moved to the top of the stairs.

"Isabella?" he called quietly.

The door opened wider and she stepped into the hall. She was wearing a pale pink cotton nightgown and he could see her figure outlined through the backlighting from the bedroom. He inhaled deeply.

"Are you all right?" he asked, unable to prevent the husky note in his voice.

"I'm fine," she replied, sounding puzzled. "Did something disturb you?"

Before he could answer, a baby started crying and Isabella hurried to the room next to hers, opening a door. He walked down the hall, every step telling himself to turn around and go back downstairs, to keep distance between himself and Boone's sister.

He paused in the open doorway. She was holding a little girl in her arms. The baby's arm was around Isabella's neck as she tried to comfort the crying child.

As she patted the little girl's back, the child stopped crying and snuggled closer to Isabella. Isabella turned around and her eyes widened.

"Is she all right?" he asked.

"She's fine. She'll go back to sleep. This is Jessie. Jessie, love," she said softly, "this is— What rank are you, Colin? The last I heard was Colonel Garrick."

"Colin is enough for a baby to deal with. She doesn't talk yet anyway, does she?"

"Yes, she talks," Isabella replied with a smile. "She has a limited vocabulary, but she talks. She's seventeen months old now."

Isabella looked beautiful in the nightgown, her hair tumbling over her shoulders, the baby in her arms. He was staring and had momentarily forgotten they had been talking.

"Did something disturb you?" she asked.

"I heard a thump," he replied, telling himself to leave her alone. Yet he could only stand and stare.

"We're fine. I dropped my book. Maybe you heard that." She looked down at Jessie who had gone back to sleep. "See, she's fine." She put the toddler back into the crib and turned to go. "She's gone back to sleep." She looked up at him. "Shall we go?"

The neck of the nightgown was high, but the top two buttons were unfastened and he couldn't keep from staring, wanting to reach out and push open the gown. It was cotton and opaque, covering her, but he knew there was nothing under it and he wanted to pull her into his arms.

He turned abruptly and left. "Just wanted to see that you were all right." He flung the words over his shoulder without looking back. He rushed down the stairs as if a demon were after him; he certainly felt as though one were. A devil of desire. Something he hadn't had to deal with in so long and that he didn't want to cope with now.

He stretched out on the sofa. While he had traveled across country for nights on end, he had been going with little sleep and catching it any way he could. Tonight, he had a plush, comfortable sofa and he should have been asleep immediately, but he knew that as long as images of Isabella tormented him, slumber would elude him.

He didn't want back into the land of the living. He put his hands behind his head, stared at a fixture and blanked out his mind as he had learned to do in prison. He repeated passages committed to memory, going over them without thinking, but keeping his mind blank until sleep overtook him.

Upstairs, Isabella sat in her darkened bedroom, her thoughts stormy as she went back over every minute of the evening.

And Colin's kiss. They had taunted each other. She shouldn't have said the things to him that she had, but she was disappointed with the man he had become. If he had been antisocial and mean, she would have left him alone about his future. But he'd once been so alive, the change seemed like a betrayal of the old Colin.

His plans for the rest of his days were grim. Going into seclusion. Giving up love and friends and family.

She touched her lips lightly, remembering his kiss again. She shouldn't have started that kiss, but what he had said had made her angry. And then after the first startled seconds, he had responded fully. As far as kisses went, his had been devastating. Just thinking about their kiss, she grew hot and ached to kiss him again. Something she couldn't do— shouldn't do—impossible.

He had come to life all right, kissing her senseless. Too vividly, she recalled each detail of his arms around her, holding her pressed tightly against him, his tongue stroking hers, his thick shaft pressing against her. And her heart pounding wildly, her breath gone, her pulse racing.

Tomorrow he would be gone forever. How long would she remember tonight?

She hurt for him and knew she shouldn't. She should let go worrying about Boone's friend. While she stared into the dark, all she could see were Colin's gray eyes and somber expression and remember how he had been a brave, idealistic man filled with vitality and enthusiasm. All of that was gone, and she could understand why from what he told her. He had mended physically, now he needed to mend emotionally.

"Right, Isabella," she said to herself. "Go save him from himself." She gave a harsh laugh. He was sexy, appealing and lost. And she wanted to save him. What a project!

The man didn't want to be saved and if she delved much deeper, she might find she had opened a Pandora's box of problems. Let him go tomorrow. Don't spend time with him. Leave him for Boone and Mike and Jonah to deal with. That's what he wants anyway.

Yet—she thought about his kiss and how full of vitality he once was. She inhaled deeply. Did she want to save him or to seduce him?

She shook her head. When had a man tangled her thoughts or her life as Colin Garrick had tonight? Never. Never once had she lost sleep over a man or argued with herself or done anything she was going through now. Even when she'd gone with Drake a year and he had proposed, she had never been tied in knots, never wanted to marry.

Forget Colin, she told herself. Blank Colonel Garrick out of mind and let him go. He's a wounded sparrow she was trying to save. Walk on by and ignore him. He doesn't want to be saved. And it wasn't "walk on by," it was "run for your life." He was a threat to her peace of mind.

She closed her eyes and gripped the arms of the chair and wished she could take back the best kiss of her life.

The very best. She inhaled deeply and wondered if she should go work out.

Reluctantly, she got up and dressed and went to the exercise room to pedal and jog, to banish the memory of Colin's searing kiss.

It was almost dawn when she fell asleep. Jessie's crying woke her and she went to pick up the baby and change her diaper. Then, slipping into a robe, she took Jessie to the kitchen to feed her.

When she entered the room, Colin was seated at the table. Seeing her, he stood with that lithe ease that indicated how strong and fit he was. Coffee was already brewing and he had made scrambled eggs and bacon. The orange juice was poured, toast buttered. Dressed in a T-shirt and jeans, he looked fit, tough and in prime condition. His black hair was combed back. Her heart thudded because all she could remember was standing in his embrace last night as he'd kissed her. And she realized she was only in her cotton gown and robe.

"I didn't know you'd be awake," she said, sounding ridiculous.

"I'm here and I can feed her while you eat, if you'd like."

"You feed her and I'll dress," Isabella said impulsively thrusting the child into his arms.

His eyebrows shot up as he surveyed Jessie. "Isabella, I don't know one thing about a baby. I'll feed her, but you need to show me what to feed her and how to do it."

"It's easy. She loves oatmeal and milk and the oatmeal is in the cabinet," Isabella instructed before she fled the room to get dressed. Let him cope with little Jessie. If he was a colonel, he was up to the task of getting breakfast for a baby. He needed a baby in his arms. Who could turn his back on life after dealing with Jessie?

She showered and dressed in jeans and a T-shirt and took her time brushing her hair and pulling on boots, wondering how Colin was getting along with little Jessie. Isabella hadn't heard any screams coming from the kitchen.

Finally she returned to the kitchen.

She had to smother a laugh. Jessie was in her high chair and she had oatmeal all over her face and in her fists and her hair. And Colin had oatmeal in his hair, too, on his shirt and face.

"How's breakfast?" she asked, holding back laughter. Colin turned to look at her and narrowed his eyes.

"You come finish this. I told you I don't know one damn thing about a baby. I think she's had about two bites of oatmeal and you can see where the rest went. Dammit, I don't have many changes of clothing."

"There's a washing machine and, as you said, clothes will wash," she said blithely, getting a wet paper towel to clean Jessie. She turned around as Colin stood and pulled off his T-shirt. His muscled body was lean and fit, but scars covered his back and ran across his shoulders, chest and arms.

Her breath caught in her throat; the scars didn't change his appeal one bit. They did remind her of what Colin had gone through, how the years had changed him.

"I told you they had to put me all back together," he said when he turned around and caught her staring.

She looked up and met his gaze. "If you think I'm staring because you have scars, think again," she whispered. The air crackled with searing heat as his eyes darkened and he inhaled deeply.

"I wouldn't have admitted that to you except you have a very mistaken notion about your appearance," she added.

Feeling as if her face were on fire from embarrassment

over her admission, she moved to the chair to finish feeding Jessie. Colin stood in her peripheral vision and she knew he hadn't moved, but she couldn't face him.

"If I weren't covered with oatmeal—" He broke off his sentence and left the room in long strides.

She closed her eyes and let out her breath. She fed Jessie, relieved the minute Jessie finished and she could clean the toddler's face and hands and escape from the kitchen before Colin returned.

Isabella bathed and dressed Jessie in a pink jumper and shirt, carrying her to the nursery and sitting on the floor to play with her, leaving Colin to entertain himself. If she had just looked away, she wouldn't have had to explain herself. But she hadn't, and that was that.

"I wondered where you two had gone."

She turned to see Colin in the doorway, dressed in clean jeans and a T-shirt, leaning one shoulder against the jamb. He held his oatmeal-covered clothing balled in his hand. "Where's the washer?"

"Come join us," she said while Jessie clapped her hands and held her arms out to him.

Isabella pointed. "Right through that door in the utility room. As soon as you put your clothes in to wash, come join us. Jessie likes you," she said, and he shook his head.

"I don't know why," he said upon his return. "Unless she hopes to throw some more oatmeal my way." He didn't make a move to pick up Jessie and she lost interest in him, turning to play with a ball that was in front of her. He looked around the pink nursery and then back at Isabella.

"You look like you belong in here."

"I should. I've been dealing with little brothers and sisters all my life."

He crossed the room to pick up a picture of Mike, Savannah and Jessie. "I like this picture. Cute family."

"Thank you for the first. I took the picture."

His eyebrows arched and he looked back at the picture again. "You're talented."

"I wish you would reconsider and let me take your picture."

He turned and shook his head. "Nope. I'd make a poor subject."

She nodded because she could understand his reluctance. She raised her head when she heard a car. Instantly, Colin moved to the window. "What kind of car does Mike drive?"

"They've taken the sports car. It's green."

"That's him," Colin said.

"Want me to go break the news that you're here? He'll be a little shocked if you meet him at the door."

"Mike can stand shock. *You* did without batting an eye."

"Come on, sweetie," she said to Jessie. "Mommy and Daddy are home. Let's go see them."

Jessie laughed, repeating Mama and Dada as Isabella carried her downstairs.

"It was interesting Isabella, seeing you again," Colin said, falling into step beside her. "I won't forget you."

She glanced up at him. "I won't forget you, either, Colin. I think I remembered you better anyway, than you did me." His gaze lowered to her mouth and her pulse jumped. Was he remembering their fiery kiss? She was and she could barely get her breath. In just minutes he would be busy with Mike and then he'd be gone forever.

Another twinge of sadness gripped her because it seemed such a waste for him to go off to some remote corner of the world to live.

He made his own choices, she reminded herself. He was no part of her life and she shouldn't worry or care what he did. He certainly wouldn't give a thought to anything she was going to do with her future.

"You're certain you don't want me to tell him?" she

asked again. "After all, everyone thinks you're dead. And you are buddies."

She gazed into his smoky eyes. They were so striking and unforgettable. Too much about him was unforgettable.

His lips firmed while he mulled over her question. "You may be right. Go ahead and break the news. I'll wait in the living room."

He turned and was gone. He moved with the silence and ease of a cat. She shifted Jessie in her arms and went to the kitchen to wait.

She could see the Remingtons heading toward the house and thought they were a striking-looking couple because Savannah was as blond as Mike was dark with his tanned skin and black hair. He was loaded down with bags and boxes and Savannah carried a few boxes, as well.

Isabella hurried to hold the door open, then followed them into the kitchen.

As they walked into the room, Jessie squealed with joy and held out her arms.

Dressed in yellow slacks and a matching yellow silk blouse, Savannah had her blond hair fastened behind her head. She looked beautiful and immaculate, too much so to have a baby in her arms. Regardless she caught up Jessie to hug her, eagerly fussing over her and laughing with the baby. Tall, black-haired Mike set down his armload of boxes and packages and bags. His brown-eyed gaze was friendly as he smiled at Isabella.

"We're here to rescue you. Bet you were counting the minutes."

"No, I wasn't," Isabella said. "Jessie's a delight and no trouble at all. Did you have a pleasant trip?"

"We had a great time," Mike said. He flung a broad-brimmed Western hat on a hook and shed a jacket. He wore jeans and a plaid shirt and radiated vitality. Smiling, he turned to take Jessie from Savannah to hug his little girl.

"How's my baby?" he asked, nuzzling her and making her squeal with laughter as she grabbed fistfuls of his hair. "We brought you something," he said, looking at the pile of luggage and bags and sacks and boxes he had carried inside and dropped by the door. He picked up a present wrapped in pink paper. "Just for you, Jessie, darlin'," he said.

Jessie grabbed the present and began to eat the paper. Laughing, Savannah took the present from Jessie. "Set her down and show her how to open it."

"And here's something for you, Isabella," Savannah said, handing a gift to Isabella.

"Thank you, but you shouldn't have," Isabella replied, taking a beautifully wrapped box of silver paper with pink roses and tied with silver ribbons. "Before I open this, there's something you two should know."

Both of them looked at her with curiosity in their gazes.

"Mike, you're in for a big surprise," Isabella said solemnly. "There's an old friend here to see you. I thought I should tell you before you saw him."

"This sounds interesting," Mike said, glancing beyond Isabella and then looking back at her again with a curious expression. "So who is he and where is he and why the fanfare before I see him?"

"Because you don't know he's alive. Everyone thought he was dead," Isabella said quietly, knowing from Mike's expression that Colin had entered the room.

"Colin!" Mike blinked and his mouth dropped open and he paled. "Colin?" The two men crossed the room in long strides and hugged each other.

They stepped apart. "I can't believe it!" Mike exclaimed, placing his hands on his hips. "You're alive and well. Damn! What the hell happened? Why didn't you let us know? Where have you been?"

"Mike!" Savannah exclaimed. "Give him a chance."

"This calls for a celebration," Mike said. "Damn, I can't believe it," he repeated, clasping Colin on the shoulder. "You're real."

"I'm very real," Colin replied.

"I keep expecting you to disappear and just be a figment of my imagination."

"No vanishing act here," Colin said.

"Let's celebrate!" Mike exclaimed, grinning broadly. "This is fantastic! Do the others know?"

"No. I wanted to see you first," Colin replied solemnly.

"I'm glad you did." Isabella could see Mike studying Colin and she could see some of the sparkle go out of Mike's eyes and concern replace it. Then Mike smiled and brightened.

"We're going to celebrate right now!"

"It's early in the day," Colin remarked. "We might wait—"

"Let's break out the champagne now," Mike decided. He looked at Savannah and put his arm around her. "Savannah, this is Colin Garrick. Colin meet Savannah."

"I'm so happy to meet you," Savannah said, extending her hand to shake hands with Colin. "Mike has told me a lot about you and about the times the two of you had together when you were growing up."

"This is our baby, Jessie, whom you've already met," Mike added.

"She's cute, Mike, but I can't imagine you a daddy."

"I'll get the champagne," Savannah offered.

When she left the room, Mike looked at Colin again. Impulsively, Mike stepped close and hugged Colin. "Damn. What happened, Colin?" He stepped away and placed his hands on his hips. "I can't tell you how much I've missed you. I'm glad to see you alive—but when that bomb went off we thought you were done for. I want to hear all about

it, but let's get the champagne. Should I call the others now
or later?''

"A little later. Let's talk first, Mike."

Mike seemed to remember Isabella and he glanced at her.
"You remember Izzie. This is great! When did you get
here?"

"Last night," Colin answered.

Mike's gaze ran over him. "What happened to you? You
look like you were in a cat fight."

"Sort of. I surprised Isabella."

When Mike threw back his head and laughed, Colin
merely shook his head and shrugged. Mike's eyes twinkled.
"So all those tricks Boone taught you really work?"

"They seemed to," she said.

"Have you gotten out of practice!" Mike exclaimed.

"Don't underestimate her. Boone taught her well."

Mike laughed. "I know Boone did. I've watched the
workouts."

Savannah returned with a bottle of champagne and
handed it to Mike to open. As Savannah picked up Jessie
to hold her, Mike poured glasses of champagne and passed
each person one. "Let's take these drinks to the family room
where we can sit and talk."

As soon as they were in the family room, Mike turned
and raised his glass in a toast. "Here's to Colin. Our sur-
vivor," he said.

"To Colin," Savannah added.

"To Colin," Isabella said quietly, and Colin looked at
her before they all clinked their glasses together lightly.

"Thank you all," Colin replied gruffly, a muscle working
in his jaw.

Isabella could see that he was struggling with his emotions. She sipped the pale liquid, feeling bubbles tickle
her nose.

"To life and Colin being back in the land of the living," Mike said, giving another toast.

They all touched glasses again and everyone sipped the champagne before setting down glasses.

"Sit, so we can talk," Mike suggested.

"I'll be right back. We need a little change here," Savannah said, taking Jessie and leaving the room.

"I'll leave you two," Isabella started to say, but Mike motioned to her.

"Sit down and join us. Savannah will be back. Come on, Izzie, we're all family."

She sat on a straight-backed chair as Mike sat on the sofa and Colin on a brown leather chair.

"Before you start, should I call the guys so you only have to tell this once?"

"No," Colin replied solemnly. "I wanted to talk to you first, but whatever we do, you can't phone them and tell them. These phones could be tapped and cell phones can be easily monitored. You'll have to get them over here for another reason. Besides, your lines are cut. I disengaged the alarm system and came in through a window. I just wanted to make certain I wasn't being followed and I could watch my back better by sneaking around late at night."

"So that's when you encountered Izzie."

"Right. I'm in hiding, Mike. I'm on the run and there's a killer after me," Colin explained.

"Go ahead and tell me about it," Mike said, crossing one long leg over the other.

Isabella listened again, watching Colin and still amazed that he was alive, just as shocked by her reaction to him. She wished she could go back and see him as she had that afternoon at the fair, just as one of her brother's friends, pleasant to be with, but just another man—who looked old to her at the time. She couldn't view him with that casual response now. He was ruggedly handsome and something in him made her want to try to reach him, to find the carefree man he once had been.

Every time she thought about him going into seclusion in some wilderness and shutting himself off from people and real living, it saddened her.

Forget it. He's doing what he wants and you can't save him, she told herself.

He glanced at her and then back to Mike. "The military asked five of us—and, with one exception, we don't know each other's identities—to work in a stealthy, covert group to try to catch the spy. I know one because at one point I worked with him. Brett Hamilton."

Mike shook his head. "Not anyone I ever knew."

"When I insisted on getting out of the military, my superior asked me to continue in the operation awhile longer," Colin explained. "They gave me a contract," Colin revealed, telling Mike something that he had not told her.

Isabella was shocked by this new information because she hadn't expected to hear that the military had wanted to keep him on in that manner.

"There is someone in the military who knows where I am now."

"Adam Kowalski?" Mike guessed.

Colin nodded. "Adam—you're on the mark."

"Kowalski is a reliable man. I can imagine either Adam or perhaps Mason VanDoren, one of the other officers we've worked with, on this case. What about Peter Fremont?"

"Our old friend with the agency," Colin replied.

Isabella remembered meeting the friendly, tall blond Fremont when he had been in Special Forces with Boone. She also recalled meeting Mason VanDoren years ago.

"I report to Adam. And I've worked closely with Peter—he's the one who pushed to get me to join the agency when I got out of the military. Even he doesn't know that I'm going through Stallion Pass."

Mike stood. "I think it's time for the next step in this operation."

Isabella watched him and wondered if another change was about to come into her life.

Chapter 4

"Let's get Boone and Jonah over here," Mike said. "I can call them on my cell phone. I think they might as well hear this now."

"I can call my brother if it would help," Isabella offered. Mike nodded.

"Tell him to bring Erin and I'll tell Jonah to bring his family—we'll throw steaks on and have a party. You can tell them I want to celebrate an investigation that I just closed."

"Did you close one?" Colin asked.

"Yep. I did, so if anyone checks out my story, it'll hold."

Isabella left the room to get her cell phone to call Boone. She went back to thrust her head into the family room. Mike and Colin were talking in low voices. "Boone and Erin are coming," she said and left to find Savannah who was in the kitchen, feeding Jessie.

"Did they run you off?" Savannah asked.

"No. I just thought they ought to be alone. Do you know you're going to have a houseful of company soon?"

"I'm not surprised. I'm sure the guys want to get to-gether.

"Right," Isabella replied. "Mike said to ask the families, so Erin and Kate and Henry are coming."

"Great! That'll be fun," Savannah said. "I'll get Jessie fed and cleaned up and then I can enjoy everyone."

"I can feed her if you want to do anything else."

"Sure. If you don't mind," Savannah said, giving the small spoon to Isabella who took Savannah's seat.

Over two hours later, after they had finished eating, they all sat in the family room while Henry played a game and Jessie dozed in Mike's arms. All through dinner the men had reminisced about good times. While most events they discussed had been comical, Isabella knew they were avoid-ing the scary and painful memories.

Mike stood. "We enjoy the wonderful company, I think it's time that Jonah, Boone and I have a chat with Colin. So if y'all will excuse us, we'll adjourn to the library."

With jokes about happy to be rid of the men, the four friends left. At the door Colin glanced over his shoulder to meet Isabella's gaze. Taking a deep breath, he turned and followed Mike to the library.

As soon as all four men entered the room, Mike closed the door. Colin looked at titles of books on the shelves, seeing many familiar ones, having buried himself in books and reading a lot of the time when he had been recuperating from his wounds.

They sat and Mike gazed expectantly at him. "Okay, Co-lin, level with us. What's up and what kind of danger are we in?"

Colin spent the next thirty minutes covering the time since the blast during the aborted mission until the current moment. When he finished, he looked somberly at his friends.

"I hope none of you is in any danger. I had also hoped seeing you might trigger my memory, but so far, it hasn't. That doesn't mean it won't."

"So you're leaving here to go to some remote spot and stay in isolation?" Boone asked with a frown.

"Don't tell me it's no way to live. I've heard that enough from your sister. I can slip out of here in the dark and be far away before dawn. You guys, just take care of yourselves and be aware there may be danger."

"I have a better idea," Mike said and all turned to him. "Stay here. Let's see if your presence draws our enemy to Texas. There are four—"

"No way!" Colin exclaimed. "I won't deliberately put y'all in danger."

"We may be in a lot of danger anyway whether you go and we never see you again or if you remain in Texas. Just listen, Colin," Mike urged. "You may draw your enemy here. None of us will be absolutely safe until he's caught, so let's flush him out. If we do, you won't have to turn into a hermit and never see any of us again or any of us ever see you."

"Yeah, that's a hell of a lot better," Jonah said.

"I agree," Boone added quickly. "I'm all for drawing him into the open."

"No damn way!" Colin snapped, standing and glaring at his friends. "You have a baby," he said to Mike. "You have Henry and another one on the way," he reminded Jonah. "Erin is expecting. No, no and double-damn no! I'm not putting little babies and kids into any extra jeopardy."

"Calm down. You can stay with Izzie," Boone suggested.

"And put *her* in danger?" Colin snapped, jamming his hands into his pockets.

Mike and Boone laughed. "Look at you!" Boone exclaimed. "Izzie isn't afraid, and she can take care of herself. She'll agree with our plan to use you as bait."

"Izzie'll protect you," Mike said with laughter in his voice.

"You won't have to be scared of a thing with her around," Boone added quickly, his eyes twinkling with amusement that Colin couldn't share.

"Y'all are hopeless! Listen, she can protect herself fairly well, but you know and I know that this is someone deadly and in earnest. And if I hadn't minded hurting a woman, you also know that I would have won the fight with Isabella."

"Well, you did a damn poor job of protecting yourself," Boone teased. "Why didn't you just draw your gun and stop her before she made hamburger of you?"

Colin glared at Boone. "You guys get on out of here."

"Why didn't you draw your gun?" Mike asked, studying Colin as he slapped his knee and guffawed. "She got your pistol, didn't she?"

"Go to hell, Mike," Colin said, shaking his head while Mike and Boone laughed. Sitting down again, Colin looked at Jonah, who was staring solemnly at him. "You're not laughing with them. You think I should go, don't you?"

"Not at all," Jonah answered quietly and the laughter died. "I think Mike's right. You should stay. Hopefully, we can entice our enemy to Texas and end this. I'm just thinking about the danger. In all fairness to Isabella, I think we should get her in here and ask her. She may not want him to be with her," Jonah said to the others.

"You're right," Mike said. "Boone, get your sister in here."

"I can answer for her—"

"No, you can't," Colin insisted, crossing the room and yanking open the door to the hall.

The moment he was gone Jonah crossed the room in long strides and closed the door. "I don't think she'll want him."

"She's not going to be afraid," Boone said. "But Izzie is full of life. She may not want to put up with Colin's gloom. He's pretty down right now, although she's a sucker for lost kittens and stray dogs."

"Look again," Jonah remarked dryly. "She's your sister and you probably can't see anything, but sparks fly every time they look at each other."

Boone's eyebrows arched. "Izzie? I don't think so."

While the men talked, Colin strode down the hall to the family room and paused in the doorway. Isabella and the other women were laughing at something Jessie was doing. His heart clenched at the sight of Isabella. Her joy was infectious.

"Isabella, will you please join us for a few minutes?"

She stood and Colin forced himself to turn away instead of watching her and waiting to walk with her. In long strides, he went back to the library. When he entered the room, everyone turned to look quizzically at him.

"She's coming," he said, turning to see her enter the room.

All the men came to their feet and Isabella waved her hand. "Oh, please," she said, entering and closing the door. She crossed the room to sit across from Colin while the men sat.

"Izzie, we're trying to talk Colin into staying here," Boone said. "There are four of us to deal with the killer who may be after him."

"Sounds reasonable to me," Isabella replied, looking at Colin who looked too dangerous for many to want to tangle with him. A glacial chill glazed his gray eyes and made her wonder why they wanted her opinion.

"He won't stay with any of us because of the babies involved," Boone continued to explain.

''So you volunteered me,'' she said, unable to keep from laughing because she knew her brother well. ''Of course, he can live at the guest house with me,'' she answered with a lightness she didn't feel. Instead panic threatened while she avoided looking at Colin.

''I told you she wouldn't be afraid,'' Boone said to Colin.

''Not so damn fast,'' Colin snapped. ''Isabella, if I'm with you, I may bring trouble to your house and most likely, it'll put you at risk.''

''I'll have all of you here, and we'll reside on Boone's ranch,'' she replied, knowing that is what the men were thinking. ''It's an intelligent solution,'' she said, realizing it was an excellent ploy to tempt the killer into a situation where all four men could deal with him. But there was little wisdom in what she was doing.

The risk would be enormous to her heart. She had been with Colin only hours, not yet a full twenty-four, and the tension increased by the minute between them and…they had already kissed.

She looked into solemn gray eyes and wondered if he was thinking the same thing. She doubted it. The combustible chemistry probably meant little to him because he was still grieving over his ex-fiancée.

''It's all right for you to live in Boone's guest house,'' she said to Colin.

He clamped his jaw shut, looked at each one of them in turn and shook his head. ''I don't like it. I didn't come to bring trouble—I came to try to help, not complicate things further.''

''We wouldn't tell you to stay if we didn't want you,'' Jonah reassured him. ''I don't think any of us would be afraid to have you with us. You must have a single killer after you, not a group. With our training, we should be able to not only cope with the danger, but hopefully catch him if he comes to Texas. You need to stop running.''

Colin raked his fingers through his hair. "Thanks. I'll stay, but I'm protesting because I've got a gut feeling that danger isn't far behind me."

"We'll be ready," Mike vowed. "If we can catch the person responsible for that blast, it's worth the risk."

"You-all have families now," Colin reminded them grimly. "It's not like it was."

"We'll be careful," Jonah replied, looking at each person in the room. "We all agree that you should remain in Texas and maybe we can catch the killer. Leave the room, Colin, and we'll take a vote—and we'll include our wives and Izzie. If it's not unanimous to keep you with us, we'll tell you and you can go…. Izzie, would you get the wives? Colin can entertain the kids."

Colin held the door for her as they left the room.

Walking down the hall together, she could sense the tension in him. "I don't like this," he repeated.

"I agree with them and I suspect this vote will be unanimous. But if it isn't, then they'll tell you. You know you can count on each one of them to level with you."

He nodded, but a muscle worked in his jaw and his eyes were flintlike.

In minutes she returned to the library with the wives. As soon as everyone was seated, Mike explained the situation and told about Jonah's idea of a vote. She saw the look that Jonah and Kate exchanged and knew that their separation had been over Kate's dislike of Special Forces. She wondered if Kate would object to Colin remaining in Texas.

"Okay," Mike said. "Any questions before we vote?"

"I want to know if it is absolutely all right with Isabella for Colin to stay," Savannah said. "Isabella may be at the most risk of all."

"It's fine with me," Isabella replied. "I'll vote for him to remain here. We'll be on Boone and Erin's ranch and I think I'll be safe."

Savannah nodded and looked at Mike.

"Any other questions?" Mike asked. Everyone remained silent. "All right. How many think Colin should live at the Double T ranch?"

To Isabella's surprise, every hand in the room went up. Kate was as quick to vote yes as Jonah, but then Isabella recalled hearing about the incident when Kate and Henry had been kidnapped and Kate had pulverized the kidnapper. Her actions had led directly to his capture.

A foreboding gripped Isabella because she suspected her life was going to change. She wasn't frightened for her life—it was her heart that was at risk.

"That settles it," Jonah said. "Colin stays. You ladies better rescue him from Henry and Jessie. I don't think Colin knows much about little kids."

The women left the room and Isabella was the first to enter the family room where Colin sat rocking Jessie while Henry leaned on his knee and looked at a book Colin held open.

Colin glanced up and arched his eyebrow. "What's the verdict?"

"You're going to live at the ranch with me," she said. "It was unanimous."

When he closed his eyes as if in pain, she wondered what was running through his thoughts. Henry asked him a question that she couldn't hear. Colin bent his head over the book to tell Henry about the story.

Kate entered and crossed the room. "I can take Jessie and I can read to Henry."

"I'll finish this story," Colin said, glancing beyond Kate at Isabella. "Tell them I'll be there in a minute, please."

She nodded and left, still with a mixture of feelings churning in her. But beneath all the wariness and dread was a strong current of excitement. Colin was remaining in Texas. He was going to live at her house!

She thrust her head into the library. "He's reading to Henry. He said to tell you that he'll join you in a few minutes."

"Come in, Izzie," Boone said. "This concerns you, so you better be in on our plans. And you better start carrying a pistol in your purse. How long since your last target practice?"

"Last month," she replied and Boone nodded. "Better brush up. I don't think you should work late at your studio in Stallion Pass unless you have someone with you and all the shops around you are open. Make sure your alarm button works. Also, call me—or any of us—at the least suspicious thing."

She nodded, already knowing what to do, but knowing Boone would feel better if he could go over the precautions with her.

Soon Colin joined them, closing the door behind him.

"It was a unanimous vote," Mike said. "You stay in Texas."

"So I heard," Colin replied with a note of resignation in his voice. "Y'all are crazy, but I yield to the majority. Now, I hope everyone will be extra vigilant because we may be stirring up a storm of trouble."

Mike nodded. "Let's plan what we do if our enemy does make it to Texas. Also, should we let the military and the agency know you're here?"

Colin stared at his hands, then looked up. "I'll let Adam Kowalski know first because I report to him. I'll see how he wants to handle it. I stay in touch with him. He'll want to let the Agency know because that's where our man works. We just can't discern which agent it is. This should flush him into the open, but he'll be dangerous. So far, he's been clever enough to avoid not only capture, but also detection."

While the men made plans and developed codes, Isabella sat quietly.

"Izzie has all our cell numbers," Boone said to Colin. "You can get them from her."

Finally she left them, knowing they would continue to plan, but she felt she was no longer needed. When Isabella entered the family room, Erin glanced up.

"They're still at it?"

"They'll probably plan for another hour," Isabella said.

"If you want to come live at our house at any time, you're welcome to," Erin said. "Or if you want to send Colin to stay with us, I won't mind."

"I'll be okay," Isabella said. "But thanks," she said, grateful once again that Erin had entered Boone's life. He had settled more than Isabella had ever thought would be possible and she already loved Erin and considered her a wonderful person. It amazed Isabella to think of Boone as a daddy, and she was thrilled for him. Her playboy brother had finally grown up and seemed devoted to his wife.

Henry had fallen asleep, curled on the sofa with his head in Kate's lap. Savannah had long ago put Jessie to bed. The women talked for another hour before the men finally showed up and everyone began to gather their things to go.

When they were leaving, Mike walked Isabella and Colin to the car. He leaned down to the open window to speak to Colin.

"Don't hesitate to call if you need me. Either of you," he told them softly.

"Don't worry," Colin replied. "You know I'm still not happy about this arrangement."

"This is the only way to catch our killer," Mike replied, and then stepped back, standing in the darkness as the two of them drove away.

* * *

"If I bring trouble to any of you, I'll never forgive myself. This wasn't why I came to Texas." Colin still sounded unhappy.

"Colin, the vote was unanimous. Even Kate. Her hand went up as quickly as anyone's. No one hesitated or had reservations."

"Oh, hell," he exclaimed as if overwhelmed.

As they sped toward Boone and Erin's ranch, Colin turned away to look out the window at the darkness.

"My brother is calling an alarm company tomorrow to get new alarms installed," Isabella said.

"I don't know whether to become your bodyguard or to stay the hell away from you," Colin said tightly.

"I don't mind you being around, and I don't require a bodyguard," she assured him.

"You don't know what you're going to need. We're dealing with someone who's dangerous and diabolical. A person who's been operating as a double agent for years and getting away with it. That takes a lot of brains and guts."

"There are four of you—when the time comes, I think you'll be more than an adequate match."

Colin gritted his teeth. He hated the thought of bringing danger to his friends and their families, but Mike had made it clear that if Colin moved on, the friends would try to ferret out the double agent without him, which could be a lot worse.

Colin gazed into the darkness and felt as if he were rushing to disaster. Adding to his worries was Isabella. Yesterday he wouldn't have thought that would matter other than for concern about her safety, but now, after their kiss, it was a monumental problem. He had known her only twenty-four hours and she already had him tied in knots. How would he manage to keep his hands to himself when they would be living under the same roof?

He turned to watch her as she drove. The bright lights from the dash highlighted her features. Her lashes fluttered and he wondered if she was aware he was studying her. He reached out to take her braid in his hand.

"Mike will be over to see us tomorrow. He's going to personally oversee the safety for everyone's place, including the guest house where you and I will be."

"So you think that will protect us?" she asked with a smile. "How long did it take you to get into Mike's house—Mr. Security himself. He's the one who's in that business."

"All right. So it was an antiquated alarm system. Neither he nor Savannah thought they needed anything elaborate. It's a gated community in a small town where the crime rate is low."

"The only flaw with that argument is the past. Anything could come out of any of your pasts and that's the problem now—danger has crawled out of your earlier life."

"A new alarm system will be better than nothing. Are you being argumentative to get me riled up or just cussed ornery?"

She smiled again. "I suppose just cussed ornery. I wasn't trying to rile you up."

"I like it when you smile," he said, tracing his fingers down her cheek.

"I smile often enough. Far more than you, Colin. I don't think I've heard a laugh from you yet."

"I don't think there's been anything to laugh about so far. You're not like your brother."

She laughed. "I hope not! At least not as you knew him. Boone was wild. Erin has tamed him some."

"I wouldn't know about that."

They turned onto the county road and soon headlights shone on an ancient concrete bridge with a metal sign that proclaimed Badger Fork Creek. They sped across and he glanced over his shoulder, relieved to see the road behind them was empty.

* * *

In a small office in a busy city, a man carefully cleaned the barrel of the pistol. In minutes he placed the weapon on a scratched oak desk. The office was high enough above the city that traffic noise from the busy street was muted. Sunlight splashed through the double windows. With patience, the man put the weapon together and replaced it in a holster, carrying it across the room to slip it into a file drawer. Closing the drawer, he turned the lock and pocketed the key.

Walking to the window, the man gazed out over the city. Colin Garrick had to die and the sooner the better. No botched attempt on Garrick's life *this* time. He should have been killed years ago by that bomb, but he had survived. He had overcome prison, poor hospitals, that attempt on the beltway last year.

With mounting anger the man turned to a desk calendar, thumbing through it and gazing intently at the page with the coming year. Only two more years and he would retire a multimillionaire. For an instant he had a flicker of regret for what he had done, but then he thought about his Swiss bank account and the home he had in the south of France, the home in Colorado that was in another name. Swelling satisfaction replaced his regret.

Everyone was scrambling to earn money to be set for life. He didn't want to risk his life and give hour upon hour for a little-more-than-adequate pension at the end of some twenty years.

With the money he was amassing, when he retired from his present job, he would be able to live abroad however he pleased.

He thought about Colin Garrick and frowned. Two years until retirement— The man clenched his fist. With only two years to go, he didn't want to have any mishaps. Colin Garrick was the wild card and he must die. Where was he?

Gone to ground here in the beltway? Had he fled to Texas to see those friends of his and hide with them? Or perhaps he had left the country? The last thought sent a chill down the man's spine.

If Colin Garrick was out of the country, he would be damned difficult to find. Unless he surfaced in some of his old haunts in Europe. Garrick was too smart for that. Still, it wouldn't hurt to put out feelers.

"Take care," the man said out loud to himself, knowing if he started asking questions, he would put himself at risk. Where the hell is Garrick? It is time for him to die.

The man shook his head. He had come too far and was in too deep to lose everything now. If those Texans were in the way, they would have to go. At this point in his life, he knew he had nothing to lose by one more killing or even two or three more. And he had everything to gain.

First, find Colin Garrick and eliminate him.

Colin glimpsed houses and buildings in the distance, but they rounded a curve and the view was swallowed up in darkness until almost a mile later they topped a rise and he looked at Boone's mansion, the guest house, the homes of employees who lived on the ranch, the stables and outbuildings and bunkhouse.

"This is a regular city! That's Boone's home?"

"Yes. Rather impressive, isn't it?" Isabella asked, circling a sprawling ranch house built of weathered timbers. The guest house had a sloping roof, a wraparound porch, black-iron furniture on the porch and a tree-shaded yard fenced with white pickets.

The moment Colin and Isabella stepped out of the car and entered the backyard, five dogs of various sizes and breeds came bounding up. Isabella leaned over to scratch the ears of two of them. "Get down!" she said to the dogs. "These are my dogs. Tiger," she said, pointing to one that resembled a Doberman. "Buttermilk." She touched a dog that probably had golden retriever blood. Then she knelt and petted a bit of fluff as she said, "This is Sweetie. Here's Topper and Snarlie," she finished about two spotted hounds. "Wait a minute while I feed and water them."

"Not exactly watchdogs, are they?" Colin said, helping her when she turned on the hose to refill one of the buckets with fresh water.

"Two of these buckets refill automatically," she explained. "And they may not be watch dogs, but they'd bark if someone came into the yard."

"They didn't bark at me."

"You're with me. They know you're one of the good guys," she said lightly, but Colin didn't smile.

"So you like dogs," he said, trying to disentangle himself from them as she poured water into their buckets.

"Actually, they're all strays that didn't have a home," she said. Colin took the hose from her while she disappeared then came back with a bag of dog food to pour into empty bowls.

"So you've taken all these mutts in since you've been here?"

"People drop animals out in the country. They needed a home and someone to care for them."

She returned the dog food to a shed and joined him again. They crossed the yard, leaving the dogs behind. Reaching the back door, she unlocked it and led Colin inside.

He set his backpack inside the kitchen door of Isabella's temporary home. Cherrywood cabinets with yellow tile in the countertops and along the wall added a cheerful enough warmth to the room, but he was barely aware of his surroundings. He looked at the alarm box. "What's the combination?"

He stood close while she explained and told him the combination and the code.

"This has to go because it's antiquated—even more than Mike's. There's probably never been any need for security here before." Colin crossed the room to the windows where he closed the plantation-style shutters.

"We're far from the highway and far into the ranch. Boone's house is only a stone's throw away. I never worry about the shutters in here."

"Start worrying, Isabella," Colin ordered. "When you brought me home with you, you placed yourself in danger. I can feel it to my toes. I think the others do, too. If you want to back out, I can go to any of their houses. They'll understand."

"No. I'm not backing out," she said.

"We won't argue about it. Just be careful."

"I'll show you around and to a room you may have," she said, placing her purse in a chair at an oval table where a green-and-gold damask runner was centered with a vase of bright yellow daffodils. "We can adjust our schedules."

"There's no adjusting, Isabella. I'll stay out of your way. Just show me my room and I'll find my way around the house."

She shrugged as she led him out of the kitchen into a dining room that adjoined a large family room. In the dining room was an oval fruitwood table that would seat twelve. Along one wall stood a credenza that held a silver tea service, silver candelabra and glistening crystal vases. Above it hung a beveled mirror in an ornate gilt frame. In the mirror he could see the reflection of an adjoining room, a living area that held armchairs, a sofa and bookshelves.

"This is an elegant guest house."

"It's very comfortable. My furniture is in storage. This was furnished so it's been easy for me to move in here," she said, walking down a wide hallway. They passed a family room, a smaller dining room and a bedroom before she motioned toward an open door.

"There are three bedrooms, but only two have adjoining baths, so you'll probably want this room," she said, stepping inside a sunny bedroom aware he had withdrawn into himself and put an invisible wall between them.

"Fine," he said without looking around. He crossed the room to the window, closing the shutters. "Just go on with your life. I'll take care of myself."

In consternation she stared at his back. She hurt for him, hating to see him shut himself off from others. Yet she knew, this was best for both of them, because she didn't want the attraction to escalate and she knew he didn't, either.

"I'll get fresh towels for you and the bed has clean linens."

Going to a large bathroom down the hall, she gathered towels from a cabinet to take them back to him. Finding his door closed, she knocked lightly.

When he swung open the door, she sucked in a deep breath. He had shed his shirt and was wearing only jeans. He was lean, solid muscles and she couldn't keep her gaze from roaming over his chest. She thrust out the towels.

"Here are your clean towels. Anything else you need?"

"I want to check the place for security," he said as he took the towels from her, his fingers brushing hers. "Mind if I see your bedroom?"

"Of course not," she replied. "It's this way," she said, thinking he might as well have let her show him around the house as she'd offered in the first place.

"This is my room," she said, entering a bedroom that was next to his and ran along the south of the house. He crossed the room to close the shutters, checking windows and looking at the locks. "This house is about as secure as a tent."

As he passed her, she saw that he had a pistol tucked into the waist of his jeans at the small of his back and she wondered if she had entered into his world of espionage and threats.

She watched him move around her room. Muscles rippled in his back as he closed shutters. His jeans rode low on his narrow hips. His scars could not detract from his sexy appeal.

"I may sleep outside tonight," he said, turning to look at her and her pulse jumped. He was acting cold and aloof, but desire burned in the depths of his eyes.

"There's a dog run at the back of the yard if you want me to pen them up."

"Nope. They'll be all right."

"You weren't this concerned last night."

"Yes, I was. That's why I slept on the sofa downstairs. Mike's house is more protected than this one—I know it's because this is on the ranch that should be more secure than living in town. I think each day that passes, the likelihood of the killer finding me increases. It wouldn't take a rocket scientist to guess that I'd come to Texas where my friends are.

"Sleep with a cell phone by your bed tonight," he added. "Do you have any flashlights?"

"Yes," she said, turning to go to the hall closet to get a flashlight for him.

"Do you have another one?" he said as she turned. He was standing right behind her and again their fingers brushed as she handed him the flashlight. She felt a tingle from the slight contact.

"I have one in my room. I keep one by my bed in case of the power going off during a storm."

"Good. I want all the shutters closed. Anybody with high-powered binoculars can see a lot from a long distance and there's no need making things easy for the enemy."

"I'll close the shutters, but I'm not the target here," she pointed out.

"Not yet. I don't want you in danger."

"I'll be careful," she said and left him to close shutters all over the house.

She didn't know when he'd gone outside, but she did see the door to his room standing open.

She went to the back door and slipped outside, closing the door behind her.

"Are you all right?" she called softly, wanting to avoid saying his name.

"I'm fine," he said only feet from her, startling her. She turned and saw him in the dark shadows of the porch. The dogs had come the minute she'd opened the door and they milled around her now, wanting attention.

"Sure the dogs won't bother you?" she asked.

"I'm sure. Go inside. It's safer than having you stand out here."

She slipped back into the house and closed the door, wondering how much he would sleep. He couldn't have gotten a lot of sleep the night before. Stop worrying about him, she told herself, going to her room and closing the door.

They might be in danger, but she didn't feel any alarm or sense of threat. Colin was standing guard. Her brother was not far away and the ranch was full of men who would help if needed. She had a pistol, but she felt no need for it. Not here on the ranch.

The threat she needed to worry about, the one that was real and intense, was her attraction to Colin. In spite of Colin's surly manner and coldness, she could still feel the sparks fly between them and there was no way to forget his kiss.

From the desire she had seen in his gray eyes tonight, he hadn't forgotten their kiss, either. She changed into a nightgown, switched off the lights and climbed into bed, wondering how Colin was faring outside. Were they really in danger this soon? She had no doubt if he stayed danger would come, but had the killer already arrived in Texas? Was he watching Colin now?

Chapter 5

Colin stayed in the shadows. There were yard lights, but not enough. One more thing that needed to be changed, but he was certain Boone hadn't had a moment's reason to worry about security here at the ranch. Under normal circumstances, why would he?

Colin's gaze searched the grounds for anything amiss. He was uneasy, unhappy with the decision that he should stay in Texas. In a way, he would be glad for a showdown, but he wished it could come a million miles from his friends and their families. He didn't want to put anyone in danger and he was certain he had just brought trouble to Isabella.

His gaze dropped to the dogs surrounding him. He idly scratched the tallest one's head as the black dog sat leaning against him. He shook his head. All of them strays she had taken in. That meant she had a heart as soft as pudding. A bunch of friendly mutts that he suspected wouldn't even bark at a stranger. Since Isabella was a softie for strays, he shouldn't be staying with her. Yet she had said she had gone with guys who had wanted to get serious and she had broken it off, so maybe her softness was only skin deep.

He groaned, thinking about her softness—too clearly he could remember holding her in his arms as they had struggled and then later, holding her close as they had kissed. A kiss that had brought him slamming back to life with an incredible jolt. She was soft, warm, luscious curves— He inhaled deeply again and tried to shift his thoughts elsewhere.

In another half hour he moved to the porch hammock and stretched out. Instantly all the dogs tried to jump up and settle with him. The two smallest made it, but the big dogs set the hammock swinging, dumping Colin onto the floor. He swore softly and rolled to his feet, glaring at them.

"Get out of here, you mutts!" he whispered, but they merely looked at him and wagged their tails.

He sat on the hammock. "Down!" he ordered. Carefully, he eased himself back into the hammock. In minutes a small dog jumped up and curled into a ball at his feet. A few more minutes and another small dog jumped on him and curled up beside him.

"Oh, hell," Colin swore. He stood and went inside, locking the back door and moving through the darkened kitchen to the family room where he stretched on the sofa and placed his pistol beneath the pillow.

"Colin?"

He sat up, instantly alert, but also recognizing Isabella's voice. "Yes."

When she stepped into the doorway, he could see her dimly in the darkness. She wore a short nightgown and her hair spilled over her shoulders. His mouth went dry, his temperature soared and his imagination ran rampant.

"I heard someone in the house and figured it was you, but I also knew you intended to sleep outside. You're staying in here instead?"

"Yes, thanks to your dogs," he answered gruffly.

He thought he heard a laugh as she turned away. "Good night, Colin." Then she was gone, leaving him in more torment than the dogs had inflicted.

He slept lightly, stirring at the slightest sound, growing accustomed to the noises of her house—the ticking of the tall clock in the hallway, the chime of the clock on the hour. Twice during the night, he awoke and took his pistol in hand to patrol outside around the house, each time sending the dogs into a flurry of wagging tails. It seemed he had only dozed off when he came instantly awake.

He sat up and saw Isabella move past the doorway. A dim light showed around the edges of the shutters.

Yanking on his T-shirt and still wearing his jeans, he hurried after her and caught up with her as she switched on a small light over the stove in the kitchen.

"Aren't you up early?"

"Good morning to you, too," she said cheerfully, turning to face him. She wore blue denim shorts and blouse that hugged her curves. She looked fresh, alert and full of energy. She flashed him a smile that made his pulse jump.

"Do you always get up this early?"

"Yes," she answered. "Nearly every morning during the week, I jog four miles."

"You can't do that now. It won't be safe."

"Oh, yes, it will. There's an indoor track, too. I'll use it."

"Wait a minute or two and I'll go with you," he said, heading toward his bedroom to change.

He wanted to gnash his teeth. He needed to jog, too, to keep in shape, but he didn't want to do it with her. He needed to keep distance between them and it was absolutely impossible when they were under the same roof. He felt a need to keep her in sight. He knew she didn't want a bodyguard, but he thought she needed one now. At the same time, he knew he was the one causing her to require protection.

He changed to cutoffs and pulled on a clean T-shirt from the laundry he had done yesterday. He tucked his pistol into his cutoffs in the small of his back and went to join her.

She was singing softly, dancing around the kitchen, her hair caught up in a clip on her head, tendrils hanging loose and swinging as she danced. He clamped his jaw tightly closed and clenched his fists as his insides did their own clenching and tightening. His gaze skimmed down her shapely bare legs and his imagination ran wild. He wanted to cross the room, to take her into his arms and kiss her.

Instead he stayed where he was. "I'm ready," he said.

"Great!" She bestowed another brilliant smile on him and waltzed out of the kitchen ahead of him, pausing only a second to reset the alarm.

He left, hearing the lock click behind him. As they stepped out into the brisk morning, the dogs swarmed them and she paused to pet each one briefly before shooing them away. Colin looked at the yard and beyond, his gaze searching for anything amiss, but no one was in sight and the surroundings appeared peaceful.

As soon as the gate closed behind them, she began to jog. He joined her, clenching his teeth for a moment as pain from his stiff knee bothered him, but he soon worked it out.

The first rays of light bathed the world in gray. Dew was thick on the grass and a slight chill was in the fresh, clear air. Colin fell into step beside her, seeing the ranch for the first time in the daylight.

"I'd forgotten the wealth of John Frates. This is some spread," he said, looking at the stables and the houses, the corral and outside track. In the distance were gently rolling green hills with tall oaks and spring wildflowers. "And it's beautiful country."

"It is at that," she said. "Boone came to Texas intending

to sell the ranch. Instead, he fell in love with Erin and that was that. He's as rooted to this place as the trees are.''

"So maybe you'll fall in love with one of these Texans and take root yourself.''

"Nah, not me,'' she said as they jogged. He noticed she could keep up with his pace and she wasn't winded. He shouldn't have been surprised because he'd already had ample evidence that she was in excellent shape.

"I want to travel, to photograph people in other lands. I have a lot of plans for my photography. I've done a few freelance jobs for magazines and I liked it. I hope to get to do more.''

"You have a studio here now, you said.''

"I do, and I have a couple of people who work for me who can keep it open and going if I'm not here.''

"So when you move to town, are you taking the five dogs with you or is Boone taking them?''

"I hope to talk Boone into keeping them.'' She extended a slender arm, pointing to a large red-brick-and-wood arena. "The track is in that building. The arena was built for the horses, but if the weather is stormy, I run there in the mornings. No one uses it for the horses this early.''

They entered the large building and he looked at a state-of-the-art arena with its built-in seats. He whistled. "This can be used for shows.''

"And it is. Rodeos, bull-riding and barrel-racing events, barn dances, all sorts of entertainment. And besides training horses here, it makes a dandy place to run in foul weather. The track is a quarter of a mile around.''

They both paused to stretch and then began to jog. He wasn't going his fastest possible, but he was going fast enough for a brisk workout. She was still keeping up with him.

"You're pretty good at this.''

"I try. The last freelance assignment out of the country

was in Patagonia and it's rugged country. I was thankful for every workout I'd done. It wasn't a place for anybody who was out of shape.''

He remained silent, trying again to raise that wall between them. He didn't want to be chums with her. And as for being out of shape—the woman had the best shape he'd seen in a long, long time.

Isabella had filled his dreams last night, added to his sleeplessness—along with her mutts—and with a start, he realized she had been the first person on his mind this morning, although, he was certain, that was because of his being in her home.

She was the first woman he had responded to physically since Danielle—no denying that one. He hadn't wanted to live, hadn't even felt alive for years now and never thought he would see the day he didn't hurt over the loss of Danielle. But he had to admit that the pain from the separation had an edge taken from it. He glanced again at Isabella who was jogging beside him as if oblivious of his presence.

Clamping his jaw closed tightly, he tried to think about securing her house, making plans on how to deal with Washington. As soon as he returned from jogging, he intended to call the general to inform him of the plans. The military would be happy about him staying in Texas. There were only five of them in the group of this covert mission to find the double agent. And the five worked independently of each other, feeding information back to Adam Kowalski unless they were instructed to work together.

Colin jogged in silence until he and Isabella had covered three miles.

''I'm speeding up now,'' he said, stretching out his legs and knowing he should push to the limits of his ability for part of the distance. He sprinted ahead and then was aware that she must have speeded up, too, because she was not far behind him. The last quarter mile, he slowed his pace, gradually winding down and falling back into step with her as she slowed.

"That's a speedy run," he said.

"There's a workout room here, too. I do that for another half hour and then get ready to go into town to work," she said.

"I'll join you and see what equipment there is."

He wasn't surprised at the array of the best exercise equipment available. "The structures on this ranch look like they were built yesterday with millions spent on them."

"It wasn't yesterday, but Boone has instigated a lot of new building. They had old stables—one is still here—and they had a fire that scared them all, including Erin, so they began to rebuild. There is a lot of money generated here. This is a world-famous horse ranch."

"I'm glad for the guys. Everyone is together again and happily married with families or one on the way."

"Sure you don't want to stay and become a part of it?" she asked, smiling at him.

"I'm sure," he said curtly, knowing that wasn't the future for him. "I may change my plans if we can ferret out the double agent. At least I could stop running and watching my back each hour of every day."

"Lighten up, Colin," she said, placing her hand on his arm. Lightning shot through him at her touch.

"Watch out, Isabella. I'm not one of your strays, happy to be picked up."

She blinked and turned away. He swore silently at himself for being harsh with her, but it was that or something neither of them wanted. She was as friendly as those mutts of hers and if she wasn't careful, that friendliness was going to complicate their lives incredibly.

His acerbic reply ended conversation and for the next half hour each of them worked out. Yet as he hoisted himself on rings, he couldn't keep from watching her on the gym horse. She was an excellent athlete and he wondered if she had taken a lot of gymnastics. She worked the horse like a pro. She had well-toned arms and her legs captivated him as she swung them around and balanced herself. His gaze roamed over her trim bottom and his body reacted, tightening and growing hard with desire.

He flipped around so he wouldn't face her and began to exert himself, doing exercises where he knew he better concentrate totally or he was going to hurt himself.

Finally they both cooled down and, at the same time, started back for the house.

"Can we take time for target practice?" Colin asked. "Boone said there was a firing range here."

"Sure," she said and shook her head. "Follow me."

"Gladly," he said, eyeing her bottom again as she stepped ahead of him. She led him around the arena to a concrete block building behind it. The long, narrow building was built solely for target practice and it was well equipped.

She reached up on a ledge and got a key, unlocking a gun cabinet.

"That's got to go," Colin said.

"What? The key up here?"

"Sure. That's about as hard to figure as hanging it on the doorknob. Take it with you when we go and I'll tell Boone."

She nodded and opened the cabinet. "Take your pick."

He picked up a Glock and watched as she did the same. He was curious about her marksmanship and shortly he saw that it was excellent, just as he had expected.

They cut short the practice, cleaned the weapons and returned them to the cabinet to lock it up. Colin held out his hand and pocketed the key when she gave it to him.

The moment they stepped outside Colin gazed around them, making certain he didn't see anyone or anything dangerous. A cowboy was near the stables with a horse. When

Isabella waved to him and he returned the wave, Colin knew it was a friend.

The sun was up now, splashing warmth over them. The dew had long since disappeared and in the distance could be heard an engine from a pickup as someone drove across the ranch. A horse whinnied, somewhere in the distance a dog barked, all sounds that were safe and normal.

"That dog sounded far from the house."

"It isn't one of mine," she replied. "There are four other dogs on the ranch and they are watchdogs—well, three of them are. One is just like mine and the cowboys all baby him. But there are dogs that will bark at strangers. And they'll bark at you, so I hope you're with one of us when you see them."

"I'll take my chances," he said, mildly amused because dogs never worried him in spite of all his years of prowling around at night in his job.

"So dogs like you," she said, looking up at him.

"You sound surprised."

"Not really. Underneath all that numb oblivion to the world, Colin, I know there's the warm, friendly man I remember."

He inhaled swiftly. "Don't bank on that one. I told you, *that* Colin died."

She stepped in front of him, blocking his path. "I don't think so. When I kissed you, you were very much alive. You're just scared to come back to life, Colin. But you may have to in spite of yourself."

"You think you're going to save me just like you have those dogs, but it's not that simple."

"You're so wrapped up in yourself you can't see beyond your nose," she said quietly. "You're not a project in my life, Colin. I regret what's happened to you, but I've got my life and I'm not letting you pull me down into your dark

world.'' She glanced at her watch. ''I'm going to fix breakfast and go to work.''

She turned and sprinted ahead of him.

Stunned by her bluntness, he walked slowly toward the
house. He was torn by emotions evoked by her words. Was
he all wrapped up in himself? Probably. But he justified his
self-absorption because he'd had to be that way for years
just to get through surgeries, therapy and to survive.

Words or no words, just now there had been a challenge
and a clash of wills. In spite of her declarations that should
have meant there was a chasm between them, he knew the
mutual attraction leaped gaps and obstacles.

He watched her take the steps to the porch two at a time.
Her long legs were enticing. Every inch of her was alluring.

He grit his teeth and tried to ignore the thread of anger
that burned in him over her accusations. She was getting
under his skin in more ways than one.

''Dammit!'' he snapped, increasing his pace. She was going to Stallion Pass and, even though he should avoid her,
he wanted to go to town and he might as well ride in with
her. ''Yeah, right,'' he said out loud, annoyed with her and
with himself.

He hurried inside, glancing down the hall at her closed
bedroom door, trying to shut out images of her in the
shower.

He stripped and stepped into his shower, turning on the
cold water, swearing and shivering as it struck him, yet
knowing if it was ice, it wouldn't cool the hot thoughts of
Isabella that burned in his imagination.

Isabella showered and dried her hair, trying to keep her
mind blank, yet failing. Colin had scars all over his body,
but he was in prime condition and all lean, hard muscle,
impossible to ignore. She shouldn't have said what she had
to him, but impulsiveness constantly got her into trouble and

that probably wasn't going to change at this point in her life.

She had a soft spot for strays, men on the mend—she had to face that fact about herself. They were keeping a wall between them or, at least, he was. Her blast had momentarily demolished that wall, but then the shuttered look had come over his features and she'd known he had withdrawn into his shell.

"Leave the man alone," she told herself, brushing her hair vigorously as she dried it and then swiftly braided it, thinking about his hands in her hair when he had unbraided it that night.

She took a deep breath and slammed her brush down. She didn't want to spend every waking minute thinking about Colin. Didn't want to, but couldn't keep from it.

She rushed around getting dressed in red slacks and a red blouse, trying to look festive because she was going to have to deal with his brooding darkness.

When she entered the kitchen, he already had coffee made and orange juice poured and was scrambling eggs. Dressed in jeans and a black knit shirt, he looked his usual handsome, dangerous self. When she tried to ignore him, he turned to look at her. The moment their gazes met, her pulse jumped and overlooking him was out of the question.

"You look great," he said in a tone of voice that sounded as if he hated the fact that her appearance was pleasing.

"Thank you, Colin," she answered with a smile, feeling as if she were winning a clash of wills here because she suspected he wanted to forget her existence. If he was noticing her, though, it meant he wasn't dead to the world, after all. And that was an improvement. The minute the thought crossed her mind, she reminded herself that she was not on a save-a-soul mission with him. Stop being glad when he responds to you, she told herself.

"Want juice, toast and eggs?" he asked.

"Yes, please," she said, pulling out the toaster and putting slices of bread into it. "And thanks for cooking breakfast."

"Sure. I want to go to town. I want to see your studio and then I'm going to San Antonio to Mike's office."

"You might as well ride into Stallion Pass with me and then take my car on to San Antonio. I'm not going anywhere until closing time," she suggested, trying to ignore the flutters that the thought of being with him stirred.

"I want to make sure that your studio is as secure as possible. While I was dressing, Mike called. He wants me to come by to meet with him. Also, I want to find a pay phone and call Washington."

"From a pay phone?"

"That can't be tapped or traced if I make it quick."

She nodded, aware when she passed close to him of his clean, soapy smell.

"When is Mike coming out to check on my alarm system?"

"Late today. He said it would be after you get home. They'll install a new system tomorrow. I can stay here for that. He wants to check out your studio, too."

"I should be safe there. It's in a string of shops and I have an alarm button and my words are falling on deaf ears, aren't they?"

"Absolutely. Do you have a busy day ahead?" he asked as he stirred fluffy, yellow eggs.

"I have one appointment this morning at ten o'clock and then two appointments this afternoon."

"I'm surprised you're so busy in a town as small as Stallion Pass."

"I close the studio on Friday even though I often go in and work. And a lot of my business comes from out of town. My ten o'clock this morning is a family flying in from Houston. My one o'clock this afternoon is a woman and her baby from Dallas. A lot of people come from Austin and San Antonio and places that are close.''

"That's impressive," he said, staring at her. "You're amazing, Isabella."

"You're still thinking about a skinny kid in braces," she replied with laughter in her voice. "Otherwise, you wouldn't be so surprised that I have a profession at which I'm succeeding."

"Maybe so," he said, turning back to dish up the eggs.

In minutes they were seated across from each other. When their legs brushed, they both moved swiftly and apologized at the same time.

"Mike said to plan on lunch, so I'll eat with him. What do you do for lunch?"

"Sometimes take my lunch. Sometimes meet a friend. Sometimes order out. Today I take my lunch because of the one o'clock appointment."

"Mike said he'll meet us here later this afternoon."

"That's all right. How long before you think someone will track you to Texas and here to Stallion Pass?"

"It's an impossible guess. The killer could be in Texas now. He failed in one attempt on my life—two if you count the blast five years ago, but that wasn't aimed just at me. I know he'll be determined to avoid failure again."

"You keep saying 'he.' What makes you so certain it's not a woman double agent?"

Colin shrugged. "Odds are a man. It isn't a woman's style to try to kill somebody by running them down with a car."

"That's true," she said. She stood to get the coffee and refill their cups. "The eggs are yummy."

"I put a load of clothes in to wash. I have to keep washing because you know how little I brought with me."

She nodded and sat facing him again. In minutes they

finished and together they cleaned the kitchen and separated to get ready to leave the house.

As she gathered her things, she heard him call to her that he would meet her at the car.

When she stepped into the garage that adjoined the guest house, Colin was bent beneath the hood.

"What's wrong?"

"Absolutely nothing that I can find," he said, closing the hood. "I wanted to check it out."

"My car is in a locked garage."

"That's right, but if you think I couldn't get in here undetected, then think again." He held out his hand. "Let me start it."

"You can drive for all I care," she said, giving him the keys and aware when their fingers brushed.

"Do me a favor. Wait outside and away from the garage."

She realized he was concerned about a bomb. "Aren't you being overly cautious?"

He gave her a level look. "After having a brother—" he started but she waved her hand and interrupted him.

"You're right, Colin. I'll wait outside, but I don't like the idea of you starting the car."

"I won't unless I think it's clean."

She left the garage and went back through the house, resetting the alarm and going outside to wait. To her relief he backed out of the garage without incident and the door automatically closed and locked behind him.

For the first time, she could sit and watch him drive. She enjoyed herself, trying to avoid staring constantly at him. "There's a pay phone a block from my shop, out on the corner in front of a gas station."

He merely nodded, seeming preoccupied, and she wondered if he wanted her to stop chattering. "Are you going to let your family know where you are?"

He glanced at her and then back at the road. "I hadn't thought about it. I'm so accustomed to them not knowing where I am, that I didn't think about telling them. But if we're leaking it anyway, there's no reason for them not to know. I'll call my dad and tell him what's up."

"If someone wants to call you, how can they if you're only talking on pay phones?"

"It won't matter with my family because we won't be discussing anything that would cause any damage if the phone's tapped. My Washington contact will know to avoid a call and I'll check in often with him."

She nodded. "So how well do you know your way around Stallion Pass?" she asked as they entered the town and passed a sign that read Welcome To Stallion Pass, Texas. "Do I need to give you a tour?"

"No. I checked that out before I went to Mike's house." He glanced at her. "There's no one even trying to date you right now?" he asked.

"Nope. Getting ready to ask me out?" she teased.

He shot her a stormy look before he yanked his attention back to his driving.

She laughed. "Forget it, Colin! I couldn't resist. You're wound up so tight and sometimes I can't keep from teasing you. Remember, I grew up with Boone."

"You know, Isabella, what happens to people who play with fire?" Colin asked in a quiet voice that should have been a warning to her.

"My simple question wasn't playing with fire. You're surely not *that* touchy!"

"All right. I'll call your bluff." His smoke colored glance nailed her and her heart hammered.

Chapter 6

"Let's go to dinner tonight. We were going to eat together at your house anyway. So will you go out with me?"

The question hung in the air and her first reaction was regret that she hadn't kept her mouth shut and not taunted him. Then her confident nature asserted itself along with the nagging wish that he would come out of his funk.

"Yes, I'll go to dinner with you tonight."

She got another quick glance with a sardonic arch of his eyebrow. "You're not afraid of the person after me?"

"You'll be there to protect me," she replied.

"I suspect that you don't know what fear is, any more than your brother Boone does."

Without directions, Colin drove unerringly through town to her studio. She liked this town and enjoyed looking around. Boone had told her that Stallion Pass was the product of both old and new money and it showed in the fancy shops, elegant restaurants and numerous office buildings. A green, tree-shaded town square with a large three-tiered fountain gushing sparkling water was the center of the business district and her shop was on the west side of the square.

"You know the way," she said as they approached her place.

"I didn't know it belonged to you. I never connected it to a kid called Izzie when I saw the name of the studio while I was checking out the town."

She looked at her red-brick studio positioned in a line of shops. A green-and-white-striped awning stood above the plate-glass windows that displayed some of her photographs. An iron scroll-work sign gave the name. Portraits By Isabella.

"Just park in back," she instructed. He drove into an alley that had been decorated by the shop owners with striped awnings above doors and windows with potted plants by each door.

"Mighty fancy alley," Colin remarked.

"A lot of these shops on both streets that back up to this alley are artists, plus a florist and a bookstore, so they got together and agreed to keep the alley attractive."

"These were established before you moved back. How'd you get a shop in here?"

"Boone heard about it before it went on the market to be leased and that's when he talked me into moving here. He leased it before he had my agreement because he knew he could turn around and sublease it if I didn't come."

"The determined Devlins," Colin remarked. "Once your brother sinks his teeth into something, he doesn't let up, and I guess it runs in the family."

"Are you suggesting I've sunk my teeth into you?" she asked, unable to resist the opening even though she knew she was flirting with him when she had promised herself she would do no such thing.

He had opened the car door and been about to step out,

but he sat back inside the car and shut the door, turning to her, and her pulse jumped.

He slid one arm along the back of the seat and placed his other hand on her door, hemming her in, and her pulse revved even more. She was looking into his eyes and he was only inches away. His gaze was hot, intense and filled with desire.

"Isabella, you can sink your teeth into any part of me anytime you want to," he drawled in a husky voice.

"You know I was teasing you," she said, barely able to get the words out, locked into his gaze that held her totally.

"Aha! You started this. Getting cold feet?"

She raised her chin and narrowed her eyes while her pulse jumped higher. "No, I'm not," she replied, leaning forward to lightly catch his lower lip between her teeth.

Her heart thudded and her pulse roared and for an instant she wondered if he was going to remain immobile and unresponsive and embarrass her to death. Then his arms wrapped around her waist and his mouth covered hers, his tongue moving over hers as he kissed her hard.

Winding her arms around his neck, she kissed him, wanting to stir him out of that cold indifference, momentarily throwing caution to the wind.

She succeeded beyond her wildest dreams. He yanked her closer, leaning over her, kissing her until all thought evaporated. She was on fire, her insides melting while she clung to him and kissed him in return. One arm held her tightly as his other hand roamed down her front over her breast, sliding down across her thigh.

His kiss devoured her; the impact even stronger than the first time he had kissed her. She shook with need that flared to life. An ache started low inside her, building with each stroke of his tongue.

Her fingers played in his thick hair and she ran one hand across his broad shoulder. She longed to twist beneath him and thrust her hips against him, but the gearshift lay between them.

She kissed him in exultation. The man in her arms now was very much alive, filled with passion, driving her to a need she hadn't felt for a long time. Her body ached and perspiration dampened her skin where she felt the heat from his body.

They should not goad each other, yet how could she resist? And no way could she regret his fabulous kisses that tore her apart at the same time they made her want him desperately.

"You're very much alive, Colin," she whispered, brushing kisses to his ear to bite his earlobe gently and then lightly nip his neck. He leaned down, kissing her breast, his breath hot even through her blouse. And even through her clothing, the kiss made her almost faint.

She caught his head, yanking it up, and they looked at each other a moment. The clash of wills was tangible. His smoldering gaze held anger and desire, but her pulse leaped because his expression was passion-filled and he was very much turning into a warm, breathing human who wanted to kiss and to love instead of the cold, walking zombie she had first clashed with.

"You minx!" he said, holding her tightly before leaning down again to kiss her.

"Colin," she whispered, twisting away from him. "Stop. We're in a very public place—my alley where a lot of people come and go and it's definitely broad daylight and everyone around here knows me."

"You should have thought of that before you taunted me, Isabella," he said, bending his head to kiss her again, another fiery kiss that blew her thought processes into oblivion.

How long they kissed, she didn't know. But dimly, after due time, she knew she had to stop him. She pushed against a chest that felt like a slab of granite. Only this was Colin, flesh-and-blood male, warm, sculpted muscles, sexy.

He continued to devour her and she struggled to get her wits together and to have enough backbone to break away from his spectacular mouth.

This time she really pushed and he raised his head again. His gaze bore through her as he wrapped his hand in her pigtail and tilted her face up to his. "You goad and taunt, Isabella. Beware. You're doing this at your own risk."

"I can take care of myself." She flung the words at him, twisting quickly so her head was out of his grasp. She pushed against his chest. "And I think I proved my point," she said smugly. "Now you move away."

For the first time since his return, he looked as if amusement danced in his gray eyes, but she couldn't be sure. One dark eyebrow arched in that manner he had. "You're still saving strays and you think you'll put another notch in your belt with me."

"And you don't want to be saved, do you? You want to stay numb and dead, right? Well, I think you're coming back into it whether you want to or not," she told him triumphantly.

"And you're going to do your damnedest to get me there, aren't you?" he said, leaning closer and looking her directly in the eye.

"Maybe there are moments, but I know you're not my project and I don't have to save a soul here."

"I don't think I'm the only one with my heart locked away. The reasons are as different as day and night, but your heart is just as off limits as mine."

"That's not—" she started, but he cut her short.

"Isabella!" he drawled, his gaze piercing her.

She raised her chin. "Get out of the car."

This time she was certain she glimpsed a hint of a smile before he turned away. Since he had not smiled yet, she almost reached for his arm to yank him back to see if he was smiling, but she knew better. She needed to learn to leave him alone because he rose to every challenge and responded to each provoked taunt.

Was she really that big a sucker for strays and lost souls?

Climbing out of the car, she didn't want to answer her own question. He stood waiting at her back door. She noticed he hadn't come around to open her door for her, but she wouldn't have waited for him to do so anyway.

She unlocked the door and switched off the alarm while he stood close enough behind her that she could feel the warmth of his body.

"This alarm is better than the one at the ranch, but not good enough."

"I think it's just like all the others in the shops on the block."

"It can be changed." He moved through the supply room and into a hallway. He paused at the door of her office and stepped back to let her enter first. He followed, walking around the room with the ease and curiosity of a cat. "Nice office," he said, pausing to look at the pictures on the wall. He gazed at one she had taken of guanacos in Patagonia. He looked back at her. "These are spectacular pictures!"

"You sound surprised."

"I'm surprised. These are excellent. You've buried yourself in Stallion Pass. You should be working in New York or L.A."

"I left California to come here and this is just fine, thank you."

"You're excellent at this," Colin said, moving around the room to look at photographs. He strolled to stand in front of another wall of framed awards. "These are national and international awards, Isabella. I'm impressed."

"Thank you. It would be nicer if you didn't sound so

tremendously surprised as if you hadn't thought I could possibly be any good.''

"Don't get touchy. I just figured you would do those sweet sentimental shots that make people warm and fuzzy. These are fantastic.''

She felt warm and fuzzy with his praise because she knew he meant it.

"Make yourself at home,'' she told him. "I need to get the studio ready.''

She left him on his own, but she was aware whenever he was in the room with her or when she could see him. In the large reception area at the front of her shop, he moved around, looking at pictures on display. "These are really great. Every one of them.''

"I'm glad you think so. I'll tell Nick when he arrives because some of those are his photos. He's my other photographer. If I can't do pictures, he can. He's very good and I don't think he will work here long at all. Except he grew up on a ranch in this area and he likes Stallion Pass.''

"Nick…?''

"Nick Warner. He'll be here soon and you'll meet him.''

Colin continued to prowl the entire shop, including climbing into the unfinished attic that could only be reached by a small opening in one of the closets.

When he came down, she was in the hall. "What did you find up there besides wires, cobwebs and insulation?''

"Fire walls for one thing. Which is reassuring. No one can get into an attic at the end of the block and come all the way down here through attics.''

His remarks reminded her again of the danger and she knew she had to warn her employees or give them some time off. "Come meet Nick and Sandy. I'm going to have to explain you to them, but I'll do that later today. I've already told Nick a little on the phone this morning.''

Colin followed her to a room where a lean, muscular man was setting up lights.

"Nick, meet Colin Garrick. Colin, this is the photographer whose work you admired, Nick Warner."

"Your pictures are good," Colin said, shaking hands with Nick. "I'm sure you hear that a lot."

"Thanks. It's still nice to hear again. I'm getting ready for our first appointment."

"Go ahead. Don't let me interfere."

"We'll leave you, Nick. Come meet Sandy," Isabella said, turning to leave the room.

"Colin," Nick said and Colin turned back as Nick crossed the room to stand close.

"Isabella said there might be some danger. Someone is after you. I just wanted you to know that I have a pistol. I know how to use it and I keep it with me."

"That's unusual in a peaceful place like this."

"I grew up on a ranch and we have rattlesnakes. Then I served a brief stint in the military—Eighty-second Airborne."

"I feel better about leaving Isabella here. That's comforting news. Although she's capable of taking care of herself."

"That she is," Nick said with a grin that had Colin wondering how Nick knew she could protect herself. He could well imagine what would happen if someone surprised her at work when the studio was empty.

"Thanks for telling me. I don't want to put any of you in danger, but I think that's already happened even though I'm the one someone is after. Isabella really has no part in it except to be in the wrong place at the wrong time if something happens."

"I'll keep my eyes open."

Colin nodded and went down the hall to join Isabella.

Behind the reception desk was a smiling blond with big blue eyes.

"Sandy, this is Colin Garrick. Colin, this is my receptionist and secretary, Sandy Holcomb."

"Nice to meet you," he said and received another big smile.

"Thanks. Isabella said you're staying in Stallion Pass for a while."

"Yes, I am. It's a nice place." Colin chatted with her a few minutes and realized Isabella had left them. He told Sandy goodbye and wandered back to Isabella's office where he found her seated behind her desk. He paused in the doorway.

"I'm going to drive to San Antonio to Mike's office now. Want to eat lunch with us? We could drive back here and meet you"

"No, thanks. I have a busy schedule."

"I'm holding you to the dinner date tonight."

"I wouldn't think of breaking it," she told him coolly and once again was certain she saw a flare of amusement in his gray eyes.

"Just in case, promise you'll give me a call if any strangers show up. I'll feel better."

"Fine. But this is a photography studio and strangers do come in on a regular basis."

"Women and children are excluded."

She nodded. "I know what to look for."

"No, you don't. And neither do I, so just be careful. Is Nick here most of the time?"

"Yes, unless he's out with a customer. We take pictures in people's homes, in parks, wherever."

"Nick is reassuring, but take care," Colin said and left through the back door.

Isabella moved to the front to watch for him because the pay phone was on the opposite corner.

In minutes Colin strolled past, along with others out shopping and running morning errands. He stood out and she saw more than one female turn to stare at him after he had passed.

In his dark clothing with his rugged handsomeness and his height, there was no way he could blend into a crowd in Stallion Pass. Besides, the locals all knew each other.

She looked at the door of her shop. She hadn't unlocked and opened for business yet and even with Nick and Sandy here, she felt very much alone for the first time in this business. An uneasy feeling bothered her and she knew that Colin had brought danger to Texas.

Trouble was coming and it was just a matter of time. She thought about Boone. She didn't want her brother in danger. When he had gotten out of the service, she had been enormously relieved—to an extent that surprised herself because she always thought she had accepted his risky lifestyle. Now they were once again plunged into danger and she had voluntarily put herself in harm's way.

Colin stood at the corner and used the pay phone to make the call that would bring the killer to Texas.

In minutes he was through on the private line to his superior, General Adam Kowalski. "Sir, Blackthorn here," Colin said, using a code name.

"Where are you?" came the familiar deep voice.

"In the destination we discussed," Colin replied. "The men want me to stay here. I'm bait to lure our catch in."

"You want to do that?"

"They said with four of us, we should be able to get what we want."

Colin listened to the pause on the other end of the line and could imagine the tall, graying military man mulling over the setup and making his own judgments. "I'll ask again. Do you want to do that?"

"Yes. There are two pluses. Get what we want and my travels would end."

"Right. If I agree, then we need to leak word of what you're doing. Won't do much good if no one knows where you are."

"That's right. So go ahead and leak. We're ready."

"Good. I'll get word to the Agency and to the others here. At least to the ones I think should know. Hopefully, the word will reach the right ears. Anything you need or want?"

"No, sir. Not at this point. The guys are all still competent at what they've been trained to do."

"We better hope to hell they are. I think I'll send a man."

"I'll call in two days to check in with you."

"Fine. Watch yourself and your friends. It may get deadly."

Colin replaced the receiver, staring at the phone as the general's last words rang in his ears. *It may get deadly.*

"No kidding," Colin mumbled to himself. He felt exposed, standing on the street corner, talking into a pay phone, yet that was probably the safest way to make contact. Now everything had been set in motion. It was only a matter of time. Time and the killer.

Isabella pressed her nose against the door and looked up and down the street. A small percentage of people were already out. There would be more in another half hour. She could name most of the people she saw, but there were a few strangers, mostly couples that she would guess were tourists. To her relief, she didn't spot any single males who were strangers, but that could change as the day wore on.

Her Glock was in her purse and she knew Colin had a pistol strapped in a holster that he wore on his leg below his calf.

Her thoughts jumped to the kisses they had just shared and all sense of danger disappeared. She touched her lips lightly. She was playing with fire by teasing him or goading him into kisses or anything else personal, yet he was not as numb to the world—and to women—as he thought he was. And tonight she was going on a date with him. There was no other way to look at it. She glanced at her watch while she thought about what she wanted to wear. Nine hours and she would go out with Colin on their first date.

She watched him replace the receiver and turn from the pay phone to walk back to the alley to get her car.

As she made her way through her studio to her office, she heard the engine of her car start up and listened to him drive away. She touched her lips again, knowing she needed to get her mind on work and off of Colin.

Returning to Isabella's car, Colin left Stallion Pass. In minutes he was on the highway headed to San Antonio. It was only when he was almost in town that he figured out he was being followed.

Colin got off the Interstate earlier than he needed to. Watching in his rearview mirror, he spotted a black sedan leave the Interstate three cars behind him. It could be co-incidence. There were a lot of black sedans and Colin knew that one could easily be headed the same direction he was.

He drove down a busy street and turned onto a wide thoroughfare. For a few minutes he thought he had lost the car, but then he saw it more than a block behind him. He turned a corner and wound around a block, taking an alley and turning another direction.

He parked three blocks away from Mike's office and walked, pausing at shops to check out the crowd, finally deciding no one was following him.

Colin entered Mike's one-story building and told a smiling receptionist that he had an appointment to see Mike.

When Colin entered Mike's office, Mike came to his feet, walking around his desk to shake hands. Dressed in a tan sport shirt and chinos, Mike closed the door and motioned Colin to a leather chair.

"I think I was followed as I drove here," Colin said. "So our man must already be here."

Mike grinned and shook his head as he settled in a chair and turned to face Colin. "You were followed all right and Boone's face is red. He thinks he's getting rusty."

"Boone followed me? Why?"

"We agreed that we'd take shifts following you—and no arguments. You're the bait and this was our idea so we're going to try to protect you."

"So that was Boone." Colin shook his head. "And somebody will follow me home from here. Now how will I know whether the person tailing me is one of you—one of the good guys—or the bad guy?"

"Just keep on with what you're doing. You spot the tail, you lose the tail. If it's one of us, we'll find you. It won't work for us to check in with you or you with us because phones can be tapped and the cell phones are definitely out."

Colin nodded. "Fine. Now down to some nitty-gritty. The guest house at Boone's has a poor alarm system. It's worse than yours."

Mike nodded. "Figures. There never has been any reason for them to have a sophisticated alarm system before. I'll be out about four this afternoon to check on it. How's that?"

"Fine."

"We'll look it over, see what we need and go from there."

"The grounds need more lights. Also, I think Isabella's shop needs better security. She's put herself in harm's way and the person we're after has no regard for life."

"I'll make the appointment now to check her studio," Mike said and pulled out his cell phone to call her, setting an appointment for three that afternoon. When he snapped shut his phone, he turned to Colin. "That covers the security. What about Washington?"

"I called Washington this morning from a pay phone on the corner across from Isabella's studio. Mike, I told you that on this mission to find the double agent, I know the identity of only one other of our group—Brett Hamilton. They might send him out here."

"You should be able to trust him."

"If this agent has succeeded all these years, then he has to be high up and he has to be someone we all know," Colin said.

"Or at least a person some of us know. He knew about us and that mission that was a death trap," Mike added.

"I have the scars to prove that. He's deadly and he's gotten away with this for a long time now. I still don't like bringing trouble to all of you and I don't like Isabella mixed into it at all. She's an innocent in this."

"Izzie can take care of herself and you know it. She knows enough to be cautious, too. And to alert you if necessary. Is she worried?"

"No, she's not."

"There you are. Forget it. She's like Boone. They're daredevils, both of them."

"I can't help feeling this is a man I know well."

"It's not one of our bunch," Mike said. "I'd swear on that one."

"I know it's not one of you guys. We went through too much together and that bomb was intended for all of us. But whoever it is, he's more than an acquaintance, he's close and trusted."

Mike nodded. "After all you've told me, I agree. That's all the more reason to be careful. How long before the killer shows up in Texas?"

"The general will contact our liaison with the Agency. I

wouldn't be surprised if Peter Fremont may come to Texas himself. Probably he'll bring another man with him.''

''Do you think we can narrow the suspect to whoever comes to Texas?''

''I think the likelihood that the killer will come to Texas and make contact is, say, ninety percent. There's that other ten percent chance that it'll be an undercover operative who'll come out of the shadows and use the other guys as decoys. We have to be ready for anything.''

Mike nodded. ''I can't tell you how good it is to have you home.''

''Thanks. It's great to be here, except I hate bringing trouble and I'm sure that I am.''

''We're ready.''

''You know the unexpected always happens.''

Mike shrugged. ''We've been through this before. We can do it one more time.''

''I'm going to call my family this afternoon to tell them that I'm here and staying for a while. They don't have to know the particulars although I imagine they might guess.''

''Let me show you my office, introduce you to the people who work for me. Colin, I have a proposition that I want you to think about. When this is over, I'd like you to be a partner with me. We can incorporate. You'd be great in this business.''

''That's a really great offer,'' Colin replied in surprise. His first thought was of Isabella. If he accepted Mike's offer, he would be able to stay near her. Colin pushed the thought aside for now. Still, he was surprised and pleased by the offer. It had been a long time since he had thought of himself with a future. ''Thanks. I'll think about it.''

''I mean it. You're an expert at this. I do more corporate and electronic security than anything else. I'm getting more and more business. Savannah knows a lot of people in these parts so I hit the ground running and it's built steadily ever since I opened.''

"Mike, I can't think that far ahead right now. Let's get this other settled first."

"I've talked to the others and we need to get together again, so can we meet at Boone's tonight? You and I will be there anyway. He said to come on over, Isabella, too. He's already talked to her and told her this meeting is necessary. She said she would be there."

"I had something I was going to do."

"Put it off. This is urgent."

"Now I'm curious. All right, I'll change my plans," Colin said, knowing that Isabella would cancel their date anyway since she had already agreed to go to her brother's house.

"That's settled. Come on. Let me show you around."

Colin toured Mike's office, met his employees, discussed security systems and went to lunch with Mike. After lunch he told Mike he would see him at Isabella's studio. Next, Colin went shopping. It amazed him to think he was no longer on the run, something he had expected to do, perhaps for the rest of his life. This might be temporary, but he needed more clothes than he had been carrying with him.

After purchasing clothing and needed items, he left San Antonio to drive back to Stallion Pass and Isabella's studio. Passing through the rolling Hill Country with its lush, verdant fields cut by ribbons of glistening streams, he thought about the morning.

Dressed in red, Isabella had looked gorgeous, and back at the house when she had first walked into the room, it had been necessary to curb the impulse to reach for her and tell her she was beautiful.

Gorgeous and pure trouble. This morning she had goaded him into kissing her, giving him a challenge he couldn't ignore. Date Boone's sister? It would be like mixing dynamite with fire. He was happy to be able to get out of the dinner date they had arranged for tonight.

Well, part of him was glad, another part of him was filled with regret. Unbidden came images of her pressed against him earlier today—their scalding kisses that had melted and seared and driven him wild. Just thinking about them made him hot again and he vowed to keep his hands to himself and to avoid dating her. The dinner date for tonight was canceled and he would let it go at that.

He hadn't been twenty minutes out of the city when he spotted a black sedan staying steadily behind him. Was it friend or enemy? he wondered. Only one way to find out.

Chapter 7

As soon as Colin exited the Interstate, he speeded up, racing to the first stop and turning, heading into Stallion Pass and turning off the highway into town to take a circuitous route to Isabella's studio.

Fifteen minutes later, he was certain he had lost the tail. Colin turned and left the residential area, driving toward town and approaching the downtown area from the opposite direction he would have taken had he not tried to shake the tail.

He didn't see a black sedan anywhere in sight when he swept into the alley behind her place.

He parked in back of her studio and had to ring a bell for admittance.

When Isabella opened the door, his pulse jumped to his mouth. Her blue eyes sparkled and she gave him a dazzling smile. "Hi."

"Hi. Sorry we had to cancel dinner plans, but those guys want to talk to me. I don't know what they have in mind, but they said we'd all go to your brother's place for supper.''

''That's fine,'' she said.

Promptly at three Mike appeared and the two men, together with Isabella, went over her alarm system and talked about what to install.

Mike then followed Colin to the ranch where they reviewed the security system for the guest house, then the two men left to talk to Boone about his house and the rest of the ranch. Isabella stayed back to get ready for the dinner at Boone's.

Shortly before seven she looked out the window and saw Colin striding toward the house. She wanted to give her hair one more pat, but resisted the temptation. It was tied behind her head with a green ribbon that matched her cotton sundress. She hurried to open the back door as Colin crossed the porch. When his gaze swept over her, her pulse speeded up.

''You look and smell nice,'' he said as he followed her into the house and closed the door.

''Thank you. I'm ready to go.''

''The wives have driven over, so it's another clambake. I don't know what this one is about,'' Colin said, sounding perplexed. ''I know it has something to do with me.''

''It must be good or all the wives wouldn't be there.''

''I agree, which makes me even more puzzled. I want to clean up a bit. I've been in attics and haylofts and I feel grubby. If you'll wait ten minutes, I'll go with you.''

She nodded and watched him walk away. He yanked his dark shirt off and muscles rippled in his back as he wadded the shirt and balled it in his fist.

In less than ten minutes he was back in fresh jeans and a blue knit shirt. His hair was wet and combed sleekly back from his face and, for the first time, she could see some tiny scars around his hairline.

"I'm ready now."

"And you look dashing and handsome, Colin. I'm sure I must have been terribly impressed when I was sixteen."

"But you don't remember for certain," he said.

She shook her head and laughed. "Sorry. You were just another old man to me then."

He groaned. "Thanks, Isabella. Let's activate this antiquated alarm system and turn loose the ferocious dogs and be on our way, secure in the knowledge that the place is well-guarded."

"The dogs might do better than you think," she said, rising to their defense.

"Yeah, right," he said and punched in the alarm code. They locked up and left, shooing away the dogs at the gate and strolling across the wide drive to Boone's mansion.

It was an April evening and the air was balmy. Colin had noticed that dusk came later each night. The ranch was quiet and still with only the songs of birds and the crunch of his feet and Isabella's breaking the silence. Boone's landscaped yard held beds of daisies and golden coreopsis. Climbing roses spilled from whitewashed wooden trellises.

"The Double T is a beautiful ranch," Colin remarked as he looked around, thinking no one would know there was danger lurking in the shadows or a life or death situation facing all of them.

At the Devlins's they ate barbecue outside on the patio under a spring sunset that was a brilliant pink splash across the sky. Horses could be seen in a distant pasture and the rolling land was verdant and in places dotted with yellow and red wildflowers. It was idyllic, belying the mounting danger.

Colin was glad to see that Jonah and Kate were back together and seemed happier than ever. Jonah constantly had his arm around her shoulders or around her waist and when they looked at each other, there was no doubt of their love. That was true of the other two men and their wives, too.

While Boone grilled ribs, Erin hovered around him and it amused Colin to see Boone so settled. A Texan now, he was dressed in hand-tooled Western boots, jeans and a Western shirt just like the others.

As the evening progressed, Colin tried to keep his attention on his friends and conversation, but he was constantly aware of Isabella.

And with the passing of time, his curiosity grew as to why the party was being held.

It was nine o'clock before Mike motioned to him. "Colin, come join us. If you ladies would excuse us for a few minutes, we need to talk to Colin."

Colin looked across the room at Isabella. If she knew what this was about, it didn't show. She arched her eyebrows slightly and shrugged.

He left, following them into Boone's study where Boone closed the door and offered to get drinks for anyone who wanted one.

When they were finally seated on comfortable leather chairs and a couple more beers brought for Jonah and Boone, Mike leaned forward, placing his elbows on his jeans-covered knees. "Colin, we had a meeting this morning and we've come to a decision we want to tell you about."

Colin gazed back solemnly, curiosity rampant because he couldn't imagine what was on Mike's mind unless it was to ask him to leave Texas.

"Now hear me out before you start protesting," Mike said.

Colin nodded, realizing they were not going to ask him to go.

"Remember when all four of us rescued John Frates, the Texas oil magnate held hostage in Colombia?"

Colin nodded. "Sure. That's something I do remember."

"John Frates put us all in his will. You were in the first will, but when John Frates got news of your death, he divided your inheritance among us. Savannah is his attorney and she knows all of this and you can discuss it with her if you want."

Wondering what was coming, Colin sat in silence when Mike paused.

"As you know, after Jessie's birth, John and his wife left for a trip to Scotland. They drowned in a boating accident off the coast there. When that happened, we each inherited a million and a third. Plus other things like care of Jessie, my home and trust funds set up for me, the ranches to Jonah and Boone. That extra third was to have been yours. None of us needs that money. We're putting it—"

"Oh, no! You'll do no such thing!" Colin said, realizing what they wanted to do.

"I asked you to wait until I'm through. Now, shut up, Colin, and listen. We're putting the third into an account for you, plus a little because you didn't get the other stuff that we did. Savannah is helping to set this up. It's a done deal and it's unanimous. Each wife agreed, too. We all want to do this. No one had to have his arm twisted. You need to make an appointment with Savannah to go in and sign papers."

"No! I won't let you do this! It's too much," Colin protested, feeling a tightness in his chest and overwhelmed by his friends's generosity.

"It's a done deal," Mike repeated emphatically. "We won't hear otherwise. It's going into an account for you whether you like it or not."

Colin was stunned and stared at them, shaking his head. "You guys—" He broke off, at a loss for words. "I don't want your money, but to know I have friends like you three…" He broke off again, choked up, remembering the days of pain and loneliness when he thought he had lost everything and didn't have a friend left in the world.

He looked at the floor and tried to get a grip on his emotions.

"Colin, we've all been through our own hells—some of us more than others. But you had the worst. We're all buddies and we want to do this," Jonah said.

"You have to take the money. It's our gift to you because you're one of us. Always have been and always will be," Boone added. "As far as I'm concerned, it's settled, and we can drink on it and celebrate."

"I still say you shouldn't. Y'all have families. Give that money to your relatives," Colin urged them.

"Stop arguing, Colin. You've lost this battle," Mike said. "I think most of us have given chunks of money to relatives. But this is money you're entitled to and should be yours. It's done and the money's already moved. You better take it or the bank will have it for the next zillion years."

"You guys are something!" Colin declared. "I'm at a loss for words."

"You don't have to say anything," Mike stated, stretching out his long legs. "Except I want you to think about staying here when this is over and going into business with me. It's great to live here and to have all of us together."

Colin raked his fingers through his hair. "'Thank you' seems damned inadequate."

"No. Thanks is plenty. We were in shock when Savannah read John's will to us. I'm with Boone—let's have a drink to this, celebrate and go join the women again."

"I'm too stunned to talk or think."

"You should've been here when Mike inherited little Jessie if you want to see someone stunned," Jonah said and grinned.

They sipped their beers and Mike stood. "Just make an appointment with Savannah."

"Yeah, and when you go into town, drive a little slower so I can keep up with you," Boone said and laughed. "Damn, I must be out of practice. You lost me as easy as a kid dodging a truant officer."

"I'll slow for you," Colin said. "I don't think you guys should follow me."

"You may be glad to have us one day," Jonah said. "We'll keep on tailing you."

Colin shrugged. "Whatever y'all do, it's just fine with me."

They all laughed and as they stood to go into the other room, Boone stopped them. He held up his hand.

"I almost forgot and I'd be in hot water. Erin wants to have a barbecue a week from Saturday night. Y'all are invited." He looked at Colin. "It's here on the ranch and you should be safe at either your house or mine."

Colin nodded. "Thanks. We'll be here."

Others accepted the invitation. As Jonah and Boone filed out, Colin stepped in front of Mike. "I think I see your fine hand in this deal about the money."

"I got everyone together and brought it up, but Jonah and Boone had both been thinking the same thing. If it hadn't been me, it would have been one of them."

"Mike, I really am at a loss. It was pure hell for several years and then to come back to friends like the three of you—" Colin choked up and fell silent.

Mike clasped his friend on the shoulder. "We're just damned glad to have you back. And you know we can spare the money."

"I'm not exactly a pauper right now," Colin said.

"Doesn't matter. Neither were we. Now you call Savannah tomorrow."

"Thanks, Mike."

Mike smiled and passed him, heading back outside to join the others.

Colin strolled out leisurely and moved across the patio to Isabella who was talking to Erin, Boone and Jonah.

"You look pale, Colin," Isabella said. "Boone told me why they wanted to talk to you."

"I'm just in shock."

"Now the next thing we need to do is foist that white stallion off on you," Jonah said.

"Say no, Colin," Isabella said. "You don't want the white stallion and besides, you're living here on the ranch so it would exchange hands in owner's name only because that horse would stay right here where he is now."

"What white stallion?" Colin asked.

"You'll be sorry you asked," Isabella said.

"Said by the woman who can't pass a stray without giving it a home," Boone teased his sister.

"I'm not any part of this," Isabella said, moving away to join Savannah, Mike, Jonah and Kate.

It was almost midnight when the group broke up and Isabella and Colin were the last to leave, walking across the road. Gravel crunched beneath their shoes.

"Erin told me what the guys did tonight. They had discussed it with their wives first and everyone agreed that's what he or she wanted to do."

"I'm still stunned. No one willingly gives away money."

"Yes, they do. They did tonight. Just accept it and make them happy. They're doing exactly what they want to do. It was to have been your share if John Frates had known you were alive. All four of you were in the original wills."

"Their generosity really gets me."

"Had John Frates known you were alive, it might have been more, but you certainly would have gotten that much. I think it's a generous and fitting thing they did."

"I'm overwhelmed," Colin said, and she glanced at him. A muscle worked in his jaw and his hands were jammed into his pockets as he walked. "I was alone a long time and now to have friends who are so generous with me is difficult to grasp.''

''Colin, you were alone because you wanted to be isolated. You could have let your family and your friends know about you much sooner than you did.''

His head whipped around and he stared at her as he walked. ''That was true the last years, but not at first. For weeks I couldn't remember any of them. I didn't know who I was. And then I was put in a prison.'' He sighed. ''I've told you all that and I suppose you're right. A lot of it was my choice.''

''Sorry if I was a little harsh there.''

''It's okay, Isabella. I deserved it,'' he said lightly, draping his arm around her shoulders and giving her a casual squeeze that surprised her because he usually remained aloof. Aloof until she provoked him into steamy kisses.

''They've already set up a bank account. All you have to do is sign papers. So now what will you do? That fortune won't be worth much if you go live in a wilderness,'' she said.

''Mike wants me to stay and go into business with him.''

''I heard him. Are you interested?''

''At this point in my life, I don't know anything about my future. Isabella, do you feel slighted because I got the money and you didn't while you're Boone's blood relative?''

''No! Not at all. Besides, Boone has been more than generous with his family.''

''It isn't just you. What about the other relatives like Jonah's parents and Mike's family?''

''I think they've all shared their windfall and they feel that you are truly entitled to this. Forget it and enjoy the money.''

''I hope the others feel the way you do.''

They reached her gate and shooed the dogs away. "I need to feed and water the dogs," she said.

"I'll help," Colin offered, and she motioned to their water bowls.

"Two of the bowls fill automatically. There is one more big bowl by the hydrangea bush that I refill."

"You do that and I'll get that fifty-pound bag of dog food you lug around."

Colin left, three dogs trailing behind him while the other two stayed with Isabella.

"You lucky mutts. You found a real soft touch. And so did I," he said. "Too damn soft in every way," he mumbled.

As soon as the dogs had been fed and watered, Colin and Isabella went inside.

"Come sit and talk," he said. "I can't sleep now. Thoughts of the job offer and the money and a thousand other things are spinning in my mind."

She nodded. "Want a glass of iced tea or a beer?"

"I'll take a glass of milk if you have it," he said, closing the kitchen shutters and crossing the room to get glasses for her. "Milk got to be a luxury for a time and now I crave it."

"It's difficult imagining you craving anything," she said lightly as she took cookies from a jar. He caught her braid and tugged lightly and she turned to see that smoldering look. Her pulse jumped.

"I crave things, Isabella," he said in a husky voice.

"Like what?" she asked softly, knowing she shouldn't inquire yet unable to resist.

He took the plate of cookies from her hands and set it on the counter. Her pulse drummed as she watched him. "You know damn well what I want. You told me to rejoin the living and stop being scared of life. I'm taking your advice."

He leaned to kiss her while he pulled her into his embrace. Isabella walked into his arms and wrapped her arms around his neck, wanting him and surprised by his response, realizing that wall he kept around himself was crumbling.

Was it the shock of the gift from his friends? Or her kisses? Or both? She would never know and, at the moment, she didn't care. Her toes curled as his tongue went deep into her mouth and fires ignited low inside her.

She wound her fingers in his hair, kissing him in return, wanting to make him burn and his toes curl.

Even though she knew she shouldn't, she wanted to break through that wall still around his heart. She wouldn't fall in love and she couldn't imagine that he would, either. But at least he was losing that cold indifference that had been so unlike the Colin Garrick she had known long ago.

His arms tightened and he leaned over her while her hips thrust against him. She felt his hard shaft press against her.

"Dammit, Isabella." He practically ground out the words as he swung her up, releasing her and turning away. His fists were clenched, and his shoulders squared.

She picked up the plate of cookies and turned away, too. He was right—they should stop. She wanted him to turn back the clock and he was changing slightly, but he probably would never again be the man she had known. He was cold, brooding, dangerous in too many ways. She didn't want to get entangled with him.

She turned to find him still with his back to her and she suspected he was trying to cool down and get a grip on his emotions.

She was a sucker for strays and hurt people and a sympathetic story and she knew it, so she needed to guard her own heart although there was very little likelihood that she would ever fall in love with a man like Colin.

"Thinking about your ex-fiancée?" she asked, suspecting

he had never talked about the breakup that obviously still churned in him and kept him in knots.

He spun around to glare at her. "Hell, no! I'm thinking about my friend, your brother. He trusts me. He would go into orbit if he knew I was hitting on his kid sister."

"'Kid sister'?" she repeated, annoyed that that was the way Colin still saw her. "I thought we laid that one to rest." She walked up to him, stopping only inches in front of him and returning his glare. "I don't believe you've been 'hitting' on me, Colin. As I recall, I've instigated most of the kissing we've done."

"Dammit, you like trouble!" he snapped. "Boone can't have a clue what a minx you are, except he's a wild man himself. Or he was until he met Erin. I hardly recognize him now."

"So maybe there's hope for me if the right man comes along and reforms me," she teased, still annoyed that Colin could only see her as Boone's little sister. "You haven't been the one who's pushed us into this, so stop worrying about my brother. I'll get your milk. Maybe it'll soothe you and calm your ruffled feathers."

Fuming, Colin watched her sashay away from him. She had a sexy sway to her hips and he wanted to give that enticing fanny a swat. She goaded him into losing control, which was something he had never experienced before.

She poured milk for him and iced tea for her and motioned to the table, arching her eyebrows in question. "Are you going to join me or are you just going to stand and glare at me?"

He shook his head. "You are a little witch, Isabella." He took his drink from her and the plate of cookies and set them on the table. He turned to hold a chair for her and she smiled sweetly up at him.

"Thanks, Colin," she said, touching his cheek lightly with her hand. It was the most casual brush of her fingers, but the contact was like a burning brand and he inhaled, his fingers tightening on the chair to keep from reaching for her again.

She sat and he walked around the table, knowing he needed to keep distance between them. He should keep the whole ranch between them.

Her question about his ex-fiancée had startled him because he was accustomed to thinking constantly about Danielle, but he had hardly thought of her today at all. Isabella was enjoying a cookie, a faint smile hovering on her face, and acting oblivious to his smoldering feelings.

She had him in knots, but he had to give her credit. She was bringing him back into the land of the living with jet speed. If he didn't just crash and burn.

The last thing on earth he wanted to do was to break the trust Boone had in him. Isabella was dynamite in too many ways. Colin knew he shouldn't touch her, much less kiss her. And he also knew he should be able to handle her taunts and challenges and keep his hands to himself.

She had been blithely ignoring him while she ate her cookie, but he knew damn well that she was aware of him. And she knew the effect she had on him, too. Sexy wench. He suspected she saw him as a project to save just as much as one of the mutts outside. Nothing more. He damn well didn't want to get over Danielle—something he had thought impossible until the past two days—only to fall for a minx whose heart was never in her kisses.

And to his shock, after spending almost five years grieving over his lost love, he realized he was getting over her. Really getting over her. He could think about her now without hurting.

It was a first and he mulled over his new status, knowing he should be grateful to the feisty woman who could kiss him into a witless state of excruciating desire.

He would never seduce Isabella. He almost laughed out

loud at the thought. He'd better worry about resisting her
when she tried to seduce him! If any seduction went on, it
would be her doing, he was damn sure of that one. She was
calling the shots and stirring him up when he didn't want
to be stirred. She looked sweet and harmless. Big, innocent
blue eyes. What a deception. A seductive, desirable woman
with an imp personality.

There was a chance he needed to worry more about the
danger inside the house than the danger outside.

"Penny for your thoughts," she said, smiling at him as
if nothing had happened and she hadn't kissed him into one
big, fiery need. "Thinking about Boone or your fiancée or
the danger?"

"Mostly thinking about you. You're pure trouble, Isabella."

"Trouble? I've given you a place to stay and I've been
friendly. A few kisses won't demolish you."

"Yeah, right."

"How?"

He glared at her some more.

"How long did you date those guys who wanted to marry
you?"

"Three years with one and two years with the other. It
wasn't serious."

"Maybe not for you. Was it serious for them?"

She shrugged. "Both times it began to get serious—but
I wasn't ready for any real commitment, so each time I
broke off the relationship. And don't lump me with your
fiancée because we were never as serious as I imagine you
two were."

"Why do I suspect you've left broken hearts behind just
like Boone used to do?"

"Not really," she said, smiling sweetly. Then she
changed topics on him. "Will you let me take your picture?

Have you changed your mind about it now that you know I can?''

He shook his head and had to laugh. ''You don't give up, do you?''

''Good gracious!''

Startled, he looked at her and his surprise grew because she was staring, round-eyed at him, her hand over her heart. ''What?''

''You actually smiled! The first! You have a charming smile.''

He closed his eyes and leaned his head back. ''Damn. Isabella, you're hopeless.'' He opened his eyes to look at her. ''Stop making me a project and getting all dithery when I smile.''

She leaned across the table to poke his chest with her forefinger. ''You, my friend, are not a project. If you were, you would definitely know it.''

He caught her braid in his hand, tugging her closer, looking into her wide, blue eyes. ''If I'm not a project, then all your efforts are aimed at getting me to kiss you.''

''Oh, my, you flatter yourself!''

''Deny that you like to flirt,'' he accused.

''So what's the harm in that? It livens things up a bit.''

''You're a hopeless romantic and another devilish Devlin.''

''I'm 'Boone's kid sister,' I believe you said. As such, you should be quite able to ignore me. And you better let go of my braid.''

''Or else?''

The challenge hung in the air and they both stared at each other. Isabella knew she should close her mouth and stop flirting and teasing him and settle back. But his gray eyes held desire and invisible, but, oh, so tangible, sparks were flying around them. Why not see what would happen?

''Or else I'll be over there in your lap in a twinkling.''

One dark eyebrow arched, giving him that I-dare-you look. "How can I possibly let go now?" he said softly, and her pulse raced.

"On the other hand, you have to let go or I can't get there except to crawl over the table, which I have no intention of doing."

He laughed and released her braid and her heart thudded because for an instant the Colin she'd known from long ago was back. And his smile made him even more handsome and appealing. His teeth were white and even; creases bracketed his mouth while a twinkle danced in his eyes.

She sat back and laughed with him.

"So, you're not heading over here." He pushed away from the table to make his lap more available, and her pounding heartrate speeded up.

"No. On second thought, I'll stay where I am. You and I both know this is better and safer, and sitting in your lap might lead to all kinds of unwanted problems."

"Chicken, Isabella? I think I can live with any problems that arise from you sitting on my lap."

"We're flirting and you said that it was dangerous. I think I should tell you good-night and get out of here right now. You can lock up and close up and check things out and do all the stuff you do. See you in the morning."

She all but ran from the room, leaving her dishes behind and her half-finished iced tea.

She needed to get away from him right now. His flirting and smiling at her had increased his appeal. He was right: she was pushing him, teasing him, flirting with him far too much. Was it the streak in her that wanted to save strays or was she really drawn to Colin?

Either way, she needed to stop and distance herself from him. Yet how wonderful to hear him laugh! How great to see him smile. His kisses—her insides heated at the thought.

She entered her bedroom and closed the door behind her.

As she moved across the room, she brushed her lips with her fingers and remembered his kisses. No one had ever touched her the way he had or caused the heated reaction he did. It was instantaneous, the moment his lips touched hers.

Why, oh, why, was there such chemistry between them when neither of them wanted it? They were poles apart in every way. Not when they touched. His kisses stirred a storm of longing in her, and she suspected it would be hours before she could sleep. Probably hours before he could sleep for a different reason. She knew he had been deeply touched by the generosity of his friends. Maybe that gesture had reached him more than anything else and had caused him to let down enough to actually laugh and smile tonight.

"Stop trying to save him from himself!" she said out loud. He wasn't a stray she could feed and pat on the head and expect to keep out in the yard.

"Colin," she whispered, desire a fiery longing that she knew she would have to battle more than ever. "Colin Garrick," she repeated, fighting the urge to go back to the kitchen where she imagined he would still be sitting. Soon he would be gone out of her life. How long would it take to forget about him? Would she ever forget him?

"I hope you can't sleep, either," she said softly, guilty to wish a sleepless night on him, yet wanting him to suffer as much as she was.

She closed the shutters, changed into a white cotton nightgown that came to the tops of her knees. She climbed into bed, switched off the light and stared into the darkness, wondering how long before she could sleep. Her thoughts jumped to Colin and the memory of his kisses.

Colin went through the house, closing shutters, checking windows, thankful Mike's crew would be out in the morning to change the alarm system.

He was only half aware of what he was doing, because his thoughts were on Isabella. He thought about her constantly and tonight he hadn't been able to take his eyes off her at Boone's. He groaned. Boone's kid sister. He had to stop flirting with her. He had to avoid her. He definitely had to stop kissing her. It was like telling himself to stop breathing.

It was three in the morning before he dozed.

He went in through a window and moved through the darkened house. He could hear men's voices, smell stale cigarette smoke. He had about two minutes' head start. In the dark room, a man was tied to a chair, an old iron bed off to one side. Colin cut the hostage free.

There were voices.

Men were coming.

Colin grabbed the man's arm to run.

Chapter 8

Drenched in sweat, Colin sat up in bed. He raked his fingers through his hair as his heart pounded. He remembered! He remembered part of that night before the blast.

He lay back down to stare into the darkness and run the memories through his mind again.

Hours later, during their morning run, he told Isabella.

She stopped in her tracks to stare at him. "Colin, that's marvelous!"

He laughed and wanted to grab and hug her. Instead, he stood with his hands on his hips. He was excited to have the stirring of memory. "Yeah. I don't know if seeing the guys triggered it or knowing you—"

"Knowing me? How would that affect your memory?"

"Maybe I'm more relaxed about my past. Maybe I have other things on my mind now," he said, his voice growing husky as he touched the tip of her nose with his forefinger.

Something flickered in the depths of her eyes. She turned and began to jog again and he fell into step beside her.

Later that morning at nine o'clock a private prop jet plane set down on the ranch runway and taxied to a stop. A brown-haired man dressed in jeans and a brown T-shirt stepped out and Colin hurried forward to meet him. Colin had seen Brett Hamilton only once before in his life. The ranch pilot passed the two men, hurrying to the plane and entering to help direct the pilot to the hangar where he could refuel before leaving.

Colin shook hands with Brett. "Glad to have you here, although you may have stepped into a hornet's nest."

"Frankly, I hope so. We want to catch this guy and be finished."

"Come with me. You can stay in the guest house, or if you think it would scare our man away, you can stay in Boone Devlin's house. He's agreed to that."

"I've been briefed that the Agency is sending two people," Brett said. "Both have impeccable backgrounds and one is an old buddy of yours. Peter Fremont."

"I got a call at five this morning from the general about them coming. I've worked a couple of times with Tyler Riordan."

"I've got a dossier on him. I don't see how either one of them could be the double agent."

"Whoever it is has cleared all intelligence hurdles. But then, the traitor would have to," Colin said. They climbed into a pickup and Colin briefed Brett on Stallion Pass, his three friends and the local situation.

"We had another agent compromised," Brett informed Colin. "The blame has to rest squarely with our man," Brett said. "We've got to hope this ploy works and we succeed. I'm your ace in the hole because no one except General Kowalski, you and the pilots who brought me, know that I'm here. That's it. Who have you told?"

"Just my friends and Boone Devlin's sister, Isabella. I'm staying in the guest house with her. Since we're in the same house, I needed to tell her. Isabella is an excellent shot and knows how to defend herself. I don't want you shot in friendly fire.''

Brett nodded. ''I'll probably stay where I draw the least attention and I don't think the best place is in the same house with you. Actually, it might be the best cover if I bunk up with the hands who work here.''

''Know anything about horses?''

Brett grinned. ''I brought my belt buckle for saddle bronc riding.''

''Great. You'll do fine in the bunkhouse with the cowboys. I don't know them, but Boone said everyone is friendly.''

''If I stay there, we need to let them know, but that's letting a lot of people in on the fact that I'm here.''

''I imagine you can trust everyone on this ranch. You know the enemy hasn't got any contact here. Except us. I still think it's going to be someone all of us who've been in Special Forces know.''

''You're probably right. It stands to reason.''

Colin parked near the back door of the guest house. ''Watch out for the dogs. They'll greet you to death.''

They entered the backyard and Colin tried to shoo away the dogs, but Brett knelt to pet them.

''You can take them home with you when you go,'' Colin said, looking at the tough Special Forces soldier kneeling and scratching one of the dog's ears.

Brett grinned. ''Who do they belong to?''

''I think Isabella will foist them off on her brother since this is his ranch, but she's the one who's taken them in. They were all strays.''

''So our hostess is a softie.''

''Just don't startle her in the dark. Come on and meet her.''

Isabella saw the men as she stood at the kitchen window.

Colin was dressed in faded jeans and a white T-shirt and looked like one of the cowboys. The man with him was less than six feet tall, much shorter than Colin, thicker through the shoulders and chest and a mass of muscles.

Grimly, she watched them approach the house. The presence of the soldier made the threat real and imminent. She could move to town and get out of this, she knew, yet she felt compelled to stay. Was that because of Colin? She didn't want to look too deeply at her reasons. She carried her pistol in her purse daily and she had added ten minutes to her running time and another ten to her workout time.

Colin opened the back door and met her gaze. He stepped into the kitchen, motioned his friend inside and closed the door.

"Isabella, this is Brett Hamilton. Brett, meet Isabella Devlin, photographer."

She shook hands, feeling hers surrounded with his thick fingers in his strong grip.

"We talked on the way here and Brett thinks he'll stay in the bunkhouse."

"I may be around on the grounds at night and I might sleep on that porch. I'll just see how it goes and how much security you have here."

"I waited to meet you, but I need to go to work now," Isabella said. "My brother will be anxious to meet you."

"Brett, you can take one of the pickups and follow us into town. I can show you around Stallion Pass or you can look on your own. At eleven o'clock we have an appointment in San Antonio with the other three guys, Mike, Boone and Jonah. They need to know you, and we need a strategy briefing."

"Peter and Tyler get in at one o'clock," Brett said.

"They're to know nothing about you. We'll have to go through another meeting with them, and it's scheduled in San Antonio at three."

"All right. Give me the keys and let's go," Brett said.

As they headed into town, Colin drove Isabella's car and she rode, watching him, occasionally glancing in the passenger's side-view mirror to see Brett in the pickup following behind them.

"Can you trust all these men who are coming to town?"

"They have the best credentials possible."

"That doesn't answer my question," she said.

He shot her a look and she had her answer. "All of us, Mike, Jonah, Boone and I, have known Peter Fremont for years. We were in Special Forces with him, but he got out long ago to go to work for the CIA. Tyler Riordan is with the Agency and I've worked with him on two assignments. Brett is military. Brett is part of this covert operation, so I trust him. I can't help but trust Peter, but logic says to not trust anyone completely, especially someone with the Agency. We've known Tyler the shortest time and the least of the three men."

"So Tyler is the most suspect?"

"Not necessarily. It may not be either Tyler or Peter. It can't possibly be Brett. It has to be someone in the CIA. Tyler's record is excellent, but then a double agent's record usually is or he would never succeed at what he does. Peter, Tyler, someone else from the CIA—I don't know the answer. But one thing I do know, the CIA has seen fit to send Peter and Tyler to Texas. That in itself sends up a tiny flag of warning."

"I'd think so. Boone knows Peter Fremont?"

"Yep. Pretty well."

"There aren't any ideas about the identity of the double agent?"

"A lot of them, but nothing that can be proven. He's damn clever to have lasted so long without detection. He has to be an insider. No one else could have known some of the secrets the killer has been privy to except someone on the inside."

She rubbed her arms. "I don't like the idea of the danger all of you are in."

"I don't like the idea of the danger you've put yourself in. Get out, Isabella. You can go somewhere else to stay."

"I don't think so," she said, watching him. He looked strong, fit and competent. Sexy and appealing. Was she being stubborn just to stay near him? Or was she curious about how their plans would play out and wanted to be close enough to see for herself?

"You can move or I can move. I'm running that past the guys again when we get together," Colin said. "I think they'll want me to stay put because they probably think that will give them the best chance at the killer. There's no good reason for you to be part of this."

"I think I'm part of it now, no matter what I do. I'm not running. I don't think anything will happen at the ranch. I think it'll be somewhere else."

"How did you come up with that conclusion?"

"With the new security system that will be put in this afternoon, the place will be a fortress. There are easier spots to get to you and the others than on the ranch."

"You're probably right, but you're in town, too. I'm still torn between being with you to try to protect you and staying the hell away from you because I put you in danger."

"That's an easy one," she said blithely. "It's much more exciting to have you with me. You're interesting, challenging, and really very sexy. I'd rather have you here with me."

"Stop flirting, Isabella," he said through gritted teeth. "Are you going to flirt with Brett now?"

"Is that worrying you?" she teased, and Colin shot her a dark scowl.

"What appointments do you have today?"

She laughed. "You're changing the subject. No, I'm not

going to flirt with Brett. I was very circumspect in greeting him this morning and I will continue to be that way. Now you, I find exciting to flirt with, but if you want me to stop, I will,'' she said lightly and, to her surprise, he laughed.

"You're asking for it, Isabella. Okay, I'll do the smart thing. I want you to stop flirting!"

"Sure 'nuff, Colin," she said lightly, knowing that neither one of them would stop. She settled back and listed her appointments.

"I'll take you to dinner tonight to make up for the canceled date last night."

"Thank you," she said, trying to bank a bubbling eagerness to go out on a date with him, "but I think you'll have to wait longer because Mike's coming out at two today to install a new alarm system."

"He told me that he and his crew will be finished by six o'clock. We can go to dinner at seven."

"So you think it's safe for us to go out?"

"We've got to go on with life as usual. The minute you want out of it, you're out. If you don't feel safe going out with me, we won't, but I'm the target, not you. Also, one of the guys will follow us. Still want to go or not?"

"Of course, I want to go."

"Where's the best place in Stallion Pass to eat?" he asked.

"Murphy's Steakhouse is excellent if you like steak."

"I'll make reservations."

She inhaled, her pulse humming over the coming dinner date that pushed danger a little farther back in her mind. She glanced at Colin. His jaw was set and he looked anything but happy. She wondered why he was taking her out because she suspected he did not want to.

Or was he just grim because of Brett's arrival and the others coming in? The wheels had been set in motion.

Now it was just a' matter of time before the enemy made his move.

They parked in the alley behind her shop and let Brett into the studio to look over the place. As soon as he finished, he and Colin left for a meeting at Mike's office.

At two that afternoon, Colin stood in the sunshine at the San Antonio airport and watched while another private plane taxied to a halt and two casually dressed men emerged.

Hurrying forward, he shook hands with tall, blond Peter Fremont, three years his senior and someone he had known for years. Looking as if he were on a pleasure trip instead of official business, Peter wore gray slacks and a plaid sport shirt.

"Glad to have you here, Peter," Colin said, gazing into cool blue eyes.

"I hope this is it, Colin. It's long overdue."

Nodding, Colin turned to greet Tyler Riordan. Shorter, sandy-haired and in his early thirties, Riordan shook hands with Colin.

Colin knew Tyler Riordan's credentials were as flawless as Peter's. He looked into hazel eyes as he received a firm handshake and welcomed the agent to Texas. It was impossible to imagine the double agent was either of these two men, yet as they turned from the plane, Colin's gaze ran over Tyler and he knew that the killer's record would be impeccable so a flawless record was no guarantee. Nor was it a guarantee with Peter, either.

Colin had already rented a car for them and they followed him to Mike's office where Jonah, Mike and Boone waited.

The men greeted their old friend, Peter Fremont, and then Tyler Riordan. As soon as soft drinks had been passed out, the six got down to business.

"We'll stay in Stallion Pass at the hotel, but we both need

to be able to come and go at your ranch so we can guard Colin and get in to see him,'' Peter said to Boone.

Colin felt a tingle of apprehension, a mere gut reaction to giving Tyler Riordan the code to the new security system. He looked across the room into Mike's dark eyes and saw the same wariness. He had known Mike long enough to know when Mike didn't like something even though there wasn't the slightest change in his facial expression.

''We've been taking turns tailing Colin,'' Mike said.

''You won't have to now that we're here,'' Peter said. ''That's why there are two of us. We'll take over watching him.'' He turned to look at Colin. ''You've set yourself up as bait.''

As Colin nodded, Mike said, ''It's way beyond time we catch this guy.''

''If we need one of you to help, we'll call,'' Peter said, ''but for the next few days, we'll tail Colin. We need a map of your ranch, Boone.''

''I've already got maps of all our places,'' Mike said, handing a folder to Peter.

They absorbed all the information given to them, made plans and broke up.

Isabella dressed in a short, simple black dress that had cap sleeves and a cowl neckline that was cut high in front and low in back. She wore her hair piled on her head and diamond stud earrings. ''Why are you doing this?'' she kept asking herself. She had promised herself to keep her distance with Colin, yet here she was going on a date with him. Going too eagerly, she knew.

She hummed as she slipped on high-heeled black pumps. She picked up a black purse, tucked it under her arm and went to find her date. Since meeting Brett Hamilton, she had never seen the man again. She suspected he was never far away, but she hadn't spotted him in town or on the ranch, yet it reassured her to know he was here.

She left her room and walked down the hall to the family room, which was empty, but saw Colin's reflection in the big mirror as he stood in the kitchen. Her pulse skipped at the sight of him. She entered the kitchen where Colin gazed out the window. He was wearing a charcoal suit and he looked incredibly appealing. Yet even in a suit, he had that aura of danger about him.

He turned and frowned slightly, his gaze sweeping over her. "You look beautiful, Isabella."

"Thank you," she said, smiling because of his compliment and the warm look in his eyes. "Don't tell me that suit was rolled up in your backpack."

The corner of his mouth lifted in a faint grin. "No. I managed to buy this in San Antonio yesterday and had alterations done immediately. Still certain you want to go out with me? It may be dangerous."

"It's definitely dangerous," she said in a silky voice.

He inhaled swiftly. "I'm talking about a life-or-death danger," he drawled wryly.

"That kind! I'll be enormously safe with you and with Brett Hamilton hovering somewhere and one of your cronies following us. We'll move in an entire entourage of guards."

"Not really. You'll be beside me and I may be a prime target. Those guys can only do so much and Peter told your brother and the others to back off. Either Peter or Tyler will be my tail. They don't know about Brett." Colin frowned. "I'll tell you, I'm having second thoughts about taking you out."

"You're not weaseling out of this date! I'm not afraid. Besides, you told me you thought you would be safe enough for a few more days. The killer has to get to Texas and get his plan in order."

Colin crossed the room and rested his hands on her shoulders. ''It's not a game, Isabella. The double agent may already be here.''

''I know the danger is real—remember, I grew up around Boone. But life has to go on and the chances of something happening tonight—I repeat, you said yourself—are not too likely.''

''That's a guess, and I'm having a lot of second thoughts about this and about taking you out and putting you at risk.''

''Stop fretting. The guys who are tailing you will protect us.'' She linked her arm in his. ''Come on, Mr. Worrier. I have my pistol and I'll guard you.''

He gave her a level look and she realized her lightness was only serving to increase his concern. She made a solemn face. ''All right. I'll worry, too. And I'll keep a sharp lookout. Which would you prefer, that I drive or that you drive?''

He thought it over. ''I'll drive,'' he said, picking up the keys from the kitchen counter.

They went outside and passed through the dogs and across the yard. Colin's gaze searched the premises, but he couldn't see anything amiss. He held the car door for Isabella and was distracted briefly by the sight of her shapely legs when she climbed inside.

Closing the door, he strode around the car to slide behind the wheel and start the engine. ''I checked the car this afternoon.''

''Checked it for what?''

''A bomb. It's not likely, but not impossible even in bright daylight. I don't like taking chances.''

She leaned closer to Colin, straining against her seat belt to touch his arm. ''Stop worrying. Do you see anything suspicious?''

He inhaled and freed his arm from her grasp. She felt rejected as she sat back, watching him. His jaw was so set he looked hard and angry and she wondered if she should have just agreed to forget the dinner date. They would have still been together at home, and he wouldn't be in such a grump. If he was angry with her and so uptight, how could they possibly have a good time?

"Colin, if it makes you feel better, turn around and go back home," she said solemnly.

He shot her a quick glance that was more of a scowl. "I may be wrong, Isabella, but I've got a gut feeling that we're in danger."

"How often do you get these 'gut feelings'?" she asked.

"Occasionally, and I have one now. I don't know whether it's from being followed or from worrying about you being with me. I'd like to see your brother following me right now."

"How'll you know whether it's Brett or one of the other men?"

"I won't. Just keep your eyes open."

They rode in silence and as they sped across the old concrete bridge across Badger Creek, Isabella looked at the woods surrounding the creek. "Anyone could hide in the shadows of the woods and no one would know." She inhaled, some of her enthusiasm for the evening cooling.

"Should we go back home?" she asked.

He thought it over and the extent of time it took him to answer her made her realize how concerned he was. "We'll go. I can't hole up on the ranch all the time, but I don't like having you out in harm's way. I may call Boone to take you home."

She had no intention of riding home with her brother, but she didn't tell Colin that. They could get into that argument later.

"Right now, it's broad daylight in early evening and nothing unusual is going on. There's little traffic so far," she said.

"You're right." He glanced at her. "Good thing this isn't a real date. I'd be a washout."

"Now there is a leading line if I ever heard one. First, it's a real date to me, Colin Garrick! Second, a washout—my friend you can never possibly be a flop."

"Careful, Isabella. You're asking for trouble again."

She smiled. "I'll take my chances."

"I've got to keep my eyes on the road, so you wait and flirt over dinner tonight."

"And you promise to flirt back?"

When he laughed, her heart turned over. Why did she have this compulsion to try to pull smiles and laughter from him?

"I'll give it a try. How's that? I've never had anyone ask me to promise to flirt over dinner."

"Well, I'm different from anyone else you've ever known," she replied with saucy assurance.

He chuckled. "That's rather an understatement. Boone should have warned me."

"About what? Me?"

"About you, Isabella. You're dangerous in too many ways to count."

She wriggled with pleasure. "I like that! I don't think I've ever had a man consider me dangerous. Now you, I'll bet every female you meet sees a streak of danger in you."

"I wouldn't hurt a woman. You should know that."

"I didn't mean danger in that sense. You're a threat to a woman's heart."

"I'm a threat to your heart?" he repeated, glancing at her. "Don't even answer me now. We'll take it up later when I won't be likely to wreck the car with one of your straight-shooting answers."

She laughed and turned to look out the back window.

"Turn around and use a mirror and it'll be a little more

subtle if we're being followed," he instructed with amusement in his voice.

"You're lightening up, Colin. Watch out or you'll thaw into a warm-blooded male."

"You're at it again."

She smiled and looked out at the side-view mirror on the passenger side of the car. There were cars strung out in the distance behind them, but nothing unusual. She couldn't guess whether anyone followed them or not. They rode in silence for a few minutes.

"You don't look as worried now," she said. "Have you relaxed a little?"

"Sure. I'm relaxed."

She didn't believe him, but he did look less forbidding. When they drove into Stallion Pass, Colin circled blocks and she realized he was checking for a tail. She watched the side mirror, but she couldn't see anything suspicious or anyone who was clearly following them.

Finally he turned a corner and drove into the parking lot of the restaurant, pulling up to the door for valet parking. He stepped out and she climbed out when a uniformed valet held the door for her. Colin came around to take her arm and whisk her into the restaurant.

The moment they entered the foyer, he moved to a window to look outside. After a minute he took her arm and led her inside the dimly lit dining area where he talked a moment to the maître d' who seated them at a table in a secluded corner. Colin sat with his back to the wall where he could watch the door, leaving Isabella wondering if she would have his attention for any part of the evening until they were back home.

The linen-covered tables held candles and tiny bouquets of fresh lilies of the valley and pink rosebuds. Beside the dance floor a piano player sang a ballad as he played. She looked around the restaurant she had eaten at before, but knew this would be the night she would always remember.

In the flickering candlelight, Colin looked dashing. Was he still grieving as much over his ex-fiancée? Isabella knew a few days probably would make little change in his feelings, yet he really did seem to be thawing; he seemed less brooding and cold.

He was not a mission for her to save, she reminded herself.

"Want a glass of wine, Isabella?"

"That would be lovely," she answered, smiling at him. To her surprise, he smiled in return. She wondered how much he still saw her as Boone's kid sister. She knew he didn't when he kissed her.

When the waiter came, Colin ordered two glasses of white wine.

As soon as the wine had been poured and they were alone once again, Colin raised his glass in a toast. "Here's to a spectacular evening. So far, we're safe."

"I'll drink to that," she replied, touching his glass lightly with hers. "And I hope that sometime during the evening you can stop watching the doorway and everyone who enters long enough to look at your date."

His gaze shifted back to her and a dark eyebrow arched. "I've noticed you. I told you that you look beautiful."

"And I thanked you, but I'm not sure you're very conscious of my existence right now."

"You're mistaken, I'm very aware of you," he murmured, giving her a heated look that curled her toes.

"If you catch the enemy agent while you're here, will you stay and work for Mike?" she asked, trying to ignore the sensation. And trying to change the subject.

"I don't have any idea what I'll do. With my new fortune, I have more options."

"So what would you really like to do?"

"At this point in my life, I don't even know the answer to that one. I haven't thought that far ahead since everything changed and I decided to stay in Texas."

The waiter returned and they both ordered the beef tenderloin with orange Bearnaise sauce. As soon as the waiter left them alone, they chatted until he brought crystal plates that held crisp green salads.

Colin and Isabella talked through dinner. Then, as more couples moved onto the dance floor, he gazed at her and finally asked, "Would you like to dance?"

"I didn't think you were ever going to ask!" she exclaimed, sliding out of the chair and taking his hand. In seconds she was in his arms. The music was a familiar ballad. Colin held her lightly, as if he were dancing with a stranger. He looked over her head at the windows that spilled light onto the terrace. Lights beyond the terrace glowed on the trees, but Colin could see that night had fallen and he wondered what dangers would be prowling the darkness.

Outside in the far end of the restaurant parking lot, in an area where employees parked their cars, a man sat in a large, black sedan. A pistol lay beside him on the front seat. He could see the entrance to the restaurant.

He had seen them go inside, Isabella Devlin dressed in black. Appropriate color for a killing. There he had been—Colin Garrick, the man with the nine lives of a cat. Yet even cats died. And often violently. Tonight would be the night.

Get it over and done with. Eliminate the one big threat to a fabulous future. Kill Garrick. Make it look like an accident if possible. And then get out of Texas. A tall order, but not an impossible one even with all the operatives here and his old buddies from Special Forces. He suspected there was someone nearby from the military, too. It wouldn't be like them to use Colin as bait and to leave him unprotected at this point.

They were no match and, by now, they should begin to face that fact. He had been slipping past them for years. Years! And in that time, he had amassed a fortune. He knew exactly how he would spend it. In a life of luxury for himself.

He jerked his thoughts back to the present and knew that none of them suspected him. He could walk right past any of them and they wouldn't have a clue. He knew them all, even Garrick. Fools and more fools! And tonight a dead fool! He wanted to get this over with.

He cared nothing about the woman; the fact that she was with him would be her misfortune. Other than that, she could live because she was no threat to him. But Colin was a growing threat with each day.

The man touched his pistol lightly, feeling the cold metal. On the drive home, he would make his move. It was all lined up, including his escape. They would never know who had been involved. Someone would be following Colin, but it would not save him. It was be a good place for the finger of suspicion to point when Colin died. Only a couple more hours and this one would be out of the way.

He shifted slightly and watched the restaurant door. It was too early for them to come out, but he wanted to be ready. He didn't want to let Colin live another day. Colin should have stayed out of this and not meddled. He had to die because he was never going to give up and go away.

The door pushed open and a tall, black-haired man wearing a navy suit strode out. There was a tall brunette on his arm and for one fleeting second the man thought he had his quarry in sight. He reached for the key in the ignition. He had this planned to the moment. When they came out to get their car, he would leave ahead of them.

Once out of town and on back roads, he could drive faster

than Colin would. He knew the place where he would run Colin into the bridge abutment—either that or run him off the road. There was an old bridge on the road approaching the ranch. It was high over steep banks down to a riverbed that looked as if it had never had a drop of water in it. Nearby, were paths fishermen had made, parking their cars and trucks near the river. Perfect places for him to wait and hide. He could park where he would be at right angles with Colin when he came up on the road.

It was a deserted area and a likely place to get rid of the man and at the same time, have it appear to be an accident.

They would know—all those trying to protect him—that it had been no accident and that they had failed, but that wouldn't help Colin.

And if one of the men followed him close enough to catch up— The man touched his pistol lightly. So be it. He would take him out, too. That would eliminate the accident theory, but he didn't really care. Just get rid of Colin and get out of the area.

This was not a night for mistakes. It was a night for dying. A night to stop the chase, to insure his future.

He had a car hidden where he could abandon this one. Then he would be safely on his way.

Dine tonight, Colin Garrick. Wine and dine and dance because it will be your last night. You should have stayed in that dark netherworld where you couldn't remember the past.

Instead, you had to go out and hunt the past and try to recreate it. Well, that past has caught up with you tonight. You won't see tomorrow. It would be over. Jubilation coursed through the man. Tonight was the night! He watched the restaurant door swing open again.

Chapter 9

In the heart of the restaurant Colin and Isabella drifted around the dance floor.

"I haven't danced in six years," he said quietly.

"Six years! Then we should dance every dance until the piano player quits for the night."

"I don't think I need to catch up for six years in one night," he replied, smiling at her, and her heart missed a beat. One of those rare, pure-gold smiles that made him more appealing than ever and brought to mind the man he had once been. She knew that man might never be back fully as he was years ago, but she had high hopes that he would approximate the way he used to be.

As they danced, Colin held her close and Isabella was aware of the brush of their thighs, their legs touching, his hand holding hers and his other arm around her waist. They moved together easily, and she loved dancing in his arms.

"For someone who hasn't danced in such a long time, you do it well," she said.

"You know that old saying, once you've learned to dance, you never forget."

"I think that was about riding a bike."

"You don't say!" he said lightly and she looked up at him. He was looking down at her and desire burned in his gaze. "Until now, I haven't wanted to ever dance again. I didn't think this could possibly happen. I shouldn't admit that to you, though, because it'll encourage you."

When she laughed, Colin tightened his arm around her waist. Every word he'd said to her had been the truth. He suspected she intended to save him from himself whether he wanted to be saved or not, but he also had to face the fact that she was succeeding and he was happier.

"I don't believe I should say thank-you to you," she replied. "You don't sound happy about enjoying life more."

"I'm an ungrateful wretch. Actually, I'm glad. Now let me see…what was it you said to me in the car? I think it was something to the effect that I'm a threat to your heart. Is that right?"

"Of course, you are."

"You've never really been in love, Isabella, and that's an impossibility with us."

"Why impossible?"

"For one thing, I know you don't want to fall in love with me because you're all wound up in that photography business of yours—right?"

"I suppose," she answered.

"Therefore, how can I be any kind of danger to your emotions?"

"I might get where I care too much about you," she replied lightly, gazing up at him. "You know I don't like to see anything lost or hurt. You admitted that you felt half dead and didn't want to live. I don't want you to go through life feeling that way."

"Just what I suspected. I rank right up there with the dogs and you are on a mission of saving me from myself. You'll always care too much about people and animals."

"There are worlds of people I don't give a rip about."

"They're probably happy, smiling souls who are busy as little bees. What about Nick? Is he one of your projects? Or Sandy?"

Isabella looked away and raised her chin. "I like to see people happy. There's nothing wrong with that."

"Of course there isn't, if they have a need," he replied, amused and knowing he'd guessed correctly. "Now if they prefer a solitary life, then it's not your place to try to change their manner of living."

"You don't say," she replied, and he knew she absolutely did not agree.

"What about Nick and Sandy? What did you rescue them from?"

"Whatever makes you think I rescued them?"

"Because you're not answering my questions about them. What was the deal with Sandy?" Colin persisted.

"If you must know, she got thrown out of her house by her alcoholic mother. Her father has long ago disappeared and Sandy wanted to go to college and needed a job. She's plenty smart and quite nice."

"See, there's someone who needed help and wanted help and I think that's admirable that you provided a job for her," he said lightly, turning Isabella, more aware of holding her in his arms than their conversation. His gaze went over her head and he glanced around the room, looking to see if anything seemed amiss, but it looked as though customers were enjoying themselves either eating or dancing, the wait staff doing the necessary services, nothing out of the ordinary.

"I think you're laughing at me, Colin."

"I thought you told me that I never laugh."

"Not out loud, you don't, but I think you're laughing right now."

"In spite of the progress I've made because of you, I'm just trying to stay out of your save-a-soul clutches. I've been saved enough."

"You're safe. You have such a wall around you, I couldn't possibly scale it."

"I think you've quite successfully scaled it several times lately. There's no wall when we kiss," he admitted, thinking that's what he would like to do right now and knowing he better not.

She looked up at him, her blue eyes plainly smoldering with desire that sent his pulse speeding.

The dance ended and he took her hand, wanting to dance the rest of the night as she had suggested, but he knew what he needed to do.

"The evening is great, but I'd feel a lot better if we'd cut it short and head home while it's still early and more people are out."

"Running from me, Colin? Or from yourself?" she asked, that flash of mischief back in her eyes and the challenge flung bluntly at him.

He inhaled and yanked her into his embrace. The music was a ballad and he pulled Isabella tightly against him, wrapping both arms around her and moving slowly while he leaned down to trace the delicate curve of her ear with his tongue.

"You like danger, Isabella," he said quietly into her ear. "You enjoy provoking me." She was warm and soft, moving with him, and he was rock-hard with desire. He wanted her and he knew that was the last thing he should be feeling. He didn't want to fall in love because he was vulnerable, on the rebound, and Isabella wasn't going to fall in love with anyone except her job. There were a million reasons to leave her alone, he thought to himself. Or if not a million, three big ones: she was Boone's sister; she would never love him in return; he would bring danger into her life—he was already doing that one.

Chemistry. Hot, intense, unwanted, but evident every minute they were together. And her constant taunting.

While he showered kisses down her throat, she wound her arms around his neck, pressing against him.

He suspected he was a game to her. He knew damn well he was a project—another stray to make happy and put back together and leave him behind when she went on to other things.

Boone had left an endless trail of broken hearts behind. Colin suspected Isabella might have done the same on a smaller scale.

Then his anger evaporated as he stopped thinking and just relished holding her close. For minutes they barely moved around the dance floor until he realized what he was doing. Playing into her hands.

But he better watch himself or he would go from one heartbreak to another. Isabella was wrapped in her own world and he was merely one of her projects, and he better remember that.

And not take advantage of it, either.

The minute the music stopped, he took her hand.

"Now we're going and you're not going to goad me into any more foolishness here. I think we're in danger and we need to get back to the security of the ranch."

"Scaredy-cat," she said softly, but she turned for their table to retrieve her purse.

Dropping his arm across her shoulders, he walked with her to the door where he stepped to one side to turn her to face him.

"Let me go out ahead of you. We're not going to argue this one," he ordered when she opened her mouth. He gave her a look that he hoped was enough to keep her safely behind him.

Colin strode ahead, opening the door to step outside.

When nothing unusual occurred, he gave the tag for the car to a valet and went back to get Isabella. They waited inside until he saw the valet arrive with their car.

"Let's go. And be quick," he said. His skin crawled and he couldn't shake the feeling they were being watched. He just hoped the person watching him was one of his friends.

Colin helped Isabella inside the car and went around to slide behind the wheel, letting out his breath as he slammed his door and started the engine. He paused at the exit lane from the restaurant to shed his coat and tie, flinging them onto the back seat. He placed his pistol on the seat between them.

They turned out of the lighted parking lot onto the street.

Isabella watched him, which she realized she could easily do all the time. "Everything's all right, isn't it?" she asked.

"I hope so."

"You don't really think it is."

He shook his head. "No. It's just one of those feelings I get that things aren't right. Call your brother to see if he can come meet us. I can pull off somewhere and you can ride with him."

"I'm not scared," she said. "You keep driving. I'd rather be with you than with Boone, Mike or Jonah. I'm not riding home with my brother like a parent and child after my first date with you."

Colin shot her a look and his pulse jumped. She had turned so she could watch him and even in the darkness of the car, there was enough light from the dials and gauges on the dashboard and lights outside to see the challenging look she was giving him.

He shook his head. "You're the feminine copy of Boone."

"And that's good or bad?"

"There are moments when it's damned exasperating. I didn't feel responsible for Boone."

She laughed. "You're not responsible for me, either!"

"I don't want anything to happen to you or to Boone, but if you're my date, I feel more protective than ever. I didn't ask you out to get you into danger or to have you get hurt."

"I know that, Colin. Stop worrying about me," Isabella said, knowing that he was truly concerned, but she didn't want to ride home with Boone or one of the others.

She knew she had taunted and teased Colin tonight. Sometimes he had been lighthearted and returned the teasing, but occasionally, she knew she'd annoyed him and the barrier between them was definitely in place.

Deciding to leave him alone, she turned to gaze outside as they left Stallion Pass. "I had a wonderful time tonight, Colin. And dinner was delicious."

He smiled. "Fine, Isabella. I'll admit, I had a grand time, too."

"I'm glad!" she exclaimed, impulsively reaching over to squeeze his hand. Instantly he caught her hand in his.

"Is this friendship or flirting?" he asked, squeezing her hand lightly in his.

"Friendship, of course," she replied.

He raised her hand to his lips and brushed light kisses across her knuckles. "Glad to know," he said in a husky voice as sparks from his feathery kisses stirred the smoldering blaze within her.

She started to pull her hand away, but Colin held it, placing their hands on his thigh. His leg was warm, his hand that held hers was warm, but nothing compared to the heat rising in her.

"All right, Colin, I started something I shouldn't have," she said, trying once again to withdraw her hand. This time he let her go and placed both hands on the steering wheel, glancing again in the rearview mirror.

"You think we're being followed?" she asked.

"I know we are, but I imagine it's Peter or Tyler. It could be Brett, but I don't think I'll ever spot Brett. And there's a possibility it could be your brother or one of the guys. We agreed today they wouldn't tail me any longer, but that was Peter's idea. Those guys might have their own ideas about it."

"So you don't have a clue who's back there. I'll call Boone to see if he knows."

"The guys need to work out a different arrangement. This isn't accomplishing anything with one of them trailing along behind me."

When she turned to look back, the next car was far behind them.

"They won't do much good back there."

"It wouldn't take long to catch up. I'm not sure it's one of them, but when we turn off on the county road, we'll know."

She called her brother but got the answering machine, so she broke the connection.

"Here's the county road," Colin said.

He didn't signal, but made a sharp turn, pulling off the road and bouncing over the rough ground. He stopped behind a cedar and cut the lights and engine. Silence enveloped them.

"You're waiting to see if you're being followed?" she asked.

"Yes. And here comes a car."

Headlights swung around the turn as a black car shot past.

"So now what do we do? And how do you know whether that was friend or foe?"

"We wait until that car is out of sight, then we go on to

the ranch. I imagine that was one of my friends, but just in case, we'll tag along behind.''

''If it was Boone or Mike or Jonah, he'll be ticked that you eluded him again. You're making them look really out of practice.''

''If that's the way it is, that's the way it is,'' he said. ''This cat-and-mouse game was their idea.''

She smiled, knowing her brother would be exasperated with himself if he lost Colin a second time.

Colin started the engine and pulled out onto the narrow asphalt county road. He switched on his headlights and slowly gained speed. ''Now we have it all to ourselves,'' he said.

Isabella sat facing him and noticed that he still watched the rearview mirror often. But, except for them, the road remained deserted.

Their lights cut a bright swath in the blackness that surrounded them and she began to feel isolated. As they approached the ancient bridge over Badger Fork Creek, she saw something moving in the darkness off to the side of the road. She twisted in the seat.

''I think there's a car—''

Lights burst on and a car raced onto the road behind them.

She glanced in the passenger side-view mirror and saw that the car behind them was gaining with amazing speed.

''Colin!''

''Dammit!'' Colin swore. ''Hang on!''

She watched as if it were happening to someone else instead of them as the car behind shot forward in a great burst of speed and pulled alongside them.

They were rammed by the other car and metal screeched against metal.

Colin had already turned the wheels. They spun out of control, going off the road and scraping the bridge abutment, smashing through a guardrail and plunging down the hillside.

Colin pumped the brakes, dodging trees, branches scrapping the car. Shots were fired and the rear windshield shattered.

"Get down!" Colin yelled, but Isabella had already grabbed his pistol. She twisted as much as possible, straining against her seat belt to fire through the open rear window at the car that had stopped on the road. The blast was deafening.

Someone returned fire. She squeezed the trigger to fire again and the car on the road sped away.

"Get down, Isabella!" Colin roared again and she turned, doubling over as much as she could with the seat belt still buckled over her. A broad cedar loomed ahead and Colin tried to avoid crashing head-on into it.

It sideswiped the car, but slowed their momentum. In seconds they hit another cedar and slammed to a stop.

"Are you all right?" Colin asked instantly, turning to her and taking the pistol from her hand.

"I'm okay if I can stop shaking," she muttered, grabbing her purse and fishing out her cell phone. "I'm calling Boone."

"Isabella, you were amazing!" Colin ground out the words.

Startled, she looked up at him. Even in the darkness, she could see a burning admiration in his expression that obliterated the danger and the past few seconds. Her heart thudded against her ribs. His hand slipped behind her head.

Before she could catch a breath, his mouth came down on hers and he kissed her. A hard, devouring kiss that turned her white hot with passion. She wrapped her arms around his neck and returned his kiss and forgot danger, her fears, the past few minutes, everything except Colin.

He leaned over her, tongues tangled, his fingers wound

in her hair as he kissed her senseless. She still trembled, only now it was different. Need escalated and she combed her fingers through his thick hair at the back of his head while she kissed him in return, yielding to all the feelings she had for him, thankful to be alive and suspecting that was what had prompted his sudden kiss.

He'd had too many near-death experiences in his life and this was just one more when he was beginning to come out of the consequences of the last one. She wanted to kiss away his past, his hurts, his depression.

After coming so close to tragedy, it was bliss to be alive, to be able to hold each other and to affirm their escape with scalding kisses that stirred up other needs and wiped out the terror of the last few minutes.

And she had been even more impressed with his swift action and quick thinking that had saved them from crashing into the bridge or being rammed off the road at a point where they couldn't have survived.

She ran her hand across his broad shoulder, down his strong arm, feeling the bulge of thick muscle. She wanted him, so much more of him than mere kisses.

He raised his head to look at her.

Dazed, she opened her eyes to find him watching her. All she wanted to do was to pull his head back down for more kisses, but she remembered how they'd gotten where they were.

"Are we safe sitting here?" she asked.

"We're safe from the killer," Colin replied solemnly. "We're not so damn safe from each other." He placed his palm against her cheek. "You really were fantastic back there, Isabella," he said in a husky voice, and there was no mistaking the sincerity of his praise. "Your warning about a car in the woods, gave me a split second to react that I wouldn't have had. You keep a cool head."

"You do, too," she replied, warming to his praise.

"I'm trained to. Let's call Boone and get the hell out of here. It isn't smart to sit here in the dark and kiss. We better move," Colin said. "The driver could come back to see what happened, although since you shot at him, I doubt that he will."

She found her cell phone while Colin turned the keys. "I'll try Boone's cell phone this time."

Colin was surprised when the car engine kicked over and started. "I didn't think the car would run after that wild ride."

He backed up, branches scraping her car. "Reliable car, Isabella. We're okay except for a flat tire or two."

She related to Boone what had happened and broke the connection. "Boone's coming to get us now," she said to Colin. "He's already on the way."

Colin nodded and turned the car. "I don't know whether we can make it back up the hill. We'll try."

The motor roared as he pressed the accelerator. Turning the car around in a slow, bumpy circle, Colin started up the incline.

The tires were flat and the rims dug into the ground.

"We're stuck," Colin said after a moment, cutting the engine. "We'll wait in the car."

"I feel safer here than on the road," Isabella replied.

"The lights are smashed, so I can't turn them on for Boone."

"He knows exactly where we are."

In minutes her cell phone rang. When she answered, she turned to Colin.

"It's Boone. He just wanted us to know that it's him. He's almost here."

"Let's go wait up on the road now. We'll be safe if he's close." Colin tried to open his door, which was smashed. "I have to get out on your side."

"I think we both have to climb out the window," she

said. "If the window opens. If it doesn't, we'll have to break it out."

Colin climbed into the back and tried both doors. "Turn on the ignition and get the windows down."

As soon as she did, he slithered out the back and dropped to his feet. He walked around to help her out.

He leaned into the car, picked her up beneath her arms and she wrapped her arms around his neck as he lifted her out and set her on the ground. For one brief moment they looked into each other's eyes. Colin leaned in to retrieve her purse and his pistol. As they climbed a hill, Isabella could hear an approaching vehicle, its beams cutting a bright swath.

Boone slowed his pickup and pulled up alongside their car.

"You're both all right?" he asked as he climbed out to meet them.

"We're fine," Colin answered.

"Thanks to Colin's driving," she added as they walked to Boone's pickup. His hair was tangled and he was wearing a T-shirt, jeans and sneakers.

"Tyler was following you and lost you when you turned off the state road. Will you stop ditching everyone? We're the good guys and we're trying to keep this from happening and catch the killer."

"Sorry, Boone, but nothing will happen if you guys are ten feet behind me. I'm just sorry Isabella was with me. I tried to get her to call you to come pick her up."

Boone shot her a dark look. "I know how likely that would have been."

"She's a chip off the old block," Colin added. "She got my pistol and fired at him, so he knows he's in for a fight."

"Did your shots hit his car or him?" Boone asked.

Isabella shook her head. "I couldn't tell. We were off the road and going down the hill. See?" She pointed to the place where they had left the road and Boone turned to look at smashed bushes, branches down, chunks knocked out of trees and ground torn up with dark tracks.

"Oh, hell!" He turned to Colin. "Dammit, stop shaking us off your tail!"

"You've got to let him try to get to me or this won't do any good."

"Yeah, but we want you alive, as much as we want to catch him."

Colin shook his head. "We've got to do something different."

"I know one thing—would you two refrain from going out dancing or dining until this is over!" Boone snapped. "It's not like you're dating!"

"Sure thing, Boone," Colin answered lightly.

Isabella thought she detected amusement in his tone. She rode in the middle of the front bench seat in Boone's pickup, ever aware of Colin's muscular body pressed against her side.

He and Boone talked about the night and the possibilities. Each one called one of the other men and she listened as Boone told Mike to try to determine Brett Hamilton's whereabouts while Colin asked Jonah to try to find out where Tyler and Peter had spent the evening and where they were now.

"I can't imagine having to check on Brett or Peter," Boone said, replacing the phone in his pocket, "but we better not overlook anyone."

"I agree with you," Colin said. "I'd rather think it's Tyler than someone we've been friends with and known for years. That would really be grim."

"Yeah, but we need to be sure. Unless it's someone here that none of us know about," Boone said.

"There's always that possibility."

"Do you think you'll be safe at Isabella's tonight?" Boone asked.

"Yes. I can't imagine him coming after me again tonight. We'll have the new alarm system in place. I think we're fine."

"Let's get together with the guys in the morning. We've got to keep you in sight, yet let him make his play. You could've told Mike your route tonight and then he could've hung back farther."

"I don't think he would have been there in time to do anything if he had been a long ways behind us. Boone, I think I'm pretty much on my own in trying to catch him unless we just get real lucky or try to set something up."

"If Mike had been there, he could have gone after the guy."

"You know he would've stopped to see about us."

Isabella sat listening, her nerves slowly calming after the night's excitement. Yet another part of her wasn't going to calm. Excitement from Colin's steamy kisses still bubbled in her and would continue to do so. She wanted more kisses, wanted to be back in his arms. And his praise was just as exciting to her.

She had had a wonderful evening with him up until the attempt on his life.

She was lost in thoughts about his kisses and remembering dancing in his arms until they stopped at the back gate at her place. Both of them thanked Boone who insisted on following them inside.

She fed and watered the dogs while Boone and Colin prowled the house and yard, checking out everything before Boone finally climbed into his pickup and drove away. Colin closed and locked the door behind him and set alarms for the yard and house.

"Let's go have some iced tea," she suggested and Colin nodded.

He reached out and pulled her into his arms. "Come here, Isabella," he said in a husky voice, and her heart thudded.

He pulled her into his embrace, wrapping his arms around her and looking at her intently. "You're some woman! That was impressive tonight."

She wound her arms around his neck and smiled up at him. "Because I didn't go to pieces or faint with fright?"

"Damn straight because of that and a lot more. You were as cool as Boone would have been, turning and firing at the guy. That was one wild ride."

"So you want to kiss me because I'm like my brother," she teased, her pulse racing because she had broken through more of the barriers he kept around himself. She was excited, wound up and she knew it was purely because of his kisses and praise and not the danger they'd been in.

"Your brother is the last thing on my mind right now." Colin leaned down to brush his mouth over hers and then to kiss her solidly.

She returned his kisses until his cell phone rang. Reluctantly, he moved away, swearing under his breath as he pulled out his phone.

The minute he began to talk she knew it was Boone again. She turned to go to the kitchen to get them something to drink. Colin trailed behind her and when she waved a cold bottle of beer at him, he nodded. She filled a glass with ice and poured her tea.

He pocketed his cell phone. "Boone hasn't heard anything yet. He was just checking on us again."

Taking the beer from her, Colin popped the top and followed Isabella to the kitchen table to sit facing her.

"You don't think there will be another attempt on your life tonight?" she asked him.

"No, I don't. If the enemy is one of the guys who came from D.C., he'll get back to cover his tracks and have an alibi for his time tonight. Even if our guy isn't one of them, his plans tonight were foiled and that has to shake him up.''

Colin took a long drink, set down his bottle and leaned on the table, putting himself closer to her to look her directly in the eyes. ''I want you out of this, Isabella. I don't want anything to happen again like tonight.''

''I got along fine and I wasn't hurt except for a few bruises maybe from jostling around in the car,'' she said, looking into his thickly lashed gray eyes and wanting to be in his arms again.

''We're not going to argue. You're out.''

''There are some things I do that you have no control over and no say so about,'' she replied coolly, getting annoyed with his heavy-handed decision to run her life even if his intentions were admirable.

''Do you know how I would feel if something happened to you?''

''You'd feel terrible, so I'll be careful and you'll protect me and everything will be fine.''

''You're out. I'm talking to the guys tomorrow and you can't change this.''

She glared at him. ''All right, we won't go on any more dates. We're not together a lot of the time and I'll be fine.''

''If we hadn't been lucky tonight, you could have been killed.''

''It wasn't luck. You did what you should've to protect us and everything was all right.''

''Dammit. You know I can't go live with one of the guys and put families and children in jeopardy. I need to find a hotel.''

''The guys won't like it. They'll ask me if I want you to move, and you know exactly what I'll tell them. I'm not scared, Colin.''

''You should be!'' he snapped, glaring at her.

''Let's go back like we were and stop arguing. There's

nothing we can do tonight and we're not going out together, except to Boone's next Saturday to the barbecue, and that's the same as staying here at my house. We're not going out together—you know we're safe here.'' She gave him a big smile and he sighed and raked his fingers through his hair, which sprang back. She wished it were her fingers moving through his hair.

''We probably are safe here. So we don't go out together.''

She nodded her head.

He sipped his beer and she watched him. When he lowered the bottle he gazed at her. ''I couldn't tell the make of the car, get a license, or anything. The car was black and driven by a man. What did you see?''

''He had on a ski mask.''

''I didn't even see that much. Get anything else?''

''It was a big, black, four-door car. Colin, that car has to be dented badly where he hit us. I shot at him. The car should be riddled with bullet holes.''

''Mike said they have the authorities already searching for the car. My guess is we'll either never find it or what we find will be stolen, impossible to trace and a worthless lead.''

''How well do you know the men who are here from Washington?''

''We've known two of them pretty damned well.'' He gazed at her with a speculative look and flexed his shoulders. ''We'll be black and blue tomorrow.''

She rubbed her neck. ''I twisted around and my shoulder is already sore. A hot shower ought to help.''

''Suggesting that for both of us?'' he asked, arching his eyebrow.

''No, I'm not. I don't know you that well,'' she replied and he smiled. He picked up his beer and walked around the table, catching her hand in his.

"Come here where it's more comfortable," he said, leading her to the living area. He crossed the room to sit on the sofa. "Turn around and I'll rub your back and neck and shoulder. Maybe it'll help get the kinks out."

She sat down close beside him and turned her back to him, setting her drink on the table. He began to gently knead her shoulders and she closed her eyes. "That's wonderful."

A ring shattered the quiet and Colin stretched out his arm to pick up the phone. "It's Mike," he said, looking at the Caller ID. He picked up the receiver to answer. "Hi, Mike. What did you learn?" he asked.

Chapter 10

Isabella moved around behind Colin and began to massage his shoulders, certain he was just as shaken from the bumpy car ride as she had been. He was solid with hard muscles and she tingled from the contact. As she kneaded his back, she could feel that he was tense.

He turned slightly to look at her, then turned back around.

She was still shaken by the attempt to kill Colin, knowing if the killer had succeeded, she would have been murdered right along with Colin and it would have looked like a wreck. Even though certain people would have known that it wasn't an accident, they would have had no proof.

She knew Colin was going to want to set up a trap and to use himself as bait and she hated that, but she could see the need for it.

She kneaded his back, feeling the warmth through his shirt while she listened to his brief answers and comments. She could tell that he was unhappy with what he was hearing.

golden bangle on her wrist. She wore high-heeled beige sandals. She hummed a tune as she pinned her hair on top of her head.

Finally she went to find Colin, half expecting him to slip out ahead of her and leave her behind to go on her own.

To her satisfaction, she found him in the kitchen. "I'm ready," she said.

He turned and his gaze went over her and then he looked into her eyes and her pulse jumped.

"You're beautiful," he said in a husky voice.

"Thank you," she replied, smiling at him. "Don't sound so unhappy about it."

She received a crooked smile. "It would be much easier to resist you if you were as plain as a mud hen."

She laughed. "Are you trying to resist me?"

"With every ounce of my being," he answered so solemnly her pulse leaped again.

"Wow! Why?"

"Let's go, Isabella. You know why I want to resist you without me telling you again. C'mon. I'll turn on the alarm and lock up."

"Where've you been all week?" she asked once they were outside and strolling toward Boone's place.

"In town," he said.

"Aren't you in a lot more danger there and coming and going?"

"Might be, but that draws danger away from you."

Exasperated, she studied him. ""Are you staying away from here to keep danger from me?"

"That's right. I don't want another incident like the one last Saturday night."

"So what do you do all day in town?"

"I joined a gym. I go work out some more. I read and do research in the library."

"You're making yourself a target."

"Might be. We all want to draw this guy into the open, get this over with and, hopefully, catch him."

"And nothing has happened all this week when you've set yourself up as a target?"

"No, it hasn't. How was your week?"

"Incredibly busy. I've done nine portraits this week."

Colin kept a space between them and resisted the urge to drape his arm across her shoulders and pull her close to his side. Once they joined the group of guests on Boone's terrace, Colin moved away from Isabella. He knew she wanted him with her, and he wanted her close, but he wasn't going to do that. He had promised himself to put distance between them and he had managed to do so all week long. He thought anyday now, the enemy would make another move.

He stood on the edge of the terrace, a beer in hand while he looked around. There were woods beyond the house and yard, and his back tingled. Anyone who could get onto the ranch and get close with a high-powered rifle could pick him off. He didn't like the idea of being here for a dinner party, but Boone and the guys had insisted and all of them were here tonight.

He looked across the terrace at Isabella. She stood in a cluster of men who were laughing at something she was saying. She was beautiful and took his breath tonight with her green blouse and slacks. She was the sexiest woman he had ever known.

The moment he made that decision, shock set in. Always, for years, Danielle had been the sexiest woman in his life.

Was he transferring his longing from one impossible woman for a second equally unattainable one? Isabella was different though. Very different.

He watched her as she laughed and tried to curb his inclinations to go stand beside her and to put his arm around her waist. Instead, he walked over to join Mike and a group of men. Peter Fremont was here tonight, mixing and mingling. They had introduced him as a business associate of Colin's from Washington and everyone had accepted him.

He waited until he was alone with Peter. "Tyler blames himself for the other night's fiasco. He's just thankful you survived, but he blames himself for our man escaping and if anything had happened to you and Isabella Devlin, he would have blamed himself for that, too."

"It wasn't his fault. We were lucky and Isabella has the same nerves of steel that Boone does."

"We should see if she wants to join the Agency."

"I don't think she'd show much interest," Colin replied with a smile. He looked across the terrace and spotted her talking to the Remingtons.

"Excuse me, Peter. I think I'll get another beer."

The sun went down, lanterns came on, a band played and a space was cleared on the terrace for dancing. And then Isabella was there beside him, smiling up at him, and his pulse jumped.

"Scared to dance with me, Colin?"

He inhaled, knowing what he should do and what he wanted to do. He took her drink from her hand and set it on a table. Then he set down his drink. Taking her hand, he led her out to the area where there were already four couples following a lively two-step. They began to dance and he was aware of her at his side, her perfume intoxicating. He turned her and moved with her and when that dance ended and a fast number began, he kept her hand in his and started dancing again, watching her as he turned her and when she moved about him. Her hips swayed and she licked her lips, watching him with a come-hither, challenging look.

There were two fast dances and two more two-steps and they danced without stopping.

"I'm on fire," Colin said. "Let's get a cold drink and wait the next one out." He wiped his brow. He was hot from the exertion of dancing, but he was hotter from wanting Isabella and trying to stay cool and keep the barrier up with her.

He got two tall, cold drinks of iced tea and handed her one, downing his swiftly.

"There's a friend. Excuse me, Colin," she said and was gone. He watched the sway of her hips. The slacks hugged her trim hips and he inhaled swiftly. He wanted her and knowing her had changed him. She was another heartbreak waiting to happen if he fell in love with her, but why couldn't he have an affair and take it as lightly as she did? Most men dreamed of a situation like that. Why was he worrying about falling in love with her?

In minutes he looked around to see her dancing with one of the local cowboys and he clamped his jaws together, knowing he had all but driven her into the guy's arms. The minute the dance was over, he was moving through the couples to stand at her side.

"I think I have the next dance," he said to her. She said something to her partner and the cowboy left. The music began and Colin took her in his arms to dance.

For the rest of the evening, he stayed at her side whether they talked with friends or were dancing. At midnight as they danced, Colin leaned back to look at her.

"Ready to go home?" he asked because already the crowd had thinned.

Her eyes widened and she nodded. "Yes, I am."

He took her hand. "Let's find your brother and Erin and pay our respects and go."

After they found Erin to thank her, they looked for Boone. When they found him and finished thanking him, he clasped Colin on the shoulder.

"I know you walked over in the daylight when people were out, but now it's night and you'll be in the lights on the drive if you walk home. You'll be a target," Boone said. "I've got a car waiting and I'll drive you to your door."

"Why don't I just take the car and bring it back tomorrow?" Colin suggested. Boone nodded, handing him the keys.

"Be careful. I want to hear from the two of you when you get home."

"Yes, Dad," Isabella teased.

"Izzie, this is serious business," Boone said solemnly. "I want to know you're locked in safely."

"I'll call," Colin said. He took the keys and put his arm around Isabella's shoulders as they left to hurry to the car. It was parked in the garage and they drove to her connecting garage.

When they were inside her house, she fixed cold drinks while Colin searched the house and checked locks and finally called Boone. She carried the drinks to the family room. As she passed through the dining room, she could see Colin's reflection in the mirror over the buffet and she watched as he turned on a small table lamp. He switched off the bright lights, put on music and turned when she entered the room.

He was talking once again on his cell phone and she suspected he was talking to her brother again. She set their drinks on the coffee table, kicked off her high heels and began to dance around him while she listened to the music.

Once she slanted him a look and her pulse jumped at the desire in his gray eyes as he watched her. A faint smile curled one corner of his mouth and his eyebrow arched in a look that speeded her heartbeat.

She tilted her head and half closed her eyes and continued to move, listening to his conversation and hearing words about guard and lights and undercover and not caring tonight what he was talking about. She had danced with him during the evening and she wanted to kiss him now. She wanted his kisses and his arms around her.

Colin barely heard Mike as he talked. Shifting his weight, Colin watched Isabella. She was an enticing fire that would burn him to cinders if he got too close. Yet she was taunting him right now and she knew it. She was going to keep at it until she got the response from him she wanted.

He tried to keep his mind on what Mike was saying about security and the coming week, setting a trap for the killer, but Colin couldn't focus on anything except Isabella. He watched her hips move.

He knew he was a project of hers, but tonight he didn't care. She had succeeded in making him savor life again and right now, she had succeeded in making him want her enough to toss aside wisdom.

She knew what she was doing. He was amused, but he also wanted to make love to her and to spend a night of passion with her. She was filled with life, eager to share it.

At last Mike signed off and Colin set his phone on the table. He stepped in front of her, gyrating with her and watching her, a seductive dance that was a hint of what was to come.

She smiled at him and turned in front of him, moving her hips and enticing him. She was throwing him a challenge that he couldn't resist. He reached for her to pull her into his embrace and they slow-danced to the soft music, barely moving while his desire heightened.

"I've waited all night for this moment," he said in a husky voice. "You're beautiful, Isabella."

Isabella looked up into smoky eyes that held unmistakable desire and her heart thudded. "Thank you. So down come the barriers for a little while, Colin?"

"I think you demolished those barriers the first few days I was here."

"I hope so. I like you better without them."

When he pulled her closer, his gaze went to her mouth

and she couldn't catch her breath. She tingled all over and wanted to pull his head down and kiss him. She longed to wrap her arms around him.

And then he did slip his arm around her waist and pull her tightly against him while his head came down and his mouth was on hers. She closed her eyes and wound her arms around his neck and trembled as he kissed her.

He tightened his arm and leaned over her as she held him tightly. Wanting to be loved and wanting to make love to him, she kissed him eagerly.

The barriers were gone and she knew it. He had changed and was kissing her senseless and she shook with an over-whelming need for all of him. She thought he was marvel-ous, sexy, exciting.

She yearned for him to be whole again and not wounded and aching and giving up on his future. The man holding her and kissing her now wasn't giving up on life. Joy bub-bled in her. Far from giving up, he wound his fingers in her hair and sent pins flying as he kissed her passionately.

Her pulse raced and she melted in his arms, desiring him with all her being. His hand slid down her back, down over her bottom to cup her and pull her tightly against him. She felt his arousal, knew he desired her.

He shifted slightly to twist free the buttons on her blouse and shove it off her shoulders. Cool air rushed over her, but she was only dimly aware of it as he cupped her covered breasts and circled her nipples with his thumbs.

She had never really been deeply in love and it wasn't going to happen now. Even if they kissed the night away, she was sure her future was secure, her heart protected.

Colin unfastened the clasp to her bra and stepped back to cup her breasts. He inhaled as she unbuttoned his shirt and pushed it away. Then his thumbs circled her nipples and she gasped with pleasure, closing her eyes and gripping his upper arms.

"You're beautiful, Isabella," he murmured and leaned down to take a nipple in his mouth. His warm tongue circled the taut peak and she shook with need. She ached for more, clinging to him and reveling in the pleasure he was giving before she opened her eyes to pull his head down so she could kiss him again.

Leaning away, she paused. "Welcome to the land of the living, Colin," she whispered.

"You little witch, you healed my heart with your magic. You don't know what it's like to hurt, but you did get me over my hurt. You're right, I'm back in the land of the living and it's glorious."

He framed her face with his hands. Surprised, she looked into his gray eyes, which had darkened with desire. The possessive, determined look she saw in his expression made her insides clutch. "Your heart may be untouchable, but I'm going to love you until you're ready to fall into a million pieces. You're going to remember this night, Isabella. I'm not going to be one of your projects that you easily forget."

"I won't ever forget you, Colin," she said, realizing that it was the truth. She couldn't forget him.

He leaned down to kiss her, slowly, with a devastating thoroughness that had her trembling and wanting him. She unfastened his belt and tugged it loose, then undid his slacks, letting them fall around his ankles.

Watching her, he released her and stepped out of his slacks and peeled away his boots and socks. He was lean, muscled and irresistible. She reached forward to tug down his briefs and free him from their constraints, taking his thick shaft in her hand to stroke and caress him before she leaned down to kiss him.

He gasped and hauled her up to kiss her hard. While he

kissed her, he unfastened her slacks. She stepped out of them when they pooled around her ankles.

As he showered kisses on her, his hands were all over her with tantalizing caresses that fanned the flames already burning in her.

His hand caressed her legs and then his fingers were between her thighs, stroking her and driving her to a new height of need. "Colin—" she gasped.

He picked her up to place her on the wide sofa and knelt to stream kisses from her ankle up her leg to the inside of her thigh. She opened her legs and he caressed her before his tongue dawdled where his fingers had been.

Dizzying sensations bombarded her and she closed her eyes, clinging to his strong shoulder with one hand, the other tangled in his short hair. Her hips arched beneath his hands and she cried out in need. When he cupped her breast, his tongue circled her nipple.

"Colin, I want you," she cried.

"We're just starting, darlin'," he whispered, showering kisses over her stomach and along her inner thighs.

He turned her over, kneeling between her legs while he kissed behind her knees and then up until he reached her nape.

She turned and sat up, gasping as she looked at him. Desire raged in her like wildfire and she didn't want to wait any longer. "Love me," she whispered, then kissed him hard. Her hands fondled him until she finally moved him between her legs as she sat on the edge of the sofa.

The soft light bathed his muscles in a golden glow, highlighting them and the shadows of the planes of his face and body. She kissed his scars lightly. "I'm sorry you were hurt. I wish I could take away all the hurts you had."

"The hurt is over," he mumbled while his fingers tangled in her hair.

Her gaze went over his magnificent body, which was so fit and virile now that the scars no longer mattered.

"You're handsome, Colin. You fascinate me," she whispered, stroking his manhood, kissing him lightly.

He slipped his hands underneath her arms and pulled her to her feet. For an instant they gazed into each other's eyes and desire was hot and intense.

This was the Colin she had known existed and tried to coax back to life. Now he was here, sexy, full of energy, demolishing her in a tantalizing way.

He leaned down to kiss her breasts again, starting an exquisite torment that escalated with each stroke of his tongue and caress of his fingers.

"I want to know every inch of you," he whispered. "I want to love you all over." He lifted her hair to kiss her nape, turning her and pulling against him while he stood behind her.

He caressed her breasts and Isabella closed her eyes, leaning back against him and winding one arm behind his head. His shaft was against her bottom and she wanted him more with each kiss and touch.

She had to turn and wrap her arms around him and kiss him. "Love me, Colin," she whispered before she pulled him close to kiss him again.

He picked her up and placed her on the sofa, coming down to stretch out on his side and hold her close. His hands were everywhere again, the sweet torment spiraling.

His fingers slipped between her legs, finding her most intimate feminine place to stroke her into a frenzy of need. She moved her hips, aching for him.

"Colin, love me!" she cried, clinging to him as he continued to caress her.

"Isabella, are you protected?" he asked. When she shook her head, he stepped away to find his slacks and retrieve a packet from his billfold.

He knelt between her legs while he opened the packet. Isabella watched him, her heart pounding with excitement. Then he lowered himself and she wrapped her long legs around him as she clasped her hands behind his neck.

He kissed her and she arched her hips beneath him, pulling him closer. His shaft touched her, entered slowly. She cried out, "Love me!"

She slid her hand down his back and over his firm buttocks, pulling him up as she arched against him. "Colin," she cried again and then his mouth covered hers.

He moved slowly, a hot, exquisite torment that drove her wild. She thrashed beneath him, kissing him, crying out, wanting him as he slowly filled her.

Colin had drawn out their lovemaking, wanting to drive her to complete abandon, wanting to know every inch of her beautiful, sexy body. He knew his control wasn't going to last, but he tried to hold on, to give her all the loving he could.

He had dreamed about this moment every night for too long now. She was a challenge and torment whenever they were together and he had wanted her more with each passing day, but he had tried to resist, to ignore her, to keep away. It was a lost cause and now she was in his arms, beautiful, hot, a dream fulfilled.

Thoughts spun away and his control went with them. He thrust swiftly and Isabella moved with him, clinging to him. "Darlin'! Isabella!" he gasped as he shuddered with release.

Dimly, Isabella heard him cry her name as her own explosive relief filled her with rapture. She held him, ecstasy pouring through every vein in her body. Her heart pounded violently while she gasped for breath.

"Colin, darling Colin," she whispered, stroking his head. He turned and they looked into each other's eyes. Her heart slammed against her ribs as she felt a bonding with him in that instant that went far beyond anything physical.

He kissed her, deep and long and she kissed him in return while her heart continued to hammer. She knew this night was special in her life and would be forever etched in her memory.

He raised his head to look at her again and smiled at her. Her heart melted at that smile that could coax the stars right out of the sky. She stroked his face and ran her hand down his back.

"You're very special," he said softly and she pulled him down to kiss him again.

Finally he rolled onto his side and kept her with him and they gazed at each other. "You're wonderful," he said.

"I seem to remember something to the effect that I'm a witch."

"That you are. You worked your magic spell on me and transformed me."

"Not from a toad. Or if I changed you from a toad, you were the most desirable, handsome toad I've ever seen!"

"Is that right?" he teased. "Well, you need to work another magic spell now because I think my bones have turned to mush."

"My magic spells have fizzled. And I'm as boneless as you. I hope we don't have to do anything for the rest of the night except lie here and enjoy each other."

"I'll second that," he said, sprinkling light kisses along her temple to her ear to her throat.

"Tonight was what I've dreamed about," she said languidly.

"It's definitely what I've been dreaming about," he said. "And imagining—"

She raised her head slightly to look into his eyes. "You didn't act like you'd been dreaming about it."

"I did try to resist your wiles and seduction and to hang on to wisdom because there was nothing wise about this tonight. It's a dangerous time, and I wanted to keep a clear head.''

''You just keep your head as clear as you want,'' she said lightly as she kissed his jaw and dressed her fingers across his chest. ''I'll entertain myself in my own way.''

He chuckled softly, a deep, throaty masculine sound. ''As soon as I get enough energy, I'll carry you to my bedroom and we can have a bed to stretch out on.''

''I'm fine here. I could stay right here for the next week.''

''I can stay right here for another few minutes and then I think I'm going to want to do other things.''

''Should I ask what other things?'' she asked, smiling at him as he brushed kisses over her temple to her ear.

''Love you all over again,'' he drawled.

Colin stood, picked her up easily, and carried her to his bathroom to set her on her feet while he ran water in the tub.

''Let's soak and scrub and see what other fun we can discover.''

''That's a deal,'' she said, lighting candles and moving around to set them close to the tub.

''Isabella,'' he said in a husky voice and she turned to look up at him.

Chapter 11

He was aroused again, hard and ready, and desire had re-kindled in his gray eyes. Her heart missed a beat as he reached for her, taking the matches from her hand and setting them down.

He picked her up and settled in the tub and she turned to straddle him while they kissed. His body was warm, wet, slippery and his hands were all over her, starting the excitement again, igniting flames that had briefly turned dormant.

She caressed him while he fondled her until he finally stood, splashing water everywhere. He stepped out of the tub and left to return with a packet. Once he put on the condom, he picked her up and she locked her long legs around him. He leaned against the door and lowered her onto his manhood and then they moved together.

She flung her head back as he kissed her throat. She was caught in another dizzying spiral of desire that spun out of control until release came and she felt him thrust wildly.

"Isabella, darlin'," he cried.

She loved hearing him say the endearment. She held him tightly. "My dear Colin," she whispered. Joy filled her not only because of their loving, but because she felt Colin was whole once again. Maybe in time he would be even more the fun-loving person he had once been, but what was important, he was no longer shut away in his own small world where no one could touch him in any manner.

Slowly, he lowered her until she stood, then he kissed her for a long time. When he raised his head again, he picked her up and they climbed back into the tub. He turned on the hot water while she settled in his lap, leaning back against him.

"Ah, darlin', this is perfection. I don't want to ever let you go."

"I don't want you to. If we could just stay right here, Colin, wouldn't that be nice?"

"It would be heaven, but a little impractical. I don't believe you could take many pictures and as for catching a killer, well, that would be definitely out."

"Mr. Practical," she murmured as she stroked his legs. "What a marvelous body you have!"

He chuckled. "I'm glad you think so, but I don't know why you do. It's been blown apart and put back together more than once."

"It was put together quite nicely. And all the necessary parts are here, I think. Let me see," she said, sliding her hand beneath her bottom to touch him high on his thigh.

He chuckled again and nuzzled her neck. "You'll start something all over again."

"Is that a promise?" she asked, turning around.

His arms wrapped around her and he leaned down to kiss her. Their kisses lengthened and in minutes he stood and helped her out of the tub, handing her a towel as he picked up one for himself. They slowly, sensuously, dried each other off in loving, light strokes that built desire again.

"You rakish rascal…" she said.

"You wanton dream come true," he whispered as he leaned down to kiss her breast. She gasped and closed her eyes, clinging to his broad shoulders and sliding one hand down to caress him.

Finally he picked her up and carried her to his bed to kneel and place her on the bed and then he trailed kisses over her, his lovemaking slow and languorous, building fires in her that raged even more than before.

They loved through the night and fell asleep in each other's arms near dawn.

Colin drifted off to sleep first and Isabella held him close, looking at his lashes feather over his cheeks, his full underlip that could be so sensual, his mouth that could drive her wild. He dazzled and excited her and tonight had been magic from the first moment. She didn't want it to end, didn't want to let the world intrude on them.

He was a wonder to her and she touched his jaw lightly, ran her fingers through his thick, short hair, traced his cheekbone and then ran her fingers across his muscled chest.

"You're wonderful, Colin," she whispered. She touched a scar along his shoulder and then wrapped her arm around him and hugged him lightly, wishing he had never been hurt or lost years from his life.

He was here now and all right, she reminded herself and she suspected he was well on the emotional mend. She smiled and closed her eyes, drifting off to sleep holding him close.

Tossing and turning, Colin came awake with a jolt. He was drenched in sweat. Staring into the darkness, he raked his fingers through his hair.

"Colin, what's the matter?" Isabella asked in a sleep-filled, throaty voice.

"I was dreaming and I was remembering," he replied.

Tucking the sheet beneath her arms, she sat up to face him. "You remember more?"

"Yes. I remember their leader. He's not the double agent, but I can identify him. I'll call Washington and let them know."

"Tell me about it," she urged.

"I freed the hostage and we started out. Three armed men blocked our way—one was the ringleader. There were words and shots exchanged and then they were gone and we ran out the front. As we ran out, a car bomb exploded."

"Then you remember it all!" she exclaimed.

He shook his head. "No. There's something that still escapes me," he said, rubbing his forehead. "There's still something."

"You've remembered this much. You'll remember it all."

"I hope," he said. He lay down and pulled her into his arms. "I still think you're the reason my memory is returning."

"If so, I'm glad."

He pulled her closer to kiss her and memories were forgotten.

In the early-morning light Colin stirred and tightened his arm around Isabella as he slowly came awake. He remembered the night, and desire rekindled as he looked down at her asleep in his arms. He held her, but he knew it was an illusion—no one could really ever hold Isabella. She was a free spirit and he better keep his heart as locked away as it had been when he arrived in Stallion Pass.

What a woman she was! Exciting, sexy, quick-thinking, brave. He stroked her hair away from her face to look at her. Gorgeous minx. Desire heated him and he let his gaze roam over her, his fingers play lightly with her breast, caressing her, watching her reaction, even while asleep. She stirred, tightened her arms around him and opened her eyes.

He looked into blue eyes that changed as he watched her. Longing filled her gaze and she slipped her slender arm around his neck.

"Come here, Colin," she whispered, and pulled him to her.

He kissed her, wanting her again more than he had during the night. She was warm, soft and beautiful, pliant in his arms as her languor transformed to eagerness and she kissed him in return.

He rolled over onto his back and pulled her across him. She straddled him as she kissed him and then scooted down. While she caressed him, her tongue flicked across his chest, going lower over his stomach, down to stroke his manhood. She poured kisses on him, wanting to pleasure him as he had her.

He rolled her over so he could make love to her, kissing her passionately while he held her in his arms.

Isabella gave herself to Colin, shaken by the intensity of his kisses while his hands worked their own magic and brought her to a bone-melting need.

Finally, sheathed in a condom, he entered her. As he prolonged his loving, he drove her wild. He was strong, fantastic; a deliberate, intense lover who made her feel as if she were the only woman who could possibly make him happy.

When release came, she was enveloped in ecstasy, lost to everything except Colin's mouth and hands and body.

As they both gasped for breath, he held her close. "This is the best possible way to wake up and start the day," he said.

She smiled. "If I were a cat, I would purr. Or if I were

a flower, I'd bloom. But since I'm a woman, all I can do is snuggle up against you and hold you tighter and smile.''

"Works fine for me," he said, holding her close against him and spreading light kisses across her temple. "Your brother will call to see if you want him to pick you up to go to church."

"No, he won't. I told him I wasn't going last night."

Colin leaned back to look at her and his eyebrows arched. "So what reason did you give?"

"That I'm staying close to the ranch whenever possible."

"I don't think your brother is going to buy that one."

"I don't know why not. Also, do you think I've never displeased my brother before in my life?"

Colin smiled. "On occasion, you probably drive him nuts."

"You and I've had about two hours' total sleep, but I don't feel sleepy or groggy."

"Neither do I, but I'll tell you what I do feel—hungry."

"Then let's go eat," she said, starting to get up.

"Come here," he said, hauling her into his arms to carry her to the bathroom where they showered together. When they started to make love again, she caught his hands and slipped away from him, tossing him a towel.

"You said you're hungry and I'm starving. Let's do something about it," she said and sashayed out of the bathroom. He watched her bare bottom before she disappeared through the door and knew his appetite for food was gone. What he wanted was Isabella. He dried himself off, suspecting she was already half dressed and headed for the kitchen.

He pulled on his briefs and jeans and a T-shirt and then went to the kitchen.

She was dancing and humming while she worked and he watched her a moment, his pulse racing. She wore cutoffs and a T-shirt. Her hair was caught up in a ponytail that swung as she danced.

She was filled with energy and vitality and he knew how she could channel that energy into passion in bed and he wanted her back in his arms, naked, responsive, eager.

Instead he took a deep breath and tried to focus on something else in the kitchen, hoping his body would cool down.

"What's for breakfast?" he asked as he got out orange juice to pour them both glasses.

"My special omelette."

"Sounds yummy," he said, nuzzling her neck and catching the soapy smell on her skin, thinking about her instead of eggs.

"Now this omelet can't wait, so you get the coffee and stop doing things that will totally befuddle me and ruin my cooking."

"This distracts you?" he asked, kissing her nape again. "I'm not even using my hands. As a matter of fact, I'm barely touching you."

"You know exactly what you're doing and you're going to ruin a good omelette and half a dozen eggs."

"I wouldn't dream of ruining anything for you," he said in a husky voice, wanting to take her into his arms. Instead he walked away to busy himself with making coffee and retrieving the bowl of fresh fruit from the refrigerator.

He returned to watch her as she cooked, standing with his arm around her waist. She thrust the spatula into his hand.

"Here, you watch. And don't ruin all my efforts."

"Never!" he said, kissing her lightly.

In minutes they were seated at the table and he took his first bite of golden omelette. "This is great," he said as he savored an omelette with thick cheese and green chilies.

"My specialty," she said, smiling at him, and when he

looked at her mouth, he knew he better keep his mind on his food.

They made it halfway through breakfast before his appetite fled and he got up to walk around the table and pull her into his arms. She came eagerly and they finally made love on the thick rug in the family room.

"Is this the way we're spending the day?"

"Suits me if it suits you," he replied, and she laughed.

"It suits me absolutely. I've been dreaming of this."

"So have I," he replied, combing his fingers through her hair and kissing her temple lightly.

"Oh, no, you haven't," she said. "You've been trying to avoid dreaming about it."

"Maybe, but I was failing miserably at that."

She laughed and hugged him and he smiled at her. "This is great, Isabella. Really great."

"I think so, too," she said, leaning down to kiss him lightly.

"I need to call Washington and tell them what I've remembered," he said, leaving her to make his call.

"They're sending pictures to see if I can identify the men from my memories," he announced when he returned. "I called Mike and told him. He'll tell the others."

"So now I have your full undivided attention?" Isabella demanded.

"You definitely have my undivided attention," Colin agreed cheerfully, swinging her into his arms to carry her into the bedroom.

The next time they ate was at ten o'clock that night. She grilled steaks after a brief argument about Colin standing outside and then they ate steaks and baked potatoes and a tossed green salad.

Isabella hummed with happiness. Colin was relaxed, smiling constantly, his dark, brooding manner gone. He was incredibly sexy and they hadn't been able to keep their hands off each other or stop kissing and loving the entire day and into the night.

She thought he was the sexiest, most exciting man she had ever known and her heart raced as she looked at him.

They fell asleep far into the early morning hours, locked in each other's arms.

She had toyed with the idea of taking Monday off, but Colin had made plans with her brother and the others so she knew she would have to leave him and go to work and the idyll would be over.

She was late to work, finally arriving at ten just before an appointment at half-past the hour. She could barely concentrate on anything except the actual photography. The rest of the time, her thoughts kept flying back to Colin and the hours of lovemaking.

She couldn't wait for evening to come and as soon as she could, she left work. She rushed into the house when she got home. ''Colin!''

He came out of the bedroom and caught her in his arms as she flung herself at him. He picked her up while they kissed and then he carried her into his bedroom to make love to her.

Later, as he held her close and played with her hair, he thought about the day. ''Mike talked to me again. He wants me to go to work with him. It would be like a partnership, although officially it's a corporation. We'd share equally in the business.''

She twisted around to prop herself on an elbow and look at him. ''Do you want to?''

''It's appealing. I like Stallion Pass. You're here. My friends are here. It's a business I know and can do.''

''It's dangerous.''

''Not too. Most of the jobs he's taking now are for corporations about their electronic security as well as their security in general.''

''So you're not going off by yourself,'' she said quietly, holding her breath, realizing that she wanted to know for certain if he had abandoned that plan.

He smiled at her and pulled her down to kiss her before he shifted back to answer her. ''No, I'm not going off to be a hermit.''

''Hallelujah!'' she said, smiling at him in return.

''One more stray you've saved.''

''You were hardly a stray. Just someone hurt. Maybe I brought some sunshine to get rid of the dark in your life.''

''That's an understatement.''

''Eat lunch with me tomorrow. We can eat in my office and no one can get to you there.''

''I don't want to expose you to danger any more than I already have.''

''I think you've exposed me plenty,'' she said, laughing and rubbing her hip against him. ''C'mon. You won't expose me—and I miss you. Just lunch. Okay? You can come in the back way. C'mon, Colin.''

''Against good judgment, all right. You know I want to be with you. I forgot an appointment yesterday with Mike.''

She giggled and he squeezed her. ''You think that's funny, but it's not. All right, lunch at noon, and I'll come in the back. I'll bring something—maybe pizza.''

''Yum. Has anything turned up about the wreck we had or that stolen car?''

''Nothing. It was stolen off the street in San Antonio. That would have been easy to do. There are no leads, but we know he's here.''

A chill ran over Isabella and she tightened her arm around Colin's narrow waist. ''If he's here, how long will he wait to do something?''

''That's the big question. I think we'll get him. He's made two attempts on my life. He'll come after me again, and I just hope we're all ready. If we can catch him, then I'll be free to make decisions about the future."

She snuggled down against him again. "The future is now and I love it!"

"Wanton wench," he teased, turning to fondle her breast as he kissed her and conversation evaporated.

Isabella was wrapped in euphoria the next day, constantly watching the clock and eager for Colin to appear. She had dressed in a tailored orange blouse and skirt and had her hair tied behind her head with an orange silk scarf.

The minute Colin stepped through the back door, her pulse jumped. From a man with rugged good looks, he was quickly becoming the most handsome man she had ever known. Her gaze ran over him as swiftly as his passed over her. Carrying a pizza box in his hand, he wore brown slacks and a tan shirt that complemented his tanned skin and gray eyes.

"Do you smell yummy! I've been counting the minutes," she said as she walked up and kissed his cheek. She took the pizza. "We'll put this in my office. Before we eat, come say hello to Nick and Sandy. Right now, clients are gone and it's quiet. Nick is getting ready to leave for a photography session on the square for the mayor."

"I don't envy him that job."

She smiled as she accompanied Colin through the office as he said hello to Nick and Sandy.

"We'll be in my office having lunch if you need me," Isabella told Sandy. "I don't have an appointment until two o'clock today."

Sandy nodded her head and Isabella took his hand to walk back to her office. The minute she closed the door, she threw herself into his arms and wrapped her legs around him.

Startled, Colin caught her and braced his feet while he kissed her hard. Desire escalated and he kept expecting her to push him away, but she didn't as he slid his hand beneath her skirt to slip his fingers into her silk panties.

In seconds she lowered herself to the floor and while they kissed, she unbuckled his belt.

He twisted away an inch to look down at her in surprise. "In your office, Isabella?"

She stood on tiptoe to kiss him. One look into her sultry, blue eyes and he had his answer. While he kissed her, he fumbled a packet from his billfold and as he put on the condom, her hands played over his chest.

He tugged away her panties and dropped them, turning with her to lean back against the door. He picked her up and she wrapped her long legs around him again.

Kissing her, he lowered her onto his thick shaft, sensations rocking him. He was lost now and beyond the point of no return as she moved with him and the world ceased to exist.

When release exploded within her, Isabella muffled a cry against his shoulder. They slowly regained their breaths and he stood while he continued to kiss her.

He raised his head to look at her, amusement, satisfaction and mischief in his eyes. "You forever surprise me," he said.

She jerked her head. "I have my private bathroom over here."

He nodded and left her and she gathered up her discarded clothes.

Shortly, they were both dressed and she had combed her hair again and retied it in her orange scarf. He watched her with amusement as she put the pizza in her microwave oven to reheat it. In minutes they had lunch spread on her desk.

"You didn't tell me the program for today. I would've been looking forward to this even more."

She winked at him. "I have to stay full of surprises to keep you interested."

He leaned closer to catch her chin. "Darlin', I'll alway be interested."

She smiled at him. "Be careful or my appetite for pizz will be gone." Her pulse skipped with his words and th unmistakable desire in his eyes. She leaned closer to hir and put her chin on both her fists. "Colin, please let m take your picture."

He laughed. "Was the lovemaking to soften me and ge your way?"

"I don't think it softened you up so much," she drawlec giving him a hot look that sent his pulse racing. "Just a fev pictures. You're being here is no secret any longer and that' the reason you gave me before."

"All right, Isabella. You may take my picture. Why yo want to, I'll never know."

She flung her arms around his neck and kissed him lon and hard before she sat down and smiled at him. "Tonigl we'll go out on the ranch. You can bring all sorts of guy to protect you and let me take a few pictures in the wood: That's wonderful. When you see your pictures, you'll kno why I wanted to take them. You have that mysteriou haunted look that is intriguing."

"Mysterious!" He shook his head. "Whatever please you, pleases me."

"So how's it going with catching your man?"

Colin shrugged and leaned back. "I think I have too man people trying to protect me. We're in an argument about i Peter and Tyler don't know about Brett who stays some where in the background. Brett is highly competent. So Pe ter and Tyler are taking turns. But that means two peopl following me and while Peter and Tyler are good at i they're not that good. They haven't been on the street or i action like Brett. They've had too many hours in the offic and I think it's easy to spot them."

"Can you get rid of them?"

He nodded. "I'm working on it. Then, even though they deny it, I think Boone and Mike and Jonah are taking shifts. That means three guys are tagging after me. It's like a damn Clouseau movie and it would be funny if it wasn't a life or death matter. I don't think our spy can risk coming after me and he's just going to wait them out."

"I take it you've talked to all of them about it."

Colin nodded and drank soda from a can, setting the cold can on a coaster on her desk. "We're hashing it out. They don't agree and your brother and those guys deny that they're following, but I know they are. I've seen them."

"So if all of them pull away, you think you'll be safe with just Brett?"

"Definitely. A lot safer than this way. This is ludicrous."

"Why won't Boone and friends agree?"

"I told you, they keep saying they're not following me. I figure a few more days of this and some of them will see it my way because the guy won't make a move with this entourage traveling with me."

"Frankly, I'm glad to hear it, but I know it just postpones the inevitable. I've lived all my life with Boone doing wild and scary things and I've accepted it—''

"And done some of them with him," Colin interjected dryly. "I seem to remember Boone talking about you two skinny-dipping in a strip mine at night one time when you were kids. That's insane."

"I didn't get my head under. Anyway, I always accepted all those things, but I'll have to admit, I'm worrying about you in a way I never did with my brother."

"Is that right?" Colin said, leaning across the desk, his lunch forgotten.

"Don't let it go to your head."

"It went somewhere else. Come here," he said, taking her wrist and pulling her into his lap to kiss her. Finally she pushed against his chest and stood up, straightening her clothes.

"I have an appointment and I can't look too rumpled."

He grinned and stood. "I'm late for my appointment with Mike, but that's nothing new." He gathered up the empty cans and she caught his wrist.

"Give me those, and you go on to your appointment."

"See you at home tonight," he said. He slipped his hand behind her head and gazed at her solemnly. "You keep alert about what's going on around you. He could snatch you to get at me."

"That just makes my day."

"You might as well have your guard up. I feel certain I'm being watched by our man."

"How on earth would you know with all these guys following you?"

Instead of answering her, he pulled her close to kiss her long and thoroughly before he released her. "That's the best lunch I ever had."

She grinned. "I hoped it would be. Eat lunch with me tomorrow."

He laughed and nodded. "Same time, same place, same menu. See you at the ranch tonight." She followed him to the door, standing in the doorway to watch him climb into his car and drive away. She looked up and down the alley, seeing someone park and go into a store, waving at another person she knew who worked two doors down. She didn't see anyone tailing Colin, but she was certain he knew what he was talking about.

A chill slithered through her as she thought about the danger he was constantly in. There were moments in each other's arms when danger seemed far removed, yet it actually wasn't. They were all so sure they could catch the killer, but she knew what danger stalked Colin.

* * *

Colin entered Mike's office and closed the door. "Sit down," Mike said, coming around his desk to shake hands with Colin. Mike, wearing a red sport shirt and charcoal slacks, looked content.

"Marriage must be good for you. You're more relaxed these days than I ever recall in the military."

"Marriage is great for me," Mike replied, amused. "There's no way to compare it to military life." He turned a chair to sit facing Colin, rather than put the desk between them. "What's up?"

"I want you, Boone and Jonah to stop tailing me. Don't tell me you're not because I'm sure you are."

"We must be getting sloppy."

"Look, Brett's tailing me and he's damn good. I haven't spotted him once, but I know he's there. He would have been there to chase the killer, but Tyler led him away from me. He followed Tyler that night, thinking I was ahead of Tyler. I'd pulled off and was hiding in the bushes until they drove past. And I don't think our man would've made a try if he had seen headlights in the distance behind me."

"Okay, I'll tell the guys. We just don't want you hurt. This was our idea to make you bait. We don't want it to end up going wrong."

"I know you don't and it was a good idea because if we can catch him, I can lead a normal life. That's worth risk. I'm counting on Brett and I keep telling you, he's good at what he does."

"Okay," Mike said, crossing his legs, "so we'll pull back. You be careful. We can't think of another thing we can do to help you."

"Just stay where I can reach you if I need you."

Mike nodded. "That's damn little, but okay. Which man is following you now? Do you even know?"

"Yes. It's Peter. We've had enough contact that I know

their schedules. One thing, we know the killer is in Stallion Pass. He's here and he's watching and waiting. Let's get him."

"You just be careful and don't take any unnecessary chances. I'm still not over letting you go in alone—"

"Forget it, Mike, for once and forever. On that mission each of us did what we thought we should. Now, think about where I can go and what I can do that might draw our guy out."

"Will do. I'm glad you're beginning to get your memory back."

"Yeah. There's still something—I just know there is. I still feel a gap."

"It'll come. Give it time."

"See you later, Mike." He stood and Mike followed him to the door where they said goodbye.

As soon as Colin left, Mike called Jonah and asked him to call Boone so they could all get together. He had a plan that he didn't want to discuss over the phone.

Late that afternoon the three met on Jonah's ranch. Mike drove his pickup beneath a tall live oak. Shade spilled over his friends and as he looked at Jonah in boots, jeans and a Western shirt and Boone in almost the same attire, he realized they were turning into cowboys.

Marriage and Texas agreed with all three of them, Mike knew, and he was heartily thankful for Savannah and Jessie coming into his life.

The three had parked their pickups far from the highway to insure no one could follow them without being easily observed. Climbing out of his pickup, Mike walked up to the other two men and greeted them.

"Colin stopped by the office today. He wants us to quit tailing him. He said that Brett always does and Peter and Tyler take shifts. Three trailing along behind him keep the killer away."

Jonah nodded. "I agree, but none of us want Colin hurt."

"How about we follow Peter and Tyler when they're off their shift with Colin?"

Jonah nodded while Boone rubbed his jaw. "If they're legit, then we're leaving Colin in the lurch."

"Not if Brett is doing his job. And the other one, either Peter or Tyler, will be somewhere in the background with Colin."

"I think you have a smart idea," Jonah said quietly. "It's something we can do, and it may turn out to be important."

"Settled?" Mike asked and the other two nodded. "Okay, let's work out a schedule. We can let whoever sees Colin next know what we're doing. I still don't think the phones are safe."

"I agree," Boone said. "I can take the first shift. Which man do I follow?"

"Peter is tailing Colin now," Mike replied. "Once we get started tailing one of them, we'll know which one is with Colin."

"Let's hope something works here," Jonah said. "Colin needs a break and he sure as hell doesn't need any more trouble or to get hurt again."

"I hope we're doing the right thing," Boone added before they broke up and each climbed into his own truck.

As Colin drove to the ranch late in the afternoon, he glanced in the rearview mirror. There was traffic on the highway and with two cars between them, he spotted the ever-present black sedan. Both Peter and Tyler had rented identical black sedans and they were incredibly easy to spot. Colin shook his head. He knew he should be glad they were back there, but he suspected they were keeping anything from happening. His thoughts jumped to Isabella and anticipation heightened his excitement over getting home to her.

Desire fanned to life, heating him while he thought about last night and today's lunch date. Was he falling in love again? He hoped to hell not because he was certain her heart was safely secured in a vault more protective than Fort Knox.

But life with Isabella was fantastic. He couldn't look far into the future and he saw no point in it. Instead, he just accepted each day and enjoyed being with her and loving her. When this was over and they had to part, they would.

He knew he had frightened her slightly at lunch when he had warned her that someone might try to grab her to get to him, but he wanted her to stay vigilant. They weren't together in public and he thought she was safe at the ranch. It was reassuring to him to know that she could react as coolly as any soldier he had ever known.

He thought about Mike's offer. Stay in Stallion Pass where his friends were. Have a job he liked and knew. Live with Isabella. That was the big one. Everything else diminished next to consideration about her. He couldn't wait to see her.

Two hours later, he couldn't believe what he had let himself in for.

Chapter 12

Some of the hands had gone with them to give Colin protection. Now they were fanned out in the woods and he was with Isabella. Boone stood nearby with his weapon tucked into his waistband.

"I feel ridiculous, Isabella," Colin complained.

"This won't take long," she said. "Sit on that rock."

As soon as he sat down, Isabella turned his head slightly, ran her fingers through his hair to muss it and stepped back, studying him.

"This is damn foolishness," he rumbled, embarrassed to have all the fuss over him while she snapped his picture. He knew Boone was openly laughing at him and some of the cowboys were grinning.

"Shh. I know what I'm doing. You'll see," she said, turning the collar of the military shirt she had borrowed from Boone. "That's perfect. Now be still."

"Dammit, you hurry."

"Do not rush me," she said in a haughty voice. "I know what I'm doing. Just sit still and do what I tell you."

One corner of his mouth lifted slightly and she frowned. "Don't smile. That ruins the whole effect." She held a camera. "There. Now look at me and think about something terrible."

"When I look at you, I can't think about anything terrible," he said softly and Boone shot him a quick look.

"Then I'll start reminding you of terrible things like when you were in the hospital and no one knew you were alive—"

"Isabella!" Boone snapped, but she waved a hand at him to shush him while she snapped pictures. "Good, that's a perfect scowl." She kept up a chatter of talk, moving around Colin and snapping pictures.

She changed where and how he sat and took more until he was exasperated.

"Isabella, I've posed and you have a million shots. Make this the last one."

"Just a couple more. Put on the navy T-shirt."

"Dammit. Boone have you done this for her?"

"Thank God, no," Boone answered, giving them a quick glance before looking away. He circled them steadily, watching the woods, moving quietly.

"Wait," Isabella said and Colin glanced at her. He held the navy T-shirt in one hand, having shed the green and brown military shirt. She clicked his picture while he was bare-chested and he wanted to gnash his teeth. He yanked on the navy T-shirt and scowled at her.

"Make this quick."

"Sure thing." She snapped more pictures until finally, she said, "Colin, smile."

He smiled and she took his picture.

"Thanks, I'm finished," she said, twiddling with her camera while he gathered up the discarded shirt.

As they rounded up the cowboys and headed back to the house, Colin chatted with Boone.

Boone told them goodbye and crossed the drive to enter his house where he tossed his hat on a hook.

Erin turned to smile at him. "My goodness! What happened? Is everyone all right?"

"Everyone is fine," he said, crossing the room to take his wife into his arms lightly. She was in a T-shirt and jeans and she looked beautiful even if she was almost at her due date in her pregnancy. "Am I glad to see you."

"I'm glad to see you, too," she said, smiling at him. "Why the grump?"

"Because I want to punch out Colin for seducing my sister. And I want to shake my sister for seducing Colin when he's on the rebound and vulnerable."

Erin laughed. "Stay out of it, buddy! It's none of your business and maybe they're falling in love."

"You know Izzie isn't falling in love—not the marrying kind of love. She won't let anything get in the way of that career of hers. As for Colin, who knows? He may get another heartbreak."

"Come sit down and forget it. It's not your problem, Boone. Izzie is grown up now and she can definitely take care of herself and Colin's a big boy. He can take care of himself. Since when do you worry about some guy you know getting his heart broken? Give me a break!"

"I know, but it aggravates me. That wasn't what I intended when I suggested he move in with her."

Erin laughed. "Stop getting bent all out of shape because Colin and Izzie have found each other. They'll work it out and no matter what, you can't change what's happening."

"I suppose you already knew all about this," he said, kissing her throat and forgetting about Izzie and Colin.

"As a matter of fact, anyone who pays any attention to what's going on around them would've noticed the sparks between those two. Particularly at our barbecue. When they danced, they were all but going up in flames."

"Miss Smarty," Boone said, sitting and smiling at her, pulling her into his embrace, forgetting all about Izzie and Colin.

Late that night as Colin held Isabella in his arms in the family room and they finished watching a movie, he clicked off the television. A light from the hall spilled into the room, giving a soft glow. He was bare-chested, in jeans, and Isabella wore one of his shirts. She had rolled the sleeves back. He brushed a kiss on her forehead. "Isabella, would you ever seriously consider getting married?"

Surprised, she twisted around, turning on her side to look at him. "Sure. I just think of it as something in the future."

"Don't you want children?"

"I used to not. Neither did Boone, but I guess we've both changed. I really don't want a big family. I've been there and done that. Boone and I had so much responsibility for our siblings. Now, I don't know. A child or two could be wonderful someday." She gazed into his gray eyes, studying him. "What about you?"

"Oh, I want a family. We had two—my brother Kevin and me. I've never thought about a number, I just know I want a family.

"I know the importance of family now." He stroked her hair away from her face. "You could marry and still keep your career."

She thought about marriage to Colin and her heart skipped. Was that what he was working up to? What did she really want? In the past, she had never wanted to get tied down in marriage, but she felt differently about Colin than she ever had any other man before.

"I suppose. I never have given the thought consideration."

"Why don't you give it consideration?"

"Now why should I?" she asked, becoming exasperated with his convoluted questioning.

"I don't know what I want," he admitted honestly. "To-morrow's a blank because I don't even know if I'll survive for to—"

She clamped her hand over his mouth. "Don't you say such a thing! You haven't come all this way to have something terrible happen now."

When she moved her hand away, he wound a tendril of her hair around his finger. "You can't predict the future. I just wanted us both to think about it."

"Colin, really! That's the most backhanded proposal—actually not a proposal. You want me to think of marriage while you're thinking of sex."

He laughed. "That's not so at all and not what I said. Shut up, Isabella, and come here." He kissed away her next words and the conversation was gone.

She didn't think of it again until the next day. Would she want to marry Colin? Was she falling in love with him? Would she know true love if she was standing in the middle of it? She couldn't answer her own questions. All she knew was that he was incredibly exciting. When she was away from him, she waited in breathless anticipation to see him. He could turn her into jelly with a kiss and his laughter warmed her more than the hottest sunshine. Was that real love? Or infatuation?

Did he mean as much to her as her career? That was the real question. He didn't know his own feelings, either. She knew one thing, he was taking too much of her attention during her waking hours because she was making silly mistakes at work. Mistakes she had never in her life made and she knew Nick and Sandy both thought it amusing.

Tuesday morning Colin drove to San Antonio, trying to lose any tail, but hoping Brett kept up with him. The thought that Brett was back there somewhere was always reassuring to him because he knew how good Brett was at what he did.

In San Antonio he saw Mike, made contact with the general, ran some errands and then headed back to Stallion Pass to have lunch with Isabella.

In town he stopped at Murphy's Steakhouse to pick up boxes of salads he had ordered. He climbed back into his car, locked his pistol in the glove compartment and began to drive circuitously through town to lose any tail.

Making certain he wasn't being followed, Colin arrived at her office on time, his blood pumping because he knew the moment they were alone in her office they would make love.

He parked in the alley and rushed inside her office. He didn't have any other appointments today and he wore his jeans and a green knit shirt.

"Isabella?" he called when he let himself inside through the back door and pocketed the key she had given him last night.

She appeared in the doorway of her office. She wore her a yellow blouse and skirt and her hair was tied behind her head.

While she talked, she motioned to him to enter her office. Carrying the sack with the two boxes of salads, he entered her office and closed the door. Her eyes were sparkling and he wondered what the call was about.

"Of course. I can't tell you how much I appreciate this and how excited I am about it. Yes." She paused and said some more yeses while he got out bottles of water and their salads.

She said goodbye, hung up, and gave a whoop of joy, flinging herself into his arms.

"Hey! I know you're glad to see me, but I suspect this is about that call."

"Right on both counts!" she cried, kissing him soundly and then pulling back. "That was the magazine I freelanced for in New York, Colin, *In Our World Today*. They've offered me a full-time job on their staff!''

She spun away from him, dancing around the office. ''I can't believe it! This is so grand!'' She flung open the door and raced down the hall. ''Nick! Sandy! Guess what that call was!''

Colin strolled after her as she told them. They all shouted with joy and congratulated her, joining hands and dancing in a circle like three little kids who'd been given a wonderful surprise.

She glanced over and saw him watching and broke away. ''Colin and I are going to have lunch,'' she called over her shoulder, taking his hand and rushing him back into her office where he closed the door and pulled her into his arms.

''So you're going to New York?''

Suddenly she sobered and looked up at him, touching his cheek. ''That doesn't have to mean the end of us.''

He wanted her and he wanted her to stay in Texas, to decline the offer, but he knew she wouldn't. He leaned down to kiss her, letting all his hungry need for her pour into his kiss. She was as vital to him as his breath or his heart. The thought shook him and he knew he had gone from an impossible love to another unattainable love. Only this time he had known better and walked into it with eyes wide open.

Tightening his arms, he leaned over her and kissed her with all the pent-up passion in him, feeling as if a volcano of need had erupted inside him.

Colin's hungry kiss stunned Isabella. They had been wildly passionate, but this kiss seared like hot flames and drove every thought from her mind except need for Colin. His kiss consumed her and at the same time stirred a rush of longing in her. Never in her life had she felt as wanted by a man.

And never in her life had she wanted a man as she did

Colin right now. She clung to him, kissing him in return until she could feel his pounding heartbeat match her own and they both trembled. Clothes were discarded and in seconds he was holding her while she wrapped herself around him. He used protection and then he was inside her, moving with her, a union that bound them body and soul.

Release came, but it didn't stop the need that she felt radiating through Colin, a hunger that went far beyond physical satisfaction.

Still stunned, she raised her head to look at him. Desire burned in the depths of his gray eyes that had darkened to the color of storm clouds in summer.

"I want you, Isabella," he said.

"Ah, Colin," she replied, clinging to him and holding him close while she kissed him again. He lowered her and in minutes released her, leaving her, to shut himself in the bathroom.

While he was gone, she had a moment to get herself pulled together. She remembered her phone call and the offer from the magazine.

What had been incredibly exciting a short time ago had paled next to Colin's dazzling kisses and hungry lovemaking. She straightened her clothes and combed her hair. When the bathroom door opened, she turned to face him.

He crossed the room to her to brush a feathery kiss on her lips.

"That was sort of overwhelming," she declared breathlessly.

"The magazine or me?"

"You, Colin. You made me forget the magazine offer— I didn't think I'd ever meet a man who could do that."

"Great," he answered solemnly. "I'd like to dazzle you and make you forget everything except me."

"You succeeded beyond your wildest imaginings." She touched her hair. "I'll be right back."

She left for the bathroom and when she stepped back out, he had their lunches on her desk.

"Now come tell me about this job offer that's got you dancing a jig all over the office."

"It's an invitation to become part of their staff. It means I'd get assignments all over the world, Colin. Since I started as a photographer, I've dreamed of this."

"Then we should go out tonight and celebrate. I'll surprise you when you get home. 'Course the circumstances sort of clip my wings about taking you out, but I'll work out something."

"No. Let's stay home and celebrate. Just the two of us. That's what I'd really like."

He inhaled and leaned close to kiss her long and thoroughly again.

When he released her, Isabella leaned back in her chair. "They're sending the papers to me about the company and they want me to come to New York next week to interview and meet everyone. They've booked my plane and my hotel and they'll meet me when I arrive in the city. They want me to stay two days."

"That's fantastic! I'm happy for you."

"So you want me to take it?"

"If it's what you've always dreamed of, sure. I'll miss you, but offers like that are rare, Isabella. And having a job you love is important."

She nodded. "I'm so excited. They said there would be a lot of traveling after this first year. The first year I would train and get to know how they work and have assignments that are local or at least, not out of the country."

Colin sat back in his chair, one foot propped on his knee as he listened to her. His gaze ran over the pictures on the wall. "You're a good photographer, Isabella. They must think you're really super."

"Don't sound so surprised," she said, smiling at him.

"I'm not. And they must think so because they're giving you red-carpet treatment."

"I'll have dinner with some of them the night I get in. I know one of the vice presidents, Natasha Harding, from conventions I've attended."

"So in the future, if I want to see you, I'll have to fly to New York," he said.

The twinkle disappeared in her eyes and she gazed at him solemnly. "Yes, you will, but you're used to going all over the world yourself and you haven't lived any one place very long in years." She leaned forward and ran her fingers along his knee. "You will come see me, won't you?"

"Of course," he answered, wondering what he would do in the future, but he knew it was the immediate future. Isabella would soon be gone from Texas. He wasn't happy to see her go, but he was glad for her sake that she was getting what she had always wanted. And he didn't want to throw a damper on her excitement.

When Isabella told him goodbye, she returned to her office, mulling over the offer as excitement coursed through her. She picked up the phone to call and tell Stacia Longstreet, one of her long-time friends in California. As soon as she finished that conversation, she called Boone to tell him. She and her brother had a close relationship and she always shared her career moves with him. He congratulated her. They talked awhile before she told him goodbye.

When she replaced the receiver, she was lost in thought, thinking about her coming trip to New York to talk to the prospective employer. She spun around, joyous with anticipation, realizing that a dream was coming true for her. She couldn't wait to get home to the ranch tonight to celebrate with Colin.

The instant she stepped into the house, she and Colin were in each other's arms and they made long, leisurely love before thinking about dinner. It wasn't until she went in to eat that she noticed the huge bouquet of three dozen red roses.

She shrieked with delight and threw herself into his arms. "You got me flowers and they're gorgeous!"

Colin was in jeans and a T-shirt and he held her tightly, kissing her again before he set her on her feet. "That I did. And I have steaks ready to grill. I ordered a cake today," he said, leading her across the kitchen.

For the first time she saw a cake box. He opened it and she looked at a dark chocolate cake with Congratulations written across it in pink icing.

"Oh, Colin, thank you!"

"There's more. Champagne," he said, producing a wine bucket filled with ice and a bottle of champagne set in it to chill.

"And for you to remember me by…" he said solemnly, reaching to pick up a box that sat on the kitchen counter. He handed it to her.

"I didn't see any of this when I came home," she said.

He laughed. "We were otherwise occupied." She wore a T-shirt and cutoffs and he placed his hands on her shoulders as she looked down at the large white box tied in a red silk ribbon.

"It's too pretty to open, but I'm going to open it," she said, yanking off the ribbon and putting it on the counter. She opened the white box, pushed aside tissue paper and then lifted out a black-velvet box. Her eyes widened with curiosity as she opened the black box. "Oh, Colin, how beautiful!" she exclaimed, taking out a gold bracelet, a chain made of dainty links.

"I love it!" she said, throwing her arms around his neck and standing on tiptoe to kiss him.

Then she stepped back and held out her wrist.

"You put it on for me," she said. Colin did so. When he

finished, his smoky gaze met hers and her pulse began to drum wildly. His arms wrapped around her and dinner was postponed for another hour.

Later that night while they were in each other's arms in the bedroom, Colin asked, "What about your house?"

"I'll sell it. It'll be easy. That area in Stallion Pass is in high demand so I'll get my money back out of it and Boone can handle it for me."

"Maybe I should buy it," Colin said lightly and she twisted around to look at him. A light was on in the bathroom and spilled slightly into the bedroom, giving enough light that she could see Colin.

"You're serious?"

"Mike has asked me to go into business with him. My friends live here—I might settle here. This isn't far from my folks and, actually, I can afford to move them here if they'd like to move."

"Well, if that's the case, I won't put my house on the market until you've made a decision."

"So I come first in one aspect of your life."

"You come first in more than one," she said and turned to kiss him. Their conversation was over.

Outside on a hill in the woods, still on the Double T property, a man stood in the darkness and gazed through binoculars at the guest house. Colonel Garrick thought he and his girlfriend were so secure, but they weren't. He knew their every move.

The Devlin woman had fired at him. For that, she would pay. Kill them both and make it look like a crime of passion.

How easy it would be to have the ex-warrior appear to be overwhelmed by emotion, losing in love the second time. An unstable man on the mend who still couldn't remember his past completely.

She was leaving Texas for New York. How easy to make

it appear that Colonel Garrick had gone to pieces over telling her goodbye, killing her and then himself.

The man touched the pistol he carried. He could commit the crime and get away and none of those fools who were following the colonel could catch him or even know about him.

With both of them dead— If the killing was done right, the military, the police and the public would accept a crime of passion. His friends wouldn't accept it, but there wasn't going to be any way they could prove differently. The man shifted weight as he swung around to view Boone's house.

He had to be patient, wait for the right moment to catch both of them.

The man smiled in the darkness. Soon, he would be rid of Colonel Garrick, the man with the nine lives.

Colin Garrick had used up all but the last.

Chapter 13

The next day after Isabella had left for work, Colin called Boone to tell him that he was thinking about buying Isabella's house. When he replaced the receiver, Colin sat in the quiet house, his thoughts on Isabella.

Next week she would fly to New York to accept the job. He wanted her to take it and to fulfill her dreams, yet at the same time, the thought of telling her goodbye hurt.

He wasn't ready to commit to a woman on a permanent basis. He shook his head at that one. This was one woman who definitely wasn't ready for a permanent commitment. No starry-eyed dreams of marriage here with Isabella!

But it hurt to think of telling her goodbye. And he knew it would be goodbye. Their lives would take divergent paths. If he lived and worked in Texas and she lived in New York and traveled, they would see less and less of each other and then they wouldn't see each other at all.

He thought he could accept that better than he was. It hurt constantly to think of losing her.

"Dammit," he swore under his breath. He knew he wasn't ready for commitment and she didn't want any, but he hurt badly. He had found joy and excitement in her.

He realized she had made him whole again. He was over Danielle, back into the mainstream of life, wanting to have friends and family around, wanting Isabella.

He passed a mirror and stopped to face himself, not thinking about his image, but about Isabella. "Don't you interfere with her happiness," he told himself sternly. He didn't want to do that, but he didn't want to lose her. He might as well book a flight to New York now because the first week she was gone, he knew he'd want to see her.

He suspected she wasn't suffering any such pangs and he hoped his faded within days. He wasn't in love—or at least he hoped to hell he wasn't—and he didn't want to be.

All through the day at work, Isabella's thoughts kept drifting to Colin. She began to make plans about the move, knowing she was going to accept the New York job, yet she constantly found she was doing nothing except gazing into space, thinking about Colin and hurting at the thought of telling him goodbye.

In spite of what they had told each other about continuing to get together, she suspected when she moved to New York, it would be farewell. Colin might sink roots in Stallion Pass, going to work with Mike and buying her house, but she didn't think he would fly back and forth often to see her and she saw no real future for them. He'd said that for a long time he wasn't going to love a woman deeply enough again to be serious, and she didn't have time for love in her plans. So why did she hurt so badly? she asked herself. And reassured herself that it was temporary and would go away. She had never wanted commitment to a man or marriage to interfere with her career.

It was six days until she flew to New York. And if she

took the job, she would probably start right away. Boone could handle things here for her. It would be easy to sell her house and to get rid of her studio because both were in areas that were in demand.

With each passing day, her feelings seesawed back and forth. She told herself that there was nothing serious between Colin and her and once she was in New York, she wouldn't hurt the way she was now over the thought of telling him goodbye.

And he had made no overtures to her for anything continuing into the future except their reassurances that they would keep in touch and still see each other. But those were vague and indefinite promises. She thought neither one of them expected their romance to continue once she left Texas.

The remaining days passed swiftly until it was the day she was to leave for New York.

The first faint rays of daylight spilled into the bedroom while outside a mockingbird chirped loudly, heralding the new morning. The world around the ranch house was still and peaceful, but Colin knew it was an illusion.

Somewhere outside a killer lurked and as long as he was free, Colin knew he was in danger and so was Isabella.

For that reason Colin was glad she was getting out of Texas. He would miss her, but he would feel better about putting her on the plane.

In the quiet of his bedroom, in the big king-size bed, Colin held Isabella in his arms while she slept. This was the morning he would kiss her goodbye. At nine o'clock, her flight to New York City was scheduled to leave. For the past week she had been as excited as a child, and Colin thought the separation might be best for both of them. He hadn't planned to go from one engagement to falling for someone else again so soon.

Making her more appealing than ever, she had been bubbling with anticipation last night. He stroked tendrils of silky brown hair from her face and kissed her lightly. A pang contracted his heart. He was going to miss her terribly, but this was what she wanted and he was happy for her. Why was it so damned hard to let her go?

He hoped he had hidden his feelings from her well enough because she was so ecstatic about the job. He wanted to share in her joy and not take one degree of it away by letting her know how much he hated to see her go.

He brushed a feathery kiss on her temple. She wound her arm around his head and pulled him close. Her eyes opened and she smiled at him before tugging him down for a kiss.

For the next hour, he didn't give a single thought to danger.

Colin drove her to the airport and kissed her goodbye, watching her as she walked along the jetway then turned to wave to him. She wore deep purple slacks and a blue-and-purple-plaid blouse and her hair was tied behind her head.

He returned the wave and watched the slight sway of her hips until she disappeared from his sight.

"'Bye, darlin'," he said quietly, knowing she had just walked out of his life.

Relieved to think she was safe now and away from the killer, and trying to keep focused on that and how happy she was, he headed back to his car.

As he sped away from the airport, a big jet roared overhead and he wondered if it was her plane. The hurt he felt was as raw and sharp as if she had been his fiancée and broken her engagement.

"Get over her," he told himself, knowing they had nothing serious between them and neither one had wanted anything serious.

Tomorrow it wouldn't matter as much and he needed to go talk to Boone about buying her house in Stallion Pass.

If he could keep himself busy, he wouldn't think about her nearly as often.

Out of habit, he glanced at the rearview mirror. He changed lanes and moved into traffic, heading north from San Antonio, back to the ranch.

When he entered the house, it was empty—a different kind of emptiness than before. He could see her everywhere he looked, remember each place in the house where they had made love, still smell her perfume.

"Get over her. She's gone," he said out loud, telling himself that he would get used to her absence and forget her in time, that he'd never been seriously involved with her anyway.

"Dammit," he said, raking his fingers through his hair. He was failing at trying to convince himself he didn't care. Give it time, he reassured himself. In a week he would be accustomed to her absence and moving on with his life.

Aboard the plane Isabella had a window seat. She knew they wouldn't fly over Stallion Pass or the Double T, but they were flying over terrain similar to the ranch.

She prayed Colin would be safe. When she got back, she would show him his photographs. She had looked at them on her computer the next day and selected the ones she'd wanted to print and frame.

She opened her purse and pulled one out, looking at his likeness and thinking his pictures might be among the best photos she had ever taken. He did have a brooding expression and was ruggedly handsome, an excellent combination for a subject.

She put his photo away and thought about her appointment tomorrow morning.

She closed her eyes. The *In Our World Today* offer was all she had dreamed of since the first photography class in college. This is what she wanted. She thought of Colin and wished he were here with her. She couldn't wait to call and hear his voice even though she just left him.

It was late afternoon when she arrived in New York. As she entered the busy terminal, she saw a chauffeur standing with a sign that read Devlin. She waved and hurried over to him. In minutes he had whisked her and her bags to a waiting white limousine.

The minute she was alone in the hotel room she phoned Colin and talked to him as she shed her slacks and shirt.

"I'm going to shower now and get a cab to meet them at the magazine office before we go to dinner."

"I wish I were there to be with you."

"Photography talk would probably bore you," she said, untying her hair.

"I meant in the shower, not while you have a business dinner," he said dryly.

She laughed and lowered her voice. "I wish you were, too. I have to go now. You can think about me, and I'll think about you."

He groaned and told her goodbye and she rushed for her shower.

When she walked into the lobby of the office of the magazine on the fourteenth floor of a twenty-story building, a short brunette with straight hair came forward to greet her.

"Isabella, we're so glad you're here," Natasha Harding said. "We're looking forward to this evening."

"So am I," Isabella said, flattered by their offer and their picking up all her expenses.

"Let me show you around our offices," Natasha offered. Isabella nodded. Excitement electrified her and made every moment memorable. She met another vice president, Jake Sargent who would join them for dinner. She was dazzled by the friendly people, the blown-up, framed copies of pictures from different issues of the magazine on display. Yet during the tour of the offices and then on the way to dinner, her mind drifted to Colin and she missed him. Each time, when she realized she wasn't hearing what was being said to her, she turned her attention to those with her.

Geena Ward from Layout and Design, joined them for dinner and over pasta and salads, they talked about their plans for the magazine.

By the time she got back to the hotel, it was almost ten o'clock. The moment Isabella was in her room, she yanked out her cell phone to call Colin who answered quickly.

They talked until she lost power in her phone, and he called her back. Then they talked for another hour before she finally told him she should get some sleep.

"You're going to tell them yes tomorrow, aren't you?"

"Yes," she said. "I've wanted a job like this since I started taking pictures. Colin, it's a fantastic opportunity."

"I know it is, but I'll be glad when you're back in Texas because I miss you."

"I miss you, too," she said softly, realizing she did miss him and when she took the job, they would part ways.

"Good night, Isabella," he said in his deep voice. "I wish I could hold you and kiss you."

"'Night, Colin." She replaced the receiver and lay in the dark, wanting his arms around her and surprised how much she did miss him.

The next morning she sat in a large corner office. Light spilled into the room. Dressed in a tailored dark brown suit, she gazed around at the gray decor with splashes of color in the pictures that decorated the walls.

Natasha Harding, Jack Sargent and Geena Ward were conducting the interview and Isabella felt at ease with all three of them after spending time with them yesterday.

"We're eager to have you join our staff," Natasha said. "The job will involve assignments abroad, but last night you said that's what you had always wanted to do."

"It is," Isabella replied.

"You'd start here your first year—let you get settled and accustomed to how we work, do your training, before there would be any assignments away from here. Those will come later."

Isabella nodded and thought about Colin. She felt a pang because she was going to have to tell him goodbye. She realized Jake Sargent was talking to her about the usual assignments with *In Our World Today,* and Isabella tried to focus on what was being said.

It was an hour later when Natasha turned to her, her pale brown eyes filled with curiosity. "We'd like to have you on our staff. If you need time to consider this because I know it means uprooting your life from Texas to New York, take the time you want. We don't have to have an answer this minute."

"The position is yours if you want it," Jake Sargent said.

"Thank you. I can say yes right now," she said, but as she gave her acceptance, a pain tore at her heart and she could see Colin gazing solemnly at her.

Breaking into her thoughts, Natasha, Jack and Geena came to their feet to shake her hand. Isabella stood. The three from the magazine were enthusiastic, telling her how happy they were to have her.

"We want to introduce you to our president, Ralph West-myer, who wasn't in yesterday," Natasha said.

Isabella went with them, meeting more employees, but all the time, she was thinking about Colin.

"How soon can you start?" Natasha asked.

For a moment the question hung in the air. Isabella rubbed her chin while she speculated. "I have a house to sell and things to wind up in Texas. This is last of April. I'd like to wait until the first of June."

"That's fine," Geena Ward said, smiling at her. If you'll come with me to our Human Resources people, I can give you a packet about the company to take back to Texas with you. You can get started on filling out papers.''

It was another hour before Isabella left the offices. They were taking her to dinner again tonight to celebrate her joining the company.

As she rode back to her hotel in a cab, her thoughts were in Texas. She missed Colin and wanted to be with him. She missed him more than she had dreamed she would and what was worse, with each hour of separation, the longing to see him grew.

The job with the magazine didn't seem nearly as wonderful as it had the day they had called to make the offer. Was this her future? Traveling from city to city, staying in hotels, being alone constantly, not seeing Colin or hearing his laughter or sharing hot kisses with him?

Growing up, she and Boone had promised each other that once they got away from the family, they would both enjoy freedom. Yet there was her brother, supremely happy with Erin and eager for his first baby.

Was she really going to continue to enjoy this freedom she had treasured for years now? At the moment it seemed lonely and less than exciting.

She'd had a wonderful business in Stallion Pass, friends, her brother was there and Colin was there and he planned to stay.

She bit her lip and watched the crowd as the taxi wove in and out of traffic. The minute her driver stopped in front of her hotel, she paid him and rushed inside, wanting to hear Colin's voice more than anything. She wouldn't go home until tomorrow, but she couldn't wait to be there and in Colin's arms.

The moment she heard Colin's voice, she sprawled on the bed and held the phone close. She missed him dreadfully, imagining his gray eyes and wishing his arms were around her.

"I did it! I took the job!" she exclaimed.

"Congratulations!" he said, sounding sincere. From his tone, he seemed happy with her decision. "You'll have to come home. How long before you start that job?"

"I asked them to wait until the first of June so I can get things wound up at home."

"Home is going to be New York, Isabella," Colin said quietly.

She gripped the phone. She ached with missing him, more so than she would have guessed possible. "They're taking me to dinner again tonight to celebrate. I'll be home to-morrow."

"But not to stay. The first of June will come quickly."

"We'll still see each other, won't we?"

"Sure," he answered lightly and she wondered if June would be a permanent goodbye between them. That notion hurt, too.

"I'll meet you when you get in and then we'll drive back to the Double T and have our own celebration."

"I'll be counting the minutes," she said, realizing she would like to go home now and be in his arms tonight.

"What's been happening?" she asked. "Anything on the killer?"

"No. Just the usual routine. Nothing at all. Maybe he gave up."

"You don't believe that," she said.

"No, I don't. I'm just surrounded with protection and he knows it."

"So are you at an impasse? And if so, how'll you change it?"

"I don't know what's in the killer's mind. If I were after somebody, I'd pull back for a while. The Agency guys will have to go back to Washington before long. They can't af-ford to keep them baby-sitting me and this case."

"It's an important one, Colin. If this is a double agent,

I'd think they'd want to keep those two guys—or at least one of them—here until this is solved. You know the killer is out there.''

"I know it. What are you wearing?'' he asked, taking the conversation on a more personal track.

She held the phone and talked, mentally seeing Colin and aching with longing to be with him.

. Colin, who had stretched out on their bed while he'd talked, didn't want to break the connection. But eventually they did, so Isabella could change, order lunch and call him back. They talked for another couple of hours, but when Colin said he could see Boone headed toward the guest house, they hung up.

That night as soon as she returned to the hotel from her dinner engagement, she called him back and they talked until half past four in the morning.

"Do you know how late it is and how long we've talked?''

"It's late,'' he said, glancing at his watch. "I don't want to break the connection. I miss you like hell.''

"I miss you, too,'' she said. "I've been thinking about it. Don't meet me when I get in. I'll stop by my office to pick up some things and then I'll come out to the ranch. I don't want you out like that. The airport seems a dangerous place because it's filled with strangers and lots of area you can't watch.''

"I can't hide in the house,'' Colin protested.

"Humor me on this one. I should get to the Double T about five o'clock and then we can celebrate. Please, Colin. That really made me nervous when you saw me off.''

"Okay, sweetie. Whatever pleases you, pleases me. At least most of the time.''

"We'll see how much we can please each other tomorrow,'' she purred in the phone.

"Isabella, damn, I want you." He ground out the words in a husky voice.

"I want you, too. 'Night, Colin."

The receiver clicked and he hung up the phone. He missed her. He wanted her in his arms every night.

He knew he had to let her go. Right now, he didn't know whether he would survive until June. If they caught the killer, Colin had thought about staying in Stallion Pass where his friends were. He had considered Mike's offer to go into business with him.

It was a business that appealed to him. Was he in love with Isabella or was this just reaction from being on the rebound?

It didn't matter. She wasn't coming back to Texas and she wasn't in love.

He was tempted when Isabella left in May to just disappear one night. He was getting tired of this killer cat-and-mouse game. He knew he owed it to the Agency, to himself, as well as to the lives of other good men to stay and try to lure the man into making a mistake.

He'd wait, but not for years. If they didn't catch the killer in another few months, then he was going to disappear one dark night, leaving Stallion Pass the way he had come, and go ahead with what he had originally planned when he'd first arrived.

As long as the killer was alive and free, Colin knew his life wasn't safe. But there were remote places in the world where he could have a good life and no one would bother to come after him. He didn't want to constantly look over his shoulder.

He thought about Isabella and he missed her. He would have to let her go, both because of his life and because of what she wanted for her life.

Every time he thought about telling her goodbye permanently, he didn't like the idea. It was inevitable, but it didn't make him happy.

He made a mental note to order flowers first thing in the morning and he planned what he would cook for dinner to surprise her. He would pick up a bottle of sparkling wine to celebrate.

He didn't want to tell her goodbye. It was dawn after a sleepless night that he came to the decision that he didn't want her out of his life.

He had all the money he could ever need now. He didn't have to live in Stallion Pass. He could move to New York, find something to do there. The instant he thought of that, his heart thudded. Was he in love with her?

He had to admit that he was. He wanted her always.

Was this just a rebound thing? Going from one woman to another to wipe out the pain of the first?

He didn't think it was. Isabella was special. Unique. Sexy. In his blood.

The minute he came to the conclusion and faced the fact how strongly he felt about her, he wanted to ask her to marry him.

Would she marry him if he moved to New York? He suspected she would not. But he was going to ask and see what she said. The minute he made that decision, he climbed out of bed. He wanted to get her a ring to give her when she got back to Texas.

His heart thudded in eagerness. At the same time, he told himself to not be shocked if she turned him down.

Even if she did say no, he could move to New York and they could continue to date and maybe in the future he would win her over.

His pulse raced at the notion and he felt better than he had from the minute she had told him about the job offer.

He glanced at the clock and decided to drive into San

Antonio to try to find a ring for her. Tonight she was coming home.

He would have to let Boone know that the deal on the house was off, but he would have to wait until Boone was awake. It was too early to call.

Colin headed for the shower, expectation and hope filling him as he counted the hours until she would be home again.

At nine o'clock, dressed in slacks and a green-and-white sport shirt, Colin stopped by Boone's house before leaving the ranch to drive to San Antonio. He knocked on the back door.

Boone opened the door and told Colin to come inside.

"Erin's sleeping in. She didn't sleep well last night and now she's catching up," Boone said, pouring a cup of coffee for Colin.

"Isabella will be home tonight."

"I know. I'm sending one of the guys to pick her up. She definitely doesn't want you to risk going to the airport—I agree with her. You'd be in a crowd of strangers and a lot harder to protect."

Colin sat at the table and Boone offered him toast or a bagel, but Colin shook his head. "I ate. Thanks, anyway. Boone, I'm going to back out of the deal for Isabella's house."

"Sure. It's early enough that it doesn't matter and she can unload that property and probably for a profit. That area gets more valuable every day that passes. Don't worry about it." Boone tilted his head to study his friend.

"Did you decide to do something else besides staying in Stallion Pass?"

"Yes, I did," Colin said, running his finger around the blue ceramic rim of his coffee cup. "I think I'll see what kind of work I can find in New York." When Boone didn't answer, Colin looked up to face his friend squarely.

"I don't want to see either one of you hurt," Boone said.

"Just remember that Izzie is not going to marry. She isn't the marrying type. Don't change the plans for your future because of my sister. If you do, you'll just get another heartbreak."

"I want to keep dating. We won't if I stay in Texas and she's in New York. That's too far and after this year she may travel to the four corners of the earth."

"True. You just watch your heart. Izzie's like the Tin Man. She doesn't have one."

"I think the Tin Man turned out to be a guy with a pretty big heart. Isabella may have more of one than you think."

"You're warned, buddy. You got over a woman before, so you'll get over this one, but I'm just telling you, don't expect much from Izzie."

"I'm going to San Antonio. Thanks for the coffee."

"Sure. Watch your back. You won't let any of us watch you."

"You're doing a great job. Just keep tailing the guy who's off duty."

"I hope to hell Brett is back there watching you."

"He checks in occasionally—in sort of a roundabout way—a note left in only a place I'd find it. He's back there behind me somewhere."

"I hope."

Colin told Boone goodbye and climbed into his car to head for the highway.

In San Antonio, he looked at dazzling rings and finally made a selection for Isabella.

As he made plans to meet Mike for lunch, he couldn't shake the feeling that he was being watched. It could just be nerves or it could be because Brett was back there somewhere, but Colin had been in too many tight situations and he knew his survival instincts were sound.

The minute he entered the restaurant where he was to meet Mike, he stepped to one side to look out the window.

He watched the street, unable to see anything unusual or to spot anyone who seemed to be watching the door of the restaurant or headed toward it.

Then he saw Mike approach. Still watching, Colin gave it up when Mike entered the restaurant and turned to greet his friend.

That afternoon Colin stood in the house at the Double T and looked at the champagne on ice, another huge bouquet of red roses. Steaks were ready to grill and he had rose petals strewn on the bed and a welcoming large stuffed bear he had bought for Isabella. He had propped a sign in the bear's paws that read I Love You.

It surprised him to realize that he loved her, but he knew he did. All the time he had thought he was doing such a good job of guarding his heart, she had stolen it away. Not deliberately though. He knew that was never what she had intended.

She had brought him back to life and then taken his heart from him. A fair enough swap, he thought, his eagerness to see her climbing.

The phone rang and he glanced at his watch. It was too early for her to be in, but maybe she was calling from the plane. He yanked up the phone and said hello.

Disappointment replaced his eagerness when he heard Boone.

"Colin, be careful. They found Tyler thirty minutes ago. He was stabbed to death in his hotel room."

Chapter 14

Coldness poured over Colin as he gripped the phone. "Who found him and what do you know?"

"A maid. The police are there. Peter was contacted and he called to let us know. You'll hear from him soon, but just be careful. Want me to come over?"

"No. Does Brett know?"

"I don't know about Brett. You're the only contact that man must have here. They've probably let Washington know by now and I'd think Washington would let Brett know."

"I'm sure you're right. Make sure Isabella is safe."

"I've called Scotty, one of our cowboys, who's picking her up. He carries a pistol."

"Dammit," Colin said, raking his fingers through his hair in frustration.

"Jonah had been following Tyler and knew he was at the hotel. He waited downstairs where he could watch for Tyler to come and go. He didn't see anything suspicious. Jonah let me know before the police arrived."

"Where's Jonah now?"

"He's still hanging around with the lawmen just in case he picks up any information. Our friend Peter may be in a lot of danger, too. As much as you are. You be careful and I'll keep you posted," Boone said.

"Thanks, Boone."

Colin replaced the receiver and looked out the window. The sun was shining. It was a beautiful April day and didn't look like a day for murder or dark deeds. Brett was out there, watching the house. Where was the killer now?

Colin walked through the house, checking locks and alarms, looking out the windows. Nothing looked out of place or alarming.

He returned to the kitchen. He had the table set for two. He'd bought candlesticks and candles and had fresh roses on the table in addition to the bouquet for Isabella.

He glanced at his watch. Her plane should have landed and she should be home within the hour. His pulse speeded at the thought. He slipped his hand into his pocket, feeling the small black-velvet box that held the ring he had bought for her.

"Come home, Isabella," he whispered. He crossed the room to put on music, turning it low.

The phone rang and he rushed to pick it up.

"Colin, I'm on my way," Isabella said.

"I can't wait for you to get here. You've heard about Tyler?"

"Boone called to tell me. I'm so sorry that happened. I don't want you to take a step out of the house tonight."

"I'm all right. You just hurry home. I have dinner and champagne and I want you in my arms."

"We're hurrying. See you soon." She broke the connection and he hung up.

He made another survey of the house, checking it over. Everything was quiet and peaceful, the house secure. He glanced at his watch again. She would be here soon. He couldn't wait to see her and wanted to dance a jig that she was finally coming home. At the front of the house he paused to gaze outside, his thoughts going back to the night of the blast.

The scene played out in his mind once again. He could remember freeing the hostage and then his brief confrontation with the ringleader.

As he recalled these images, more details came to mind. The images fell together and the last puzzle pieces clicked into place. He knew who the killer was.

Now he had to get to Mike and warn him.

Chapter 15

Colin was heading for the phone when Peter stepped in from the adjoining living room.

Colin froze.

Peter held a gun in his hand and it was aimed at Colin.

"I was just going to call and warn the others," Colin said. "The memories finally came back." A burning rage filled him when he thought of all he had gone through and the lives that had been lost because of the perfidy of the man.

"I knew the day would come when you would remember. Yes, I'm your spy. You should have died in that explosion five years ago. How much simpler it would have been."

"How could you?" Colin asked, realizing Isabella was on her way home. Scotty would let her out and not come in with her. She only had two small carry-ons.

Where was Brett? With a sinking feeling, Colin knew Brett probably didn't have a suspicion of anything happening; his friends had been following Tyler, not Peter.

"I could because I'll earn more wealth than you inherited. Soon I'll be gone," Peter said. He was in tan slacks and a brown knit shirt and Colin saw the gun had a silencer.

"It's a standard line to say you can't get away with it."

"Oh, yes, I can. I got in here without your shadow, Brett Hamilton, knowing, or any of your friends. Besides, now with Tyler out of the way, I'll be the one who is supposed to tail you."

"Why did you kill Tyler?"

"He discovered my plane ticket that I carry in case I need it. It's to leave the country. We got into an argument. I knew he was suspicious and would try to contact General Kowalski. I couldn't risk that at all."

"You're scum, Fremont."

"I don't care what you think. After I kill you, I'll get back to one of the barns and then give a false description of the man I saw running from your house, sending everyone off on a wild-goose chase."

"I'm surprised Brett didn't see you come into the house."

"Your man is very good, but I happen to know where he is today and he can only be in one place at a time. He's seen me, but it was when I came on duty. He'll see me again, but he'll be like the others and think I was following you as I'm scheduled to do, watching the house from the barn. Your guys are gone because of Tyler's death."

"Get this over with, Peter. Isabella is coming and I don't want her to walk in on us."

"On the contrary. They will think you killed her in a fit of passion and then committed suicide because she's the second love to leave you—" He bit off his words as a car stopped outside.

Colin's mind raced as he gauged the distance to try to jump Peter. Colin didn't want Isabella to come into the house. "That's ridiculous," Colin said, trying to keep Peter talking and distracted as much as possible, wanting to yell to Isabella the moment he heard her enter the kitchen.

He heard the key turn and he watched Peter, ready to jump him because he didn't want Isabella hurt. He opened his mouth to yell but before he could, she screamed, a blood-curdling, ear-piercing cry that made the hairs on the back of his neck stand on end.

As her scream filled the air, Colin, who had been watching Peter, saw him glance at the kitchen.

The moment Peter took his eyes from him, Colin leaped behind the sofa and yelled at Isabella, "Get out! Get out of here, Isabella!"

Peter fired at Colin and Colin felt a hot sting graze his arm. As he whipped out his own pistol, he heard Peter run from the room.

Terrified for Isabella's safety, Colin vaulted the sofa and raced after Peter.

When he dashed outside, he took in everything at once. The gate was open, the dogs running loose and barking. Colin saw Isabella, cell phone in hand, sliding behind the wheel of her car. She dropped the phone to start the engine and started to yank the door closed.

Peter grabbed the door and shoved her aside, sliding in behind the wheel. Everything in Colin seemed to freeze in cold terror that she would be hurt.

Acting automatically without thinking, Colin took aim at the tires. Through the car windows, he glimpsed Isabella's feet and legs as she kicked at Peter.

Colin steadied his hand and fired as Peter began to pull away. The passenger door opened and Isabella spilled out, rolling in the dirt. Colin raced toward her, praying she was all right. Someone else could catch Peter.

As dogs came bounding to lick Colin's face and hers, Colin knelt to scoop her into his arms. "Izzie—"

She flung herself at him and sobbed. "You're all right."

He heard more shots and looked up to see Boone in his car, heading after Peter. As Peter roared away, Colin saw Brett positioning his car to face Peter's farther down the road.

Peter swerved and turned as Brett raised his pistol and fired.

Boone also fired. Peter already had one flat and now another tire went. He lost control of the car as it spun around, hit a tree and then rolled. Peter was flung out and tumbled across the ground, his car smashing against a tree and bursting into flames.

Colin didn't care what happened. All he wondered about was Isabella. He framed her face with his hands. "Are you all right?"

"You're bleeding!" she gasped, looking at her bloody hand and then at his arm where she had touched him.

"Damn him," Colin growled, studying her scraped cheek. Her blouse was torn and she had a cut on one arm.

"Colin, you've been shot!"

"It's just a graze, Isabella. I'd know if I was shot, believe me." Shoving a dog out of the way, Colin leaned down to kiss her and she turned her face up to him, holding him tightly. His heart pounded with relief that she was all right. He shook, feeling weak in the knees, terrified when he had seen Peter slide into the car with her.

"Hey, you two," Boone called.

Colin raised his head as Boone rushed up. Sirens blared and one police car had already arrived and two uniformed men spilled out.

"Are you all right?" Boone asked.

"Isabella, these damn mutts," Colin muttered. He stood, lifting her into his arms as dogs milled around his legs.

"He's shot," Isabella said, and Boone looked at Colin's wound.

"I'm all right," Colin declared.

"It's nothing," Boone said. "Might help you if you'd set her down. Look—Erin just called. She's got contractions so we're off to the hospital."

"Call and let us know," Isabella said.

Boone was already running for the house.

"Thanks, Boone," Colin called, turning to carry Isabella inside. He glanced back to see the two police officers holding Peter between them. Brett, striding toward Colin, was talking on his cell phone.

"Colin Garrick, you have to see a doctor about your arm. If you don't go to the emergency room in Stallion Pass—" Isabella said.

He kissed her to make her to stop talking, then set her on her feet. "Here comes Brett. I think I need to talk to him. We'll go to the emergency so you'll be happy, but you'll see. If you let me clean this up, I'm just barely scratched."

"Are you all right?" Brett asked.

Colin nodded. "We're both fine. Scratches and bruises. Thanks."

"I didn't know he was inside with you until all hell broke loose. I heard the shot, saw Isabella come running out and I knew he'd gotten to you in spite of my surveillance. I failed on this one."

"He's good at what he does. He's gotten away with his double life for years," Colin said. "I remembered everything. On the night of the blast the ringleader found me and gloated, telling me, 'Your friend set you up.' Shots were being exchanged and we ran. Then the bomb exploded, and you know the rest. I knew the ringleader had to mean Peter. When the memories came back, I was on my way to call Mike and warn him. But Peter got here first."

"Damn. What an evil man. I saw him, but it was his shift to tail you, so I didn't think a lot about it. I thought I knew where he was, but he slipped away without me seeing him."

"I had the alarm off because I was in the house and expecting Isabella to arrive."

"He's caught now. They're sending a chopper to pick me up. I'll be going soon. Someone will come for a statement from you."

"Thanks, Brett," Colin said, extending his hand to Brett.

"I didn't do what I should have."

"That happens to all of us and you stopped him from escaping. If you hadn't stepped out and fired at him, he might have made it away from here."

"He couldn't have gone far. Good luck. Nice to know you, Isabella. Your scream brought me on the run."

Colin looked at her. "Why did you scream? You hadn't seen Peter, had you?"

"You weren't there to meet me when I came in the door." She raised her head. "I have instincts, too. But then I looked in the mirror and saw a man with a gun, so I just screamed to distract him and I ran."

Colin hugged her. "I told you that you'd make a good soldier."

They could hear the sounds of a helicopter and all three turned to look. A black military helicopter swept over the ranch and settled on the ranch runway. Brett turned to jog away. "Y'all take care," he called, waving at them. "I'll miss this place."

"Come back and visit," Colin called after him.

"How on earth did they get a helicopter here so soon?" Isabella asked.

"There's a base at San Antonio. It wouldn't take any time to get from there to here." Colin looked down the road to see the police putting Peter into a car. A lawman was striding toward Colin and Isabella.

"Here comes an official who'll probably want a statement. Go on inside and I'll get rid of him. We can give him a statement tomorrow."

"I'm not moving without you," she said in a low voice and he looked down to smile at her.

"Colonel Garrick?" the officer said, extending his hand. Colin shook hands with him as he introduced himself.

"I'm Larry Norris. Are you folks all right?"

"We're fine. Nothing big, except shaken up. I know you need a statement, but can we come in tomorrow and give it to you?"

The officer's lips firmed as he seemed to mull it over, but then he nodded. "Not exactly following procedure, but you've been through this before. Do you mind coming first thing in the morning?"

"Sure, and thanks," Colin said. "Where do we go?"

"Stallion Pass courthouse. Nine o'clock. Just ask for me."

Colin nodded. Just then Boone and Erin drove past and waved. Isabella and Colin waved in return.

"I can't believe my brother is about to become a daddy," Isabella said.

"You better get used to the idea soon. You're going to be an aunt before long."

"That I can imagine much easier. Come inside and let me clean that wound. If it's the least bit deep, off we go to the emergency. When did you last have a tetanus shot?"

"You sound like an army nurse. I had one last year and don't need another now. And I sure don't need one for this. Isabella, these damn dogs," he said, trying to get to the house, but the dogs were still milling around his feet.

"The gate's open," she said, and started back to close it, but Colin held her arm.

"I'll get it, but they're not about to run away. These mutts have sense enough to know a good thing and they're not leaving you."

He hurried to close the gate and returned, shooing the

dogs away as he and Isabella went inside. The moment the door closed, he pulled her into his arms to kiss her.

Isabella stood on tiptoe, wrapped her arms around his waist and kissed him in return.

She raised her head after a moment. "We clean your wound. I don't want you bleeding to death in my arms."

"No danger." They started across the kitchen and she caught his wrist. "See, when I was right here, I could see the reflection in the mirror of Peter standing there with a gun."

"That scream saved the day."

"Thank goodness," she said.

They went to the big bathroom and she began to rummage in the cabinet for antiseptic. Colin's hand closed over hers.

"I've got a better idea. Let's get in the shower and wash all these wounds and scratches and see how bad the injuries are."

Her eyes darkened, and she got that sultry look that heated his blood.

She nodded and he began to unfasten her buttons as she twisted his free. They undressed each other and stepped into the shower and he turned on warm water.

In seconds she was in his arms. Isabella clung to him, relishing his strong arms around her, overjoyed to feel his bare, warm body, hard and strong, pressed against her.

Desire raged, burning away control as she moved her hips slowly against his arousal. He groaned and combed his fingers in her hair. "I've missed you more than I ever thought possible," he declared and her pulse jumped with excitement.

"All I could think about all the way home was you, Colin. I couldn't wait to get here."

"I have an evening planned for us."

"Your arm!" she gasped, remembering and pulling back

to look at him. His skin was torn, but it was minor, looking as if it were no more than a scrape from a branch.

"See, I told you it was nothing."

"I was so frightened for you."

"I was damned terrified for you. You got right in the thick of it. But that scream was marvelous. It startled him and gave me just enough of a chance to get away from him."

"It's over, Colin. You don't have to worry about being a target any longer and you have your memory back." She gazed up into eyes that were filled with desire and a hunger that was mutual.

"I missed you so much," she whispered.

"Darlin'," he said, then leaned down to kiss her. They forgot the water pouring over their naked bodies as they clung to each other and kissed endlessly. He stepped out of the shower stall to retrieve a packet of protection. But when he returned, they dried each other off and kissed once more before he finally picked her up to make love to her.

Colin carried her to bed to hold her close in his arms.

"I've been dreaming of this since the moment you waved goodbye," he whispered. "Wait a minute and I'll be right back," he said, getting up and leaving the room.

Isabella smiled in contentment. She knew what she wanted for her future and she knew she was making the right decision.

She watched Colin walk back to bed. He was nude, aroused again, all lean, hard muscles.

"You're beautiful, Colin."

"Hardly. But you probably think all those mutts out there are beautiful, too. Darlin', I've come to a decision about the future. I missed you every second you were gone. Isabella, I love you."

Her heart thudded. The words were magic, important

when they came from Colin, and she wrapped her arms around him to kiss him passionately.

His arms banded her waist and he held her against him. Their bare legs tangled while they kissed. He raised his head and brushed her hair away from her face. "Darlin', I made a decision. I don't have to live in Stallion Pass. I can live in New York. Will you marry me, Isabella?"

Her heart thudded against her ribs and joy filled her. She threw her head back. "Colin! Yes, yes, yes!" She laughed with joy and showered him with kisses and then kissed him on the mouth, a long, steamy kiss.

When she pulled away. "Marry you! Yes! Oh, Colin, I'm so happy."

"What about 'I don't ever want to marry because it will interfere with my career'?" he asked, gazing at her solemnly.

She laughed and pushed him down as she straddled him. "You think a career is better than this?"

He grinned and pulled her down into his embrace to kiss her and the question was forgotten for a longer time as Colin stroked and kissed and then made love to her again.

It was an hour later as they lay in each other's arms that she turned to him. "Colin, I thought about us while I was in New York."

"And—" he said warily.

"Don't sound so worried. I want you and a family more than that career. I have a perfectly fine business right here and I'll have a beautiful new home and a sexy husband. I don't want that job."

He raised up so swiftly, she fell back against the bed. He pulled her up to look her directly in the eyes. "That's all you've wanted all your adult life. You've told me that repeatedly. Your brother has told me. Since when did this change of heart happen?"

''When I was away from you,'' she answered solemnly. ''I hated it.''

''Isabella, I don't want you to wake up one day and realize that you tossed aside a fantastic career to marry me. You can do that and marry me. I'm not objecting to your job.''

''Aren't you getting argumentative!'' she exclaimed. ''I'm not going to wake up one day and wish I'd done something else. I know my own mind and I know how I felt when I was away from you. I know what I want.''

''You want to get married and live in Stallion Pass for the rest of your life?''

''If it's with you. Don't you want to stay here?''

''You're sure?'' he asked.

''Since when did you think I don't know what I really want?''

''You must not have known when you went to New York,'' he pointed out.

''Well, I figured it out quickly when I got there. How long are we going to argue about this? You just proposed and now—''

He kissed her and ended the conversation, and his kiss confirmed how much he wanted her. He broke free and reached over to the bedside table. He placed a black-velvet box in her hand. ''For you.''

She opened the box and looked at a dazzling emerald-cut diamond flanked by two smaller diamonds. ''Colin!'' she gasped and threw her arms around him, knocking him flat as she kissed him.

In seconds she raised her head and pulled up the ring to look at it again. ''It's gorgeous.''

He took it from her. ''Will you marry me?''

''Yes, I will,'' she said, gazing into his sexy gray eyes, her heart pounding with joy. ''Oh, Colin, how I missed you and dreamed about this!''

"I wish I'd known. I've been in hell while you were gone. Isabella, darlin', I love you."

She hugged him. "Goodness knows, I love you!"

He leaned back to look at her. "I heard you say something about wanting a family. Isn't that a big change, too?"

She smiled at him. "I think having a little Colin would be the most wonderful thing possible."

"I'd like a family. I take it you also know exactly what you want on this issue, too."

"Certainly," she replied smugly. He grinned. "All right, but let's not start on the family for a little while. For a few months I want you all to myself."

"I think that's a splendid idea."

"And how soon can we marry? Make it soon, darlin'."

"This is April. How about the middle of June? I think that's soon."

"Not soon enough, but I'll settle for that. Now come here and let's make up for lost time," he said in a husky voice, caressing her breasts as he pulled her to him.

A ringing broke the stillness. Colin stretched out his arm to pick up the phone, placing it on the bed before he answered.

He glanced at Isabella, then handed the receiver to her. "Your brother."

Colin toyed with her hair and caressed her back, leaning forward to lift her curtain of silky hair while he kissed her nape.

Suddenly she shrieked, nearly toppling him off the bed. "I'm an aunt!" she cried, turning to look at him. "They have a little girl. Seven pounds. They named her Mary Isabella Devlin and they're going to call her Mary."

"Great," he said, leaning over again to kiss her ear.

"We'll be there," she said, replacing the receiver and handing him the phone, which he set back on the table.

"I told Boone we'd come see them and little Mary."

"Uh-huh," Colin said, cupping her breasts as his thumbs circled her nipples.

"Oh, you wicked man," she purred, leaning forward to kiss him.

Epilogue

Isabella gazed at herself in the mirror, still unable to believe what she saw. She pushed back the bridal veil. The simple white silk dress had tiny sleeves and a plain skirt with a train that could be removed. Tiny pearls beaded the lower part of the dress and along the straight neckline.

"You look beautiful!" Erin said, standing nearby.

Isabella turned to her matron of honor and squeezed her hand.

"So do you. You don't look as if you could possibly have had a baby a little over a month ago."

"I feel like I did," Erin said, laughing. "Right now, Boone has her. At least I know she's in good hands and he's experienced at this."

"He's a pro when it comes to babies."

"I'm glad you're marrying Colin," Erin said. "Your brother didn't think you'd ever give up a career, but he's glad you did."

"I didn't give up a career. I have my studio, but I know

what you mean. I'm so happy, I could fly," Isabella said, and Erin smiled.

"You *do* look gorgeous," Stacia Longstreet confirmed.

Isabella turned to her friend. "Thanks again for being in my wedding. Thanks to all of you," she said to her sister Emily, a tall, slender brunette, and to another sister, Cathy, a shorter brunette with hazel eyes.

Emily smoothed the skirt of her black dress. "A black and white wedding—this black dress is great, Izzie, because I can actually wear this dress again to parties."

"Good!"

At a knock on the door, Isabella called, "Come in," and her brother Zach thrust his head in the door. "The minister said it's time. Don't be late for your wedding," he teased, closing the door quickly.

"Your family was blessed with looks," Stacia said, still gazing at the door. "Your brother Zach is as handsome as he was in college."

"Zach?" Isabella repeated, straightening her skirt and not thinking much about Stacia's remarks. "Boone's the handsome devil."

"Well, he's married and Zach isn't."

"Shall we go?" Emily urged, handing Isabella her bouquet of white tulips and roses.

They left, and Isabella waited while her sisters and friend walked down the aisle.

Colin's father, Stuart, was to walk Isabella down the aisle. He linked her arm through his. "Isabella, I'm happy for both of you. You've been great for Colin. You've given our son back to us."

"I love him very much," she said, patting Stuart Garrick's arm.

And then it was time for her entrance. The moment she started down the aisle, her gaze flew past their guests to Colin. In a tuxedo, he looked more handsome than ever and her heart skipped beats as she moved closer to him.

She barely heard the words said to them, repeated her vows, and all the time couldn't take her gaze away from Colin's.

And then the minister finally pronounced them husband and wife. Colin kissed her lightly. "You're mine, love," he whispered and smiled at her.

He took her hand and they walked back up the aisle. Surprisingly, she was able to keep up with his long-legged stride.

After posing for pictures, they left in a limousine for the Stallion Pass Country Club for the reception.

Garlands of greenery were strung around the large reception room and bouquets of flowers were banked near the bridal table while a fountain ice sculpture was centered on the table.

As children ran underfoot and guests continued to congratulate the bride and groom, the band began to play and Colin took Isabella's hand.

Having shed the train to her dress, she turned to dance with him, gazing up at him. "You are the most handsome man on earth!"

He grinned. "That purely isn't so, but I'm glad you think it. Hon, I'm all sewed back together like the scarecrow in the Oz story."

She poked his hard, flat stomach. "Doesn't feel to me like you're stuffed with straw."

"After a while you can take a peek and see."

She laughed. "I can't wait."

"You think you can't wait! In that yummy dress you look good enough to eat. How long before we can get out of here and I can get you all to myself?"

"We have to be nice to our guests for a couple of hours and then we can disappear. You never have told me where we're going for our honeymoon."

"I want to surprise you."

"You can at least give me a hint."

He shook his head. "Nope. You have to wait until we leave here."

"Okay."

"Our families work well together. Kevin is dazzled by your sister Cathy, but then I think Kevin is dazzled by most females at this point in his life," Colin said as he pulled her closer in his arms.

Dancing with Colin was bliss. Isabella closed her eyes and leaned her head against him, knowing she had made the right decision when she'd returned to Texas and agreed to marry Colin. It was a decision she would never regret.

Later, as Colin stood in a group of his friends, talk came up again about the wild white stallion that had been passed from groom to groom. When Mike mentioned it, both Boone and Colin said no at the same time.

"I thought we settled that at my barbecue in April," Boone declared.

"That horse is going to wear out with you guys moving him around," Colin added. "With all the strays Isabella takes in, we don't need one more animal," Colin added. He gazed at his friends in the circle, Mike, Jonah and Boone. "Guys, thanks to you, I did get my life back. I'm glad you talked me into staying and catching Peter."

"I still can't get over that it was Peter Fremont," Jonah said. "The headlines have died away now, but they'll flare up again when his trial comes up."

"All those years of deception," Jonah said.

"All the lives lost," Boone added.

"Well, once more, I appreciate what all of you did," Colin said.

"We're glad he's caught and you don't have to worry about him," Mike said.

"Here comes my doll baby," Boone said as Erin walked up to hand Mary to him.

"Can you hold her a minute?"

"'Course. Come here, sweetie," Boone said to the baby. His brother Zach joined them.

"Now, here's the guy that told me for years he would never marry," Zach said. "Look at him now."

"I'm a happy man," Boone said, grinning. "And, little brother, you can get in some practice," he said, putting Mary into his brother's arms.

The men laughed and Zach grinned as he adjusted Mary in the crook of his arm. She snuggled down and closed her eyes and Zach gave Boone a smug grin. "See—who's the expert here?"

"You guys excuse me," Colin said, leaving them and searching for Isabella. As soon as he could, he pulled her aside.

"I haven't kissed you in far too long. It's been three hours and I've shared you with too many people."

"All right. Where's that limo that you said was waiting to whisk us away?"

"Just come out on the terrace with me," he said, strolling with his arm lightly around her waist. "Now this way, my darlin'." They turned a corner. "Come on. We'll make a break for it."

He took her hand and she picked up her skirts and they ran to the parking lot, where they climbed into a waiting limo. She fell against the seat laughing and trying to catch her breath while Colin spoke to the driver. They were off to Austin to spend the night in the bridal suite of a luxurious hotel.

"Look in my coat pocket," Colin told her, holding her close in the back seat of the limo.

Isabella reached into his pocket and pulled out plane tickets. She turned them over and threw her arms around his neck. "Switzerland!"

"I told you to pack your camera. We're going to a beautiful place that I saw a long time ago and from there we can pick some remote, rugged places where you can shoot pictures to your heart's content.''

"Oh, Colin, that's fabulous!'' she exclaimed, kissing him soundly.

When he started to slide his hand beneath her silk skirt, she caught his wrist. "Wait for the hotel.''

He inhaled and leaned back, pulling her into his arms.

"Colin, when they finally finish building our house in Stallion Pass, can we take the dogs with us?''

He grinned. "Why am I not surprised by this question? I don't care what you do with the dogs. Just try to keep the number of them down below a dozen.''

She smiled. "Are you going to grant my every wish?''

"I hope I always can. I'll try.''

The minute they were in the bridal suite and the door closed behind the bellman, Colin shed his coat and tie and turned to look at her. She had crossed the room to look at the view. It was still afternoon and she turned back to Colin as he crossed the room.

"This is a beautiful view of the city.''

"You don't say,'' he said, never taking his eyes from hers. He wrapped his arms around her. "I love you, Isabella, more than anything on earth.''

"Ah, Colin, how happy you make me,'' she said, winding her arms around his neck and standing on tiptoe. She pulled his head down to kiss him.

Colin's arms tightened around her waist and he pulled her closer against him, his kiss deepening.

In love with her tall husband, Isabella hugged him. She leaned away and combed her fingers through his hair. "Colin, I'll love you forever. You're mine now and that's not going to change.''

"I don't want it to change, darlin'. I love you.'' He tightened his arms again and kissed her.

Isabella's heart filled with joy and she knew this night she and Colin were starting a new life together with a love to last a lifetime.

* * * * * *

COMING NEXT MONTH